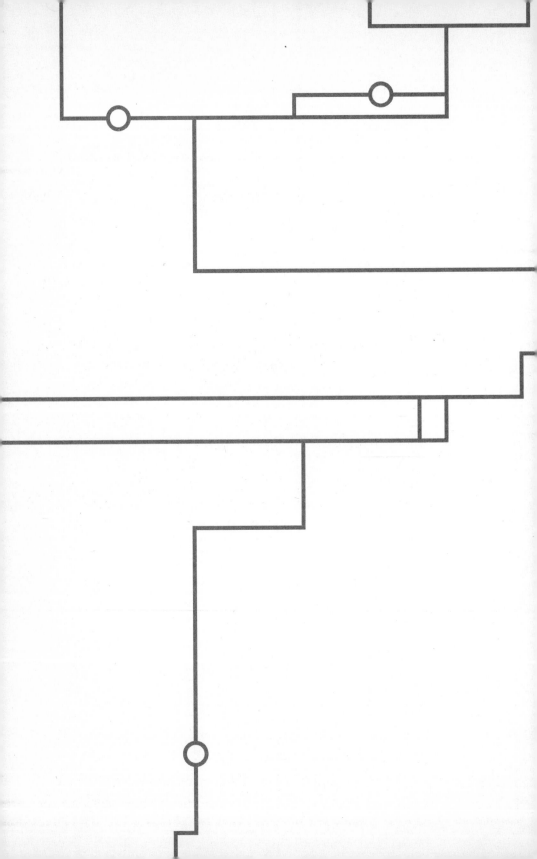

HAZZARDOUS UNIVERSE 2

OTHER BOOKS AND AUDIO BOOKS
BY JULIE AND KEVIN:
Hazzardous Universe (Book 1)

BY JULIE:
Olivia

Cross My Heart

Eyes Like Mine

HAZZARDOUS UNIVERSE 2

THE MAGICIAN'S LAST WORDS

JULIE WRIGHT & KEVIN WASDEN

Covenant

Covenant Communications, Inc.

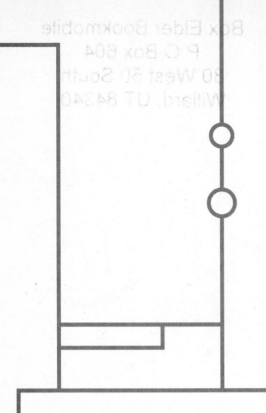

Cover and interior artwork copyright © 2012 Kevin Wasden

Cover and book design copyright © 2012 by Covenant Communications, Inc.

Published by Covenant Communications, Inc.
American Fork, Utah

Printed in the United States of America
First Printing: March 2012

19 18 17 16 15 14 13 12   10 9 8 7 6 5 4 3 2 1

ISBN 978-1-60861-967-2

To McKenna, Julia, and Lily,
because life is full of adventures to be had,
and there is a universe of opportunities waiting for you.

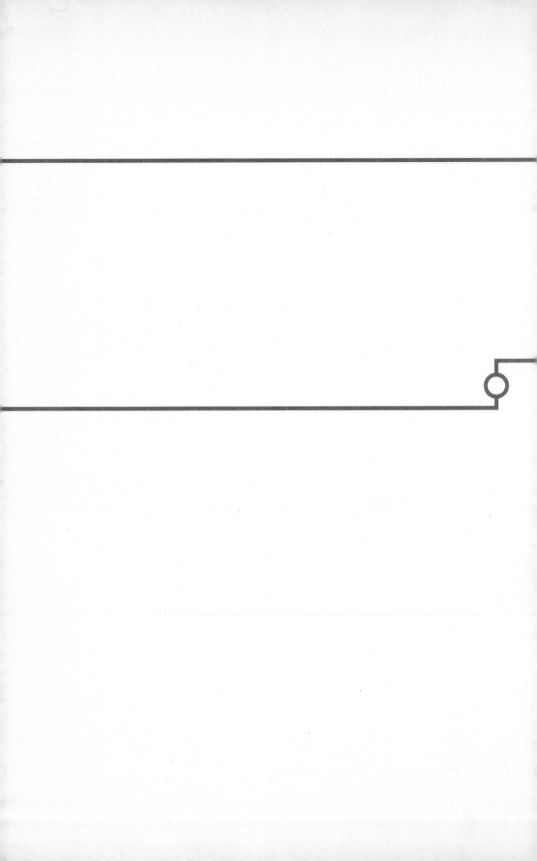

ACKNOWLEDGMENTS

Thank you to:

Chandler Wright, Scott Wright, and Nathan Davenport for catching things we missed while still in the drafting stages and saving us from feeling silly about those things later.

Jeff Savage, Jen Savage, Jessica Day George, Howard Tayler, Heather Moore, Josi Kilpack, Annette Lyon, and James Dashner. Great friends are the finest treasure of the universe. Thanks for all your support in helping us achieve our dreams.

Kirk Shaw, Kathy Jenkins, Robby Nichols, Mark Sorenson, Margaret Weber, Ron Brough, Kelly Smurthwaite, and the rest of the Covenant family who approved, designed, and breathed life into this expanding universe.

The Wright and Wasden families, who put up with us during the creative process. No artist of any kind is worth much without a strong spouse to support them. Scott and Michelle support us and keep us balanced. In the creation of the Hazzardous Universe, one thing has become clear—there really is a universe of possibilities out there. And our children inspire us with their potential and wonder every day.

1. The Lizard Comet

Landing on the Lizard Comet made Hap's top-five list of "coolest things ever." All the glowing bits of dust made it feel like they'd flown through a glitter storm. Amar had described it as a foglike cloud of ions. The description meant absolutely nothing to Hap, but Svarta had taken over and explained that it was the same as going into outer space—no breathable air. Either way, it looked cool.

"It's amazing!" he said for the zillionth time to Mosh. "You should've seen it!" They sat in Mosh's room where Mosh watched Gygak—the Gygan who tried to get them all killed back at Stupak's Circle. "I'll watch Gy-geek if you want to go look out the port windows."

Gygak rolled his eyes several times at Hap's excitement, and he blew out several snorts through his nose holes. Mosh smiled, showing all of his stumpy teeth, and shook his head. "I'll stay. Gygak is my friend—my responsibility."

Some friend, Hap thought. Gygak had tricked Hap and Tara into stealing the Hira—the crystal pyramid that allowed the nine books of power to be read. Then he handed over the Hira, the last of the nine unknown scientists, Hap, Tara, *and* Mosh to Don Nova, intergalactic criminal mastermind.

Friends did not turn friends over to the bad guys. Hap was certain it was written down in the friendship rulebook somewhere. It was a totally uncool thing to do. And Don Nova was the ultimate in bad guys—even if Amar said there were far worse out there. Amar had said that the Dark Ones who'd hired Nova . . . they were worse.

Hap shuddered and turned back to the task at hand—letting Mosh see something he'd never seen before. "But you've never been on a comet," Hap said. "What if this is your only chance in your whole entire life?"

Mosh shrugged. "I will stay with Gygak."

Hap looked doubtfully at the Gygan. "But he's boring. You've got to be out-of-your-mind bored right now. I'm bored just looking at you looking at him."

Gygak glared at Hap. "Then you should leave. Go get into trouble somewhere else, little alien boy."

Gygak called Hap little alien boy a lot because he knew it bugged Hap to have to consider himself the alien in a universe full of such strange creatures.

"At least I'm one of the sentient aliens, Gy-geek. You would *absolutely* survive the zombie apocalypse, because you don't have enough brains for the zombies to bother with you."

Gygak struggled to get up and likely blacken Hap's eye for the comment, but he was strapped in pretty securely.

Hap grinned then looked again at Mosh. "You sure?"

"It's my job," Mosh affirmed.

"Okay. I'll bring you some real food when we get back. None of those nutty paste things." Hap jumped to his feet and went to the door, turned back briefly, and said, "What does Gy-geek have in common with the scarecrow from *The Wizard of Oz*?"

"What?" Mosh, who usually liked Hap's trivia, asked.

"No brains." Hap laughed as the door to Mosh's room swished open.

Gygak struggled again, and Nana, the sentient ship, tsked at Hap as she swished the door closed again.

"That was an uncalled-for insult, Hap," Nana said.

Hap shrugged at her. "He deserves it. He almost got us all killed. *And* we lost the Hira because of him . . . well, because of me too, but he tricked me." Hap still felt awful about how things had turned out on Stupak's Circle. He'd do anything to change things—to fix them—if he could. "I'm sorry," Hap said to the ship as he made his way down to where preparations had been made for them to disembark the ship onto the comet's surface.

Nana didn't ask what he was sorry for. She never asked him to elaborate on anything. She always just knew what he meant. "I know you're sorry about the Hira. Don't dwell on what you can't change."

Hap nodded and turned toward the exit.

Everyone else was already there—Tara, Svarta, Laney, Amar, and Tremble. They'd all spent a long time studying the maps and debating the locations of the rest of the missing books of power. They also had a team of people back on Earth who were experts in the missing books and the Nazca lines and knew the general locations of each and every one. The specifics were a little more complicated, but Hap was grateful that Amar's contacts on Earth had been right so far.

They'd taken a detour on their trip to the comet when Amar had been contacted about a breakthrough discovery about a place called Anansi, and they'd ended up on a planet full of horrific spiders. But they'd secured one of the books on that detour. That meant they had two—one on gravity and one on propaganda. Nova had the one that taught how to turn metals into gold. They'd have to do something about that. Seven books more and a crystal pyramid to go. And then Hap could see his family in person again.

No one planned on being on the comet for very long. And after that, they were heading to some planet called Koda.

Lame name, but Hap was still curious about it. Amar said it was a planet rich in a rare blue gemstone that could fuel the electricity of one planet for centuries but that something had happened to it when a mining company set up an entire operation on the planet. All their mining equipment and several entire colonies were still there—abandoned to rust. All the people had disappeared. A planet full of abandoned junk could be pretty cool.

But Hap was even more excited to explore a comet. The idea that he was hurtling through space on a glowing ball of ice—well, that had to go on his top-five list as well. And the comet itself promised a lot of fun and adventure . . . *if* Laney would ever let them leave the ship, that is.

"Can I trust you guys to behave yourselves?" Laney had her hands on her hips. She started lecturing as soon as Hap showed up to the exit hatch and didn't stop for a full twenty minutes. "I want promises from both of you." But she pointed at Hap specifically.

She'd gotten more bossy and motherly than even Nana during their hops across the universe, trying to get to the books of power before Nova and the Dark Ones. He didn't know what she was so uptight about. They'd already successfully found another book of power.

And yes, finding that book had been a little freaky, but everyone survived with all their fingers and toes—and in Tremble's case, antennae and tail—intact.

That book had been on the bottom of the ocean on Anansi, which didn't sound too bad, except it turned out that *Anansi* was another word for "spider." Tara and Hap hoped the name was figurative. Except it *wasn't.* The place was overrun with gigantic mutant spiders that were as cunning as they were creepy. Hap had looked forward to getting to the ocean where the spiders couldn't follow, except . . . the ocean wasn't filled with water but *webs.* Spiderwebs to be exact. The king spider, Anansi himself, thought Hap's alarm at seeing the ocean of webbing had been hilarious. Who would have guessed that spiders had a pretty wicked sense of humor?

But it had been *awful.* Laney had grounded both Hap and Tara to their cabins for a whole day of travel afterward, where she made them study. That was Laney's answer to everything. *Be armed with information.* Hap didn't know why she'd gotten so mad. They'd ended up with the book—wasn't that the important thing?

Laney had started out bossy from the moment she found them in the cargo hold after they'd been accidentally abducted into the spaceship back on Earth. But something had changed on Stupak's Circle. Laney had saved them on that first adventure—even after they'd messed up and delivered the Hira to Nova. Svarta had taken a flame bolt to the back for them. Svarta and Laney had both confronted Nova and a bunch of Servien soldiers to make sure that Hap and Tara got out safely.

Then again, on Anansi it had been Laney who'd almost sacrificed her own life to get them out of the webbing. From there, Laney had gone from bossy to impossible. She had a lecture for him every time her eyes landed on him. Hap sometimes wished he didn't have the translation bugs in his system, converting any alien's language in a way he could understand—not that Laney was an alien—but even when Laney was muttering at him in her native Spanish, he understood.

Laney's mothering and smothering meant that she cared. She'd actually shed *real* tears when she'd thought Hap and Tara were goners.

And with Hap's own mother on the other side of the universe, he kind of didn't mind the idea of an adult caring about him.

Kind of.

Not that he'd ever tell Laney that. Admitting such a thing could get all kinds of weird.

The last thing Hap wanted was her treating him like a kid. He was fourteen, which was totally *not* a kid. And he'd agreed to help save the universe, which ought to earn him some sort of respect. If he admitted he liked her obvious display of concern, she might get even worse. She might start trying to tuck them in for sleep cycles. Or worse yet, she might decide they needed to stay on board Nana while everyone else went out hunting for the books of power.

"Promise me," Laney said again.

"I promise." Hap raised his arm and put up three fingers in the air. "Scout's honor."

Svarta blew the bangs out of her eyes. "They let you into Scouts?" She grunted. "That's proof they'll take anybody."

Tara laughed at that.

Laney allowed a small smile. Tremble and Amar kept out of the conversation, since neither of them knew anything about Boy Scouts.

"Why is my being a Scout so funny?" Hap demanded to know.

"Because," Svarta said, "if anyone let you go to some Scout camp, you'd likely burn down all the cabins."

"We never got cabins at my camps. We had tents—even in the rain."

"Probably a good thing," Svarta said, "since tents are cheaper to replace when you burn them down."

"Catching the paste tube on fire was an accident!" Hap had only tried to heat up the protein rations of nutty paste that they'd fed him for every meal. Was it a crime to want something warm in his stomach?

And no one mentioned that water was scarce in outer space either, or he never would have filled the buckets of water and dumped them on the blaze. Tremble had pointed out that no one should have had to tell him that water was scarce since it should have been obvious. Laney had tried to ground him to his cabin for the mess, but Svarta wouldn't hear of it. She'd made him stay and clean it up.

Amar had chuckled. Tara had scowled.

The bad thing about being stuck on a small ship with all those people was that when you did something dumb, there was nowhere to hide until things blew over. Everywhere Hap went, he was tripping over people in the narrow hallways and rooms. The only place he had any sort of privacy was in his own cabin, which was little more than a glorified closet with a bed.

And his own cabin wasn't really private either. Nana, the ship's computer, hated it when he stomped away to pout. Her voice followed him everywhere, trying to offer guidance and advice—trying to make him feel better, or coax him into apologies he didn't think anyone deserved. Nagging, nagging, nagging. They should have named her Nagga instead of Nana.

There was no privacy at all on the ship. Which was why he *needed* to get out. If he had to put up with some teasing and promises of good behavior in order to get access to the outside—he'd grit his teeth, pretend to smile, and deal with it.

Besides, if Laney thought she could keep him from something as cool as exploring a city on a comet, she didn't understand him at all.

"I mean it. I promise not to get into any trouble." He'd already made this vow three times.

"I'll keep him out of trouble," Tara said, which only made Hap grind his teeth a little harder. Half the trouble Hap was dragged into had been Tara's fault.

Well, maybe not *exactly* her fault, but she'd been there for it and hadn't managed to stop him from getting into it.

"And you have your link keys?" Amar reminded them. It seemed to Hap that Amar said it to remind Laney, too—to help her know that she still had a way to contact them and that they had a way to contact her if anything bad should happen.

"You do have your link keys, don't you?" Laney asked, suddenly panicking that they might have forgotten them.

"Right here." Hap dangled his in front of her.

Tara patted the pocket of her jeans where she'd tucked her link key.

Hap didn't have jeans anymore, thanks to his run-in with the neubins and their red needles of death. He was still stuck wearing the silky green pants he'd found in the room he'd stayed in at the Rissan's Neswar. That was part of the reason Amar was determined to get them on the comet surface. He wanted them to get some new clothes.

"Well, I guess you can't get into too much trouble if you keep those link keys on and you promise not to lose them." Laney looked doubtful.

Hap now promised several times that he would definitely *not* lose the link key. He sneaked a glance at Amar, who offered over a wink and a thumbs-up.

"And if I link to you, you have to answer. No matter what. You don't get to ignore me."

Svarta rolled her eyes and stood in front of the door leading to the Lizard Comet's only landing bay. "Let's go, Laney, before you start bugging them about brushing their teeth and talking to strangers."

Laney's eyes widened, and she pulled down hard on the bill of her baseball cap. "Don't talk to strangers! I mean it! There are some seriously seedy people who hang out at Bo Shocks's concerts. The last thing I need is you guys taking off on some stranger's ship."

"Oh my stars, Laney! You've only gotten worse as you've gotten older. Lighten up already!" Svarta said.

Nana swished open the door and lowered the ramp as Svarta shoved at Laney to get her to stop lecturing Hap and Tara. Amar patted Hap's shoulder as he followed the group out.

"Remember who you are," Amar murmured, which was the equivalent of at least two hours of Laney's lecturing.

Hap grunted. "Honestly, people! I think I can handle a walk on a comet! You'd think I was an idiot with the way you're all acting."

Everyone stopped and turned as one to look at him. Svarta laughed and turned away, shaking her head.

"Stay away from the bars! And the credit tables! I mean it!" Laney shouted one last command as Svarta and Tremble dragged her away.

Hap rolled his eyes now that they were all far enough away they couldn't see him. "I'm not an idiot," he muttered.

"Whatever gets you through the day, Hap Hazzard," Tara said. She shouldered her backpack, which had a few aluminum water sleeves and a few mat paks in case she couldn't stomach the food served in the restaurants on the comet.

Hap had already teased her about throwing up when Nana had landed on Stupak's Circle. He said he'd made bets with Tremble *and*

Googool, twin souls in the same body, as to whether or not she'd throw up again. Tara had to have known that he hadn't really made any such bet, because Tremble terrified Hap when she was Googool. Tremble terrified *everyone* when she was Googool.

Because they'd landed on a comet, which had very little gravitational pull, the landing was smoother—less traumatic on Tara's sensitive digestive system. Tara didn't vomit on the comet, after all.

But she had taken the opportunity to slug his arm when Nana released the straps holding them into their silver beds.

"I'm not an idiot," Hap grumbled as they stomped down the ramp and onto the landing dock. The dock was awesome. It was paved with multicolored flat rocks and decked out with lots of planted trees and flowers. He felt like he'd landed on a five-star resort.

"I didn't say you were an idiot. *You're* the only one who even used that word." Tara turned from him to smell one of the flowers but not before Hap caught her smiling. She let go of the flower and sighed. "Flowers. How do they get these things to grow on a muddy snowball?"

"Ask Nana when we get back. She can pull down the history of the comet for you." Laney had insisted on "education time" for a couple of hours every day to "fill in the places where earthside education failed." She'd insisted on exercise time, too, so their muscles didn't flab or sag.

"It's really lame that we can't look for the book with them," Hap grumbled. He'd wanted to help, but Laney said he was helping enough by not making them go to Earth first. She also said he'd be an even bigger help if he could just stay out of stuff.

She acted like all he did was get into stuff—which he totally didn't.

Tara stood up and brushed off her jeans. "At least we aren't stuck on the ship anymore. I was starting to get claustrophobic. No offense to Nana, but there's only so many times you can walk around that ship without going crazy."

They turned to the right and started walking. Each step felt a little like hopping in spite of the astronomically expensive false gravity on the comet—which it had to have to keep the high paying customers coming back and not leaving, unintentionally, too early. The Lizard

Comet was apparently famous for its bars and credit tables. Laney had called it a Las Vegas of the stars. Only this place didn't have any age restrictions, so Hap and Tara were on their honor to not enter the bars or to gamble away any of the credits Amar had put on their individual scan cards. Amar threatened punishment worse than anything they could imagine if they even *thought* about going into the bars or gambling at the tables.

Hap wondered what could be worse than anything he could imagine, because he could imagine quite a lot.

Amar had also paid to install a link plate on board Nana so they could contact their families again and so Amar could contact people working within the society on Earth to help him decode the Nazca lines and figure out where all the books were.

Even with the link plate directly installed aboard the ship, the cost was still so high that Hap and Tara had only been able to call a couple of times, so they worked hard to make the links last as long as possible. Hap and Tara ate until their stomachs felt ready to explode so they could have enough energy to lengthen the calls.

Tara's call was pretty typical for girls. Tara and her mom blubbered and said they loved each other a million times. Tara explained that it would be a while before she could come home and told her mom to visit the Hazzards for more information because she didn't want to waste *her* time explaining all the details.

That meant Hap had to be the one to waste all of *his* time.

Not that Hap really minded. He loved explaining all the details to his family. Grandpa Hazzard had been a war hero. Hap's dad had also been decorated in the military. Hazzard men were men of honor, and for the first time in Hap's life, he felt he really belonged in his family. The way his grandfather and father had straightened their shoulders and looked him in the eye with those nods of, "You're doing the right thing, Hap." Hap knew he'd made them proud. His mom blubbered, and his sister, Alison, blubbered, but Hap didn't.

Well . . . not a lot anyway.

Laney had left them detailed maps of where they could go on their link keys. It reminded Hap a little of his dad's GPS in his car. Tara bumped his arm. "You owe me an apology."

"For what?"

"For making fun of me when we entered the comet's debris tail."

"I wasn't making fun of you," he insisted.

"Oh really? Making retching sounds when I said I might get sick isn't making fun?"

"But you didn't get sick. You held up really well, even when all those little dust and ice particles pelted the ship."

"Don't even try to kiss up now. You were a total creep, and you owe me an apology." She looked up to the clear dome that kept them safe from the vacuum of space and the zillions of dust specks that flew off the surface of the comet as they hurtled through space. The sun's light glowed off the dust, making the particles glitter and shine as they flew past the dome.

It was like being on a reversed snow globe. Instead of shaking the globe and watching snow fall inside, Hap was inside the globe and watching the glittery snow swish by *outside.*

"We really need to get a camera," he said, still looking up.

"A camera would be pretty cool. But you know ICE will take away any camera or pictures we might get as soon as we dock back on Earth. They're never gonna let us tell anyone about what we've seen."

Hap sighed, unable to deny the truth in Tara's words. ICE, Intergalactic Communications Enforcers, was a government agency on Earth that prevented the world's population from ever knowing about space travel and extraterrestrial life. But Hap figured he had enough time before going home that he'd surely be able to think up some way to sneak things past a silly little government agency.

"Let's go to the causeway," he said. "I need new pants. Maybe we can buy a camera there too."

Tara didn't start walking again when he moved forward. He turned to see what her problem was. She stood with her arms crossed over her chest and her glare all the way up to the "furious level." He managed to hit the "furious level" a couple of times a day with Tara. "Apology?"

Hap groaned. "Fine. I'm sorry."

"What exactly are you sorry for?"

"Really? Tara, you *know* why I'm apologizing. You were the one who told me I *had* to apologize. Why do I have to explain it?"

She tapped her finger on her arm impatiently. "I hope that by explaining it, you'll actually think about it, and maybe if you think about it, you won't do it again."

"Aw, c'mon! You're like a school teacher. No, worse. You're like a principal! You know, fine. *Fine.* I am sorry I made vomit noises while landing on the comet. There. Happy?"

"I guess it'll do." She fell into step beside him and glanced at his link key map to make sure they went in the right direction.

"I know where I'm going," Hap assured her.

"I didn't say you didn't." But she smiled in a way that indicated he might *not* know where he was going.

He almost stopped to make *her* apologize to *him,* but he let it go. Besides, he had to peek down at his link key too—just to make sure.

"Whoa!" Hap whispered when they went through the airlocks that led to the causeway. "Awesome."

"Totally awesome!" Tara agreed.

The causeway was amazing. The path was cobbled together with the same multicolored paving stones that were on the docks. Trees and flowering shrubs ran straight down the center of the wide aisle. Carts filled with vendors' wares were evenly spaced, and the windows to the shops along the sides were tricked out with all kinds of things Hap had never seen before.

It was sensory overload.

He almost couldn't take it all in. Entertainers of all kinds performed in the causeway. But it wasn't until Tara mumbled, "They're not real," that Hap noticed the glowing quality of the entertainers. They were life-sized holograms. But they weren't fuzzy like the ones sent through the link keys. These were high-quality holos.

Holographic dancers in twirling snowflake costumes flitted and jumped along the cobbled stones. Some of them were human-formed— two legs, two arms, one head. Others . . . well, others *weren't.* A couple of the holo dancers were Gygan. One was Rissan, and several others were creatures Hap couldn't identify. The Rissan stood much taller than the others, her wings adding to the delicate quality of her dancing.

A human guy holo wrestled what looked like a dragon. Hap stopped, unable to move another step. "Do you think all the things in the holograms are real somewhere?" he asked Tara.

"They look real." Tara said, still watching the dancing snowflake people.

"I hope so," he breathed. "How cool would it be if we got to see a real dragon before going home?"

Tara noticed the wrestler and the huge winged creature and backed up behind Hap with an exclamation of surprise. "Maybe it's just like a movie," she said, completely unwillingly to hope the dragon really existed somewhere.

Hap nodded, his excitement taken down a notch. It *was* just a holo, after all. Dragons probably didn't exist anywhere.

Bummer.

A fire-breather holo blew directly out at them while Hap still watched the dragon. He jumped back into Tara, who'd squealed when the flames shot out of the holo's mouth.

"Tickets!" A tall, lanky guy appeared out of nowhere, waving tickets in Hap's and Tara's faces. The tickets glowed at the edges and had red-lined circuitry glowing along the face of each one. "Tickets to see Bo Shocks live! Don't miss it!"

Hap wanted to see the concert. Svarta had raved about Bo Shocks, but Amar said they were absolutely, in no way, allowed to use *his* credits to see such an absurd excuse for music. Since all the credits uploaded on the link keys Tara and Hap now held were given to them by Amar, and since Amar would know exactly where those credits were spent, Hap knew buying tickets was out of the question.

The ticket salesman put his arm right through the holo fire-breather's face. Hap waved the tickets away. "No, thanks. We're not interested." Hap moved to walk around the holo, unnerved by the way the guy with the tickets moved through it, making the image blur and fragment where he touched it.

Hap didn't know why, but it seemed rude to interrupt a performer by walking through him—even if it was just a projected image.

"Not interested?" The guy's eyebrows shot up. He maneuvered himself directly in front of Hap, forcing Hap to focus on him. "How can you *not* be interested?"

The ticket guy wasn't much older than Hap—maybe seventeen or eighteen. He had a slight Asian accent—Chinese maybe. He had black hair with that messy styled look and dark, almond-shaped eyes. A scruff of whiskers lined his upper lip. Hap thought he heard Tara sigh, and not one of her impatient sighs that she used with Hap. This was the sort of sigh he'd heard when girls gathered together and talked about boys they thought were hot. Hap couldn't explain exactly why Tara's doing the sigh-over-hot-guy thing bothered him, but it *did* bother him—a little, anyway.

"We're just not." To prove his point, he took Tara's hand and tried to lead her around both the ticket guy and the fire-breathing holo.

The ticket guy didn't take the hint and fell into step next to Tara. "Bo Shocks? What galaxy are you from that you aren't interested in Bo Shocks?"

It was a rhetorical question—the kind his mom would always ask and his dad would carefully avoid. But Tara answered it anyway. "The Milky Way. We're from Earth."

Hap was ready to remind Tara that Laney said they shouldn't talk to strangers—especially ones who were trying to scrounge up ticket sales. They were probably counterfeit tickets, anyway.

But the guy stopped short upon hearing Tara's answer, which made Tara pull away from Hap.

"What's wrong?" she asked.

"You're from Earth?" He lost his used-car-salesman tone. His voice actually cracked when he said the word *Earth*.

Hap felt a bit embarrassed for the guy. He hated it when his own voice cracked like that. "Yep. And we gotta get shopping. So it was nice to meet you and all, but—"

Tara didn't budge when Hap tried to pull her along. All of her attention stayed on the ticket guy as he became agitated with excitement.

"I'm from Earth, too! Wow! I've never met anyone from home who was my age! Actually, I've never met anyone from home at all. How'd you get here? I'm Confucian, by the way."

"I'm Tara."

Hap scowled, not offering his name and not intending to. And what kind of name was Confucian? It almost sounded like he'd said *confusion*.

Confucian seemed not to care or even notice that Hap existed. He practically bounced with excitement. "Whoa! Earth! I haven't been there since I was twelve. Seeing you two—well, that's the zanest thing that's ever happened to me!"

Tara finally took her eyes off Confucian to shoot a look of, well, *confusion* at Hap. Hap shrugged.

"What part are you from?" Confucian asked.

"Utah," Tara said.

He looked confused. "I've not heard of this Utah." He sounded out the word *U-tah* as though it was hard for him to say.

"It's in America," Tara added.

He still looked confused.

"Where are you from?" Tara asked, likely trying to figure out how to help him understand where she was from.

"China. Qufu, China. Born in the Kong family mansion." He sighed and shook his head. "I tell you, much is required when you're born in such a place. This," he waved his hands at the causeway, "is freedom."

"What year were you born?" Tara asked. Hap, already bored of the conversation, only barely paid attention while he fiddled with the wares on a vendor's nearby cart. He turned over the object in his hand before he realized they were sunglasses for someone who happened to have four eyes. Seriously. He hadn't seen anyone with more than one pair of eyes, but he knew they existed because of the stuff Laney had been explaining during their voyage here.

"I was born in the eighth year of the Han Dynasty."

"Oh." Tara's furrowed brow and defeated tone indicated she had no idea what that meant. Hap snorted lightly and put back the sunglasses.

"When were you born?" Confucian asked.

"I think . . . much later than that," she answered.

Confucian nodded. "Likely. I jumped off planet on the wrong ship. They were scavengers and weren't very smart. None of them knew a thing about gates, drops, and wormholes. I didn't know—didn't understand time and space until I tried linking back home. No one's there anymore—not for me." Confucian's voice cracked again. And his eyes watered. He shook himself as if trying to erase painful memories. "Anyway, traveling's much easier now that I know what questions to ask before just accepting passage."

The wrestler holo lassoed the dragon's head and jumped up on its back. Everyone watched the dragon try to escape its bonds and shifted uncomfortably in the silence that followed Confucian's admitted sadness over the loss of his family and home. Hap couldn't think of any way to exit the encounter with Confucian without being a complete creep. But he couldn't think of any way to lighten the mood either.

"You could always go back to Earth . . . start over, maybe?" Tara's gentle suggestion along with her hand now on Confucian's arm snapped him out of it.

"Oh no!" I've found my place here with Bo and the band. Life's beyond zane now."

"Zane?" Hap repeated, wondering why his translation crawler didn't always work. Figures that he'd get a broken one.

"You know, great. Good. Wonderful. Happy." Confucian smiled wide.

"Well, that's great!" Hap gave Confucian a friendly slap on the back and pulled Tara away so her hand wasn't on Confucian's arm anymore. "Happiness is really . . . zane. Good luck to you, *man*."

Hap guided Tara around the guy, but Confucian yelled out, "Oh! I just got the iciest idea ever! You guys have never been to a Bo Shocks concert, have you? I mean, of course you haven't, or you'd have bought the tickets right at the first."

This time, it was Hap who stopped. He really did want to go to the concert, and even though there wasn't any way he could buy the tickets without getting skinned when he got back to the ship, he still wanted them.

"You can't come to the comet and miss out on the only icy reason for coming to the comet. You *have* to see Bo Shocks! You just have to!" He held out the tickets. "You guys take these, my treat."

Tara looked at Hap as if to say, *Don't even think about it.*

He looked at her as if to say, *You're the one who stopped to chitchat, not me.*

He hurried to look away to avoid interpreting any other looks she might shoot in his direction. He didn't see any reason to be rude by not accepting a perfectly harmless gift now that they *were* stopped.

Amar had said they couldn't *spend* their credits on concerts. But he'd never said they couldn't go to a *free* concert. Besides, Tara was the one who'd bonded with the ticket guy and got his life story and everything.

She should stop being so friendly to people if she wasn't really planning on being friends. And the only friendly thing to do here was accept the gift their new friend had offered.

"Seriously? You're giving them to us?" Hap palmed the tickets before he even finished the question, ignoring the fact that, just a moment before, he'd figured the tickets were fakes. "That's awesome! Thanks!"

Confucian smiled at Hap, looking genuinely happy to have made a friend, which made Hap feel guilty for being kind of a creep at the beginning. Not guilty enough to apologize or anything, but guilty enough to act nicer from then on. He hoped Confucian wasn't weird enough to make him apologize out loud like Tara always did. Why couldn't it be enough to simply feel sorry? Why did he have to say it out loud all the time?

Girls.

They were more alien than *anyone* Hap had met in this universe.

Hap glanced up to notice Tara's glare and hurried to turn his attention back to Confucian. "So when's the concert?"

"At 7:20 solar."

Hap blinked. "Uh, yeah, I got no clue what that means, dude."

"The Lizard Comet goes by the Elektra solar system's time. Lots of comets follow the time of the star in their elliptical. Some don't, but the Lizard Comet does. You got a link key on you?"

Hap showed him the link key Laney had given him.

"Most link keys tap into the local time. It's right there on the screen."

Confucian pointed to Hap's screen.

"Oh, cool. Thanks." Hap felt stupid that he didn't know this already. Laney had really only given instructions on things that had to do with her rules. According to the numbers on Hap's link key, it was only 4:50. He still had more than two hours, or solars, or whatever people on the comet called them, to get to the concert, which meant he had time to buy pants that didn't make him feel lame.

"I better get back to work. I gotta sell enough tickets to earn my way. If you want, you can meet me after the concert, and I'll give you a tour of the stage, and maybe you'll get a chance to meet Bo Shocks." He looked hopeful that they'd say yes.

"Totally! We'll be there!" Hap said over Tara's, "I don't know that we can."

Both Hap and Confucian pretended not to hear Tara's protest, and they made plans to meet up as soon as the concert was over and everyone cleared out of the concert hall.

"Don't be late. Man who is always late is never on time! See you soon!" Confucian said and bowed to Hap.

Hap hesitated a moment before bowing back. Confucian bowed to Tara as well and then went off to sell tickets to a few older girls of a catlike species.

"Did you get that weird little proverb thing at all?" Hap whispered to Tara as they watched Confucian with the girls.

"Nope," she said.

"Of course you're never on time if you're always late," he muttered, noticing the way the girls sighed the same way Tara had when she'd first seen Confucian.

Hap shook his head and rolled his eyes. Confucian wasn't *that* good looking.

Girls.

Totally alien.

Tara waited until Confucian was out of earshot before voicing her disapproval. "Amar won't be happy with this."

"Why not? He's not paying for it. He only said he didn't want to pay for it. He never said we couldn't go for free." Hap nodded toward a shop that sold clothing, and they moved in that direction.

Tara laughed. "Tents on fire, Hap. You're a tents-on-fire kind of guy."

"I'll have you know I never caught a tent on fire—not once!" He didn't mention that he *had* caught a picnic table on fire, but that was because it was plastic and no one had told him that using a charcoal grill on plastic wasn't the best idea.

Tara was still laughing but stopped when she looked up to see why Hap had suddenly become so still.

The shopkeeper who greeted them made Hap's top-five list of scariest things ever—which was saying something, since he'd faced space mafia with guns, neubins, and the entire Anansi planet. And the way she smiled made Hap wonder if he hadn't been safer left on the ship.

"You two are dead meat," the woman with the blood-red eyes said.

2. Rocking Out on the Rock

Hap was pretty sure he let out a squeak.

The woman put her face right up to his and said, "Boo!" Hap and Tara stumbled back as the woman started laughing.

"Gotcha!" She grabbed them each by a shoulder and herded them to the back of the shop. "Just joking around. Trying to liven things up," she said, all the while herding them back farther from the causeway—farther from anyone who might help.

"Joking around?" Tara sputtered. "You just said we were dead meat! How is that funny?"

"You two have the look of crop kids. You totally stand out. You've never left the farm, have you? Your clothes are just awful." This statement she directed to Tara. "Anyway, what can I help you find?"

An exit, Hap thought. He tried hard not to assume the woman was a mass murderer just from looking at her. *I'm in a different solar system. For all I know, everyone here looks like this.* Only most aliens didn't creep him out the way this lady did.

The shopkeeper was human. But all similarities ended there. Even the kids in school who wore dog collars and black eyeliner looked like nice, sweet kids compared to this lady.

Her blood-red hair was braided in a couple of dozen different strands. It would have probably looked cool if the many braids went down her back like gravity dictated—even if it was fake gravity—but somehow the foot-long braids fanned up from her head, sticking straight out like a bizarre sort of crown. Her lips matched the color of her hair, which was anything but natural. It really looked like blood and made him swallow hard when she met his gaze with her eyes—which matched her hair and lips.

How she got her eyes the same color as her hair totally baffled him. It shouldn't have been possible. And it wasn't with contact lenses; the eye color didn't change at all when her pupils dilated in the light as she looked at him. She really did just have freaky eyeballs.

And her cheeks.

Criss-crossed patterns worked along her cheekbones, looking like some sort of metallic yarn had been sewn into her cheeks. It gave her face a skull-like appearance. Those cheek stitches, along with the hair and the eyes, sent a shudder through him.

I'm in a different solar system. He repeated this several times before finding his voice again. "Uh . . . hi there. I'm looking for a new pair of pants. Can you point me in the right direction?"

"You looking for more of the Rissan style, or are you wanting to try something new?"

He looked down at his silky pants. *This was a style?* "Something new. Something kind of like her pants." He pointed at Tara's jeans.

The lady scowled and pursed her lips, stretching the stitches out. "You want to buy pants like that on purpose?"

Hap shrugged. He did want to buy pants like that on purpose, but with her looking at him that way, he wasn't sure he wanted to admit to it. Tara made a noise low in her throat, obviously insulted.

The lady shook her head. "No idea where you'd find pants like that. We've got these . . ." She led him over to a rack with a bunch of things on them, though none of them looked exactly like pants.

She pulled out a pair of pants that looked like tights—the kind Gygak wore under his flight uniform . . . the kind that Hap had already decided looked lame, lame, lame. They looked like something figure ice-skaters wore. And he didn't care what galaxy he was in, he would never wear tights. He shook his head as she put them against him to see if they were his size.

She shrugged and put them back, pulling down another pair of pants that were better—not great, but better.

They were black and had a sort of vinyl feel to them. They had pockets, which was totally important because Hap liked pockets. Pockets were useful. She told him the price, but Hap had nothing to really compare it to. Were the pants cheap? Were they expensive? Were they astronomically priced so that Amar would be broke if Hap bought them? He had no way of knowing. But he'd pretty much decided to buy them just because the shop owner freaked him out; he feared leaving empty-handed.

He glanced at Tara, who lifted a shoulder.

"Do you want to try them on?" the lady asked.

The idea of undressing anywhere near the lady with the stitched cheeks unnerved Hap in a way he knew to be entirely irrational. "No, thanks. I'll just buy them." They looked like they'd fit, and that was good enough. He really wanted out.

"There's no returns. You better try them on." She practically dragged him to a little closet space and shoved him inside.

"Want me to wait in the causeway?" Tara yelled, sounding very much like she had no desire to stay alone in the store front with the creepy lady.

"No! You stay!" Hap demanded.

With his heart racing, he hurriedly pulled the pants on.

"Do they fit?" the stitched-cheek lady called out.

"Um, yeah."

"Then you can wear them out if you want."

He took her up on that offer, wadding the silky pajama bottoms into a ball and carrying them to the register. The new vinyl pants made a snicking noise as he walked.

He'd been told to never hand off the link key to anyone—even though it was biocoded and no one else could make it work. He blew over it to make it work then gave it permission to talk to her register and take credits to pay for his pants. He tried not to look impatient for the several seconds it took to process. He wanted out as fast as possible.

Outside the store, they broke into a run to get some distance from the shop.

"I don't think she was joking about killing us. I bet she really does eat kids. She's like the witch you hear about in the stories with the house made out of candy, fattening up kids so she can make a brunch out of them later," Tara said as she sped down the causeway, ignoring the salespeople trying to catch her attention.

They stopped moving only because they were nearly trampled by a holo marching band. They tripped over each other to get out of the way.

Tara laughed. "We're trying to get out of the way of light," she said. "As if light can do anything to us."

Hap, for once, didn't laugh. The memory of the dream he'd had after he'd linked home the first time rushed back into his thoughts. The world had exploded. Everything he loved—gone. "According to Amar, light is something to take seriously." He frowned.

She stopped laughing then bumped his shoulder gently with her own. "Put the green pants in your backpack, you leprechaun. Let's get some real food. I'm starving."

They watched people ordering at the food court for a long time before they felt brave enough to attempt an order on their own. They waited until someone walked away from the counter holding food that looked edible and then ordered the same thing.

Tara didn't complain about any of the stuff on her plate and finished every bite. Hap suspiciously eyed the goo that had looked like mashed potatoes. It tasted like hot radishes—like the kind his mom sometimes put in salads. It was awful. But everything else on his plate was okay.

Tara waited until he'd pushed his plate away, indicating he was done. "I really don't know that we should be going to this concert. What if we end up getting in trouble for being out too late?"

Hap pointed at her. "You worry too much."

"Only because you don't worry at all."

He leaned back in his chair and watched the holo of the dancing snowflakes float gracefully by. "We can't get in trouble for being out late when they never gave us a curfew to begin with. And if they'd wanted to keep tabs on us, then they should've let us go with them."

"It's not like they're going on vacation. This is serious stuff. We'd just be in the way, and they can't afford to waste time in finding the books."

Hap scrubbed his hand over his head. "You're just repeating what Svarta said."

"I'm repeating it because she's right."

"Tara, you do know you're a teenager, right? You do know that it's against the code of youth to always agree with adults."

She gave him a smile, pulling her napkin off her lap to wipe her fingers then tossing it down on her plate. "You just hate not being in on everything. Laney and Amar are smart. They can do this on their own, you know. They don't need us—more specifically *you*—to find the book. And if we slow them down . . ."

She didn't have to finish the sentence. They couldn't afford to make mistakes, couldn't afford to let Nova get the books first.

"Candle flame to parchment . . ." he said softly.

"What?"

"Just what that Tolvan guy said to Grandpa Hazzard. He said if the wrong people got the books, everything we held dear would be like candle flame to parchment—nothing but ashes."

"We'll get the books. We will." She nodded as if she'd made the decision and that was the end of it.

Hap hoped she was right.

Amar had said there was a network of caves in this comet, and he felt certain the book was in one of these. He said all of the brothers had stored their books in stone boxes before leaving their homes with them. The lid of the box had a picture of a lotus flower carved into the stone. He'd said they'd all agreed to store the boxes in caves—far away from prying eyes.

The caves on the Lizard Comet couldn't be accessed without a space suit, which was the excuse they used for Hap staying behind and hanging out in the causeway. They didn't have an extra suit and didn't have the time to teach him how to read the monitors on the life support in the suit even if they'd had an extra one.

Hap could not think of one way to get around arguments like those, though he still tried.

"Do you think the book is still here?" he asked. His fingers tapped out a random rhythm on the table.

"And you say my nail clicking is obnoxious." She put her hand down on top of his to make him quit tapping. "Stop worrying. Amar thinks the book's here. That's good enough for me."

"A little contradicting, aren't you?"

She moved her head to the side in that mock inquisitive way she had. "About what?"

"You tell me I never worry and then tell me to stop worrying . . ."

She patted his hand affectionately and shook her head. Hap was sorry when she moved her hand, though that was another thing he wasn't willing to admit. "Want to see where our seats are for the concert?" he asked.

"It's too early. Let's just walk while we have the ability to walk more than a few feet." They stood, dropping their plates into the heat bins for sanitizing. Hap had learned in the homework Laney gave them that water was too great a resource to waste on the comet because the production of it was so expensive, and it was even more expensive to ship it in. All cleaning and sanitation was done by heat. Hap had thought he understood water conservation, having grown up in the Utah desert, but after living on a spaceship where all water was recycled, and then visiting a comet where water was basically mined from the icy rocks or imported, he'd realized he didn't know anything.

The snow and dust debris continued to fly past outside the dome. Hap and Tara walked down the causeway, avoiding the holos wherever possible, and avoiding people with link boxes wherever possible. People with link boxes were always so busy paying attention to whomever they were linked to that they had a tendency to not pay attention to anyone else. Amar thought linking while doing other activities was rude.

The boxes didn't allow for super-long-distance calls—not like the plate Hap and Tara had used to link home when they were in Nova's lair, but Hap had discovered that long-distance was relative when the universe was never-ending. Hand link boxes couldn't pull enough human energy to link beyond the caller's solar system. Link plates were the only way to move beyond the solar system you were in.

A salesman who'd been standing next to his cart stepped in front of them. "You kids going to the Bo Shocks concert?"

"We already got tickets," Hap said, dismissing the guy.

"But do you have something to remember the event by? You don't want to leave the Lizard Comet without some token that proved you were here!"

"Are you selling cameras?" Tara asked hopefully.

The guy stuttered a moment before saying, "We can do better for you than that!"

Hap snorted. The guy didn't know what a camera was. It was totally obvious in the look he'd given Tara.

"We've got comet dust!" The guy opened his fist and two necklaces dropped down, dangling from his fingers. At the end of each necklace was a little glass ball. Inside each ball, powder glittered and swirled around as if in its own miniature cyclone.

Tara whined a little, which meant she was about to cave. "You don't need one of those." Hap tried to steer her away.

"You got new pants!"

"Yeah. I got new pants because Amar told us to buy new clothes so we didn't smell the ship up. He wanted us to get stuff to *wear*."

"Well, I *can* wear this! And it's gorgeous!" She shoved Hap aside and gingerly cradled one of the necklaces.

"How is that supposed to help her remember Bo Shocks?" Hap figured the question would stump the salesman who didn't know anything about cameras.

It didn't.

The salesman pulled a small glass stopper out of the top of the ball, and the swirling dust swirled right out of the ball. Music immediately began playing. It sounded vaguely familiar—probably because Svarta had been singing Bo Shocks songs for the last three days to annoy Amar.

When the salesman tipped the ball so the stopper side was facing down, the dust swirled back inside.

Tara had her link key out faster than Hap could blink and was already fastening the necklace around her neck while the salesman synced his machine to scan the credits on her link key.

Hap shook his head as they walked away. "You have no idea what you paid for that."

"I'll bet it was cheaper than your leather rock star pants."

"These aren't leather. I don't wear leather pants. They're plastic, or something." Not that plastic was any better.

"I bet your sister would love one of these," Tara commented while playing with her new necklace. "You *did* promise to get her a present the last time you linked home."

Hap grumbled but went back and bought another one for Alison. He *did* promise her a present, and she *would* probably like the stupid little thing.

They shopped some more. Tara got a new shirt that seemed like it might be on sale, but they couldn't really tell for certain. It was shiny green and long, kind of more like a short dress than a shirt. A cape thing wedged out from her shoulders, trailing down to her elbow. "What do you think?" she asked.

"It's cool," he said.

"Is it concert cool?" She smiled.

Tara worrying about fashion while careening through space on a comet made Hap laugh. "You are such a girl. It's completely concert cool."

They'd wasted enough time that they only had a few minutes to get to the concert hall. They had to run the whole way, tripping into holos and working not to run into actual people. Luckily, most of the people were gambling at the credit tables, which were strictly off limits to Hap and Tara.

The concert coliseum was on the far side of the dome. They reached the ticket taker and slapped the tickets into his hands.

Or *its* hands.

It was a robotic looking thing with a tuxedo on. The bowtie seemed entirely wrong against the metallic neck.

"You're almost late," the robotic voice said with an echo.

"We still have three minutes," Hap insisted as he took the stubs and moved past the metal man and into the coliseum.

"Holy Houdini," he breathed.

The sun, the Elektra Star, blazed on the comet's horizon behind the glass dome—or whatever the material the dome was made of. The stage was set against the dome so Bo Shocks and his band could take full advantage of the natural lighting and effects provided by the solar system. The stage was made out of glass or something shiny and clear that glinted in the sunlight.

"Beautiful," Tara whispered in agreement.

The glass acted as a prism, casting rainbow shadows all over the vast seating space full of people. It reminded Hap of the Hira—the crystal pyramid he'd handed off to Nova during his first adventure with Tara. Guilt pricked his conscience every time he thought about doing such a stupid thing.

A blast of music blared from the stage as the overhead dome lights dimmed. Hap pulled Tara along to find their seats.

"Excuse us," Hap whispered as he and Tara crawled over people to get to their seats in the middle of the row. Hap had to hand it to their new ticket salesman pal—the seats were awesome: close to the stage but not so close that they'd kink their necks trying to look up.

"Sorry," Tara apologized to the guy next to her who hadn't stopped glaring at her since they'd jostled him while getting to their seats.

Glass pillars rose from the stage, reflecting even more of the sun's light, until the entire stadium was washed out in golden rainbows. The music blared loudly, which made the pillars seem to tremble under the power of the sound.

A loud announcer voice called out over the music, "Bo Shocks and the Sungrazers!"

The crowd went animal.

Screaming, catcalling, swooning, clapping, jumping up out of their seats as though that extra little bit of height might make Bo Shocks and his band closer. Hap jumped out of his seat too. He didn't want to miss a thing.

He really, really wished he'd had a camera.

Out of the center stage rose a stone pedestal, like a throne. A man sat hunched on the throne, looking like bored royalty. The white cloak covering the bored prince's shoulders hurt to look at because it was so bright. When the stone pedestal came into line with the rest of the stage, the man threw off his cloak, jumped to his feet, and started singing.

Bo Shocks.

Totally cool.

Bo Shocks's white hair was spiked on top and matched his white shirt. He had black pants that looked a lot like the ones Hap wore, except Bo's pants had sequined suns stitched all over them, which caught the light and reflected it back.

All of the band members wore a kind of flame-colored uniform. They looked like living fire.

"Do you think those are just costumes?" Tara yelled the question right into Hap's ear to make herself heard over the music.

Hap jiggled his head in what could have been a nod or a shake. He had no idea. The band members had *feathers*. Not hair, but feathers. He didn't know why that felt stranger than some of the other things he'd seen, but it did. They seemed to have regular skin except their eyes were rimmed in feathers that swept back from their heads. And instead of hair, they had a mane of feathers that stood on end when they hit higher notes. The feathers on the girls were bright blue. The guys were golden.

It could have just been costuming . . . really good, really expensive costuming. But Hap suspected that if he were to pull one of those feathers, it would be the same as pulling on a girl's braid in school—there would likely be an, "Ouch!" and a slap to follow.

The guitar bodies were in the shapes of stars, and the neck of the instrument was designed to look like the tail of a comet.

And the music . . . Hap clapped, Tara whistled. Hap smiled enough that his cheeks hurt.

The beat thrummed through Hap's chest, and he sang along to the lyrics he knew from Svarta's singing on the ship.

The Sungrazers, led by Bo Shocks, sang on. Hap hoped the concert would never end. When the concert did finally start to wrap up, a beam of light shot from the dome into the actual comet, which exploded a hunk of dirty ice from the comet, sending it spraying into space, reflecting all the glory of the sun's light—looking like a small fireworks display.

Tara grabbed Hap's arm and frowned, her eyes widening.

"What?" Hap yelled, though he doubted she could hear him over all the screaming fans.

She pointed to where the last shiny bits of ice floated away into space and shook her head as if to say, *Did those idiots really shoot at the very rock we're standing on?*

"Yep! They did. And wasn't it so cool?" he shouted. But she didn't hear that either, which, considering how irritated she looked, was likely a good thing.

They sat back down in their seats to wait for everyone to clear out when Tara's link key blinked and beeped at her. She blew over the screen to activate the biometric lock.

Tara squinted at the screen, which meant that Laney had sent her a text message instead of sending a voice communication.

"What's she say?" he asked.

Tara smiled. "They found inscriptions on the cave walls. She said they're in the right place and should have the item soon."

"Awesome! That means we have enough time to do Confucian's backstage tour before we leave!" He stood and scanned the area, which had mostly emptied of people, to see if he could find Confucian. "There he is! Let's go."

Tara groaned but stood as she shoved her link key back into her pocket. "But we have to go as soon as Laney contacts us." She smoothed her hands over her new shirt. "Do I look okay?"

Hap stopped and stared at her. "Yeah. You look like you always look. Why?"

"Never mind. Asking you a question like that is pointless."

"How is it pointless?" he said, spreading his hands wide while she gathered her stuff and started toward Confucian. "You asked a question. I gave an answer."

Tara ignored him.

"So icy that you guys could make it!" Confucian all but beamed at seeing him. Hap felt really guilty about being kind of mean earlier, especially after Confucian had given them the tickets to the most awesome concert ever—well, the *only* concert Hap had ever seen. His mom and dad weren't exactly pro-concerts unless it involved music from some long-dead composer.

"You're not going to get into any trouble for this, are you?" Tara asked.

"Me? Trouble? Naw. Bo likes me. He thinks of me as the baby brother he never had. And I sell a lot of tickets for him, so I'm useful. C'mon. Let me show you around."

He took them up on the stage and explained how everything had been designed to utilize the sun's light to the fullest. No matter what angle the sun was at, all the pillars, instruments, and even the stage were meant to catch and reflect the light. The dome was actually a big sun catcher that gathered energy and powered the entire comet with electricity.

Confucian talked about all the technology, none of which Hap understood, and spoke with some great degree of pride that he had helped design certain elements.

"You didn't design the big explosion at the end of the concert, did you?" Tara asked.

"No. That was all Bo. He thought it added a special something . . ."

Tara sniffed. "Special, all right. He could have knocked the comet out of its elliptical with a stunt like that. He could have also made the comet unstable and crack it or something. Seriously. That kind of stupidity is begging for catastrophe."

Confucian smiled. "So you're smart."

Tara blushed deeply.

Confucian must not have noticed the blush, because he went on about the comet and the band. "Bo signed an agreement with the Lizard Comet's management. He can't do anything that will damage the comet's existence. All of the explosions are really minor, and they're strategically timed and spaced to keep everything balanced. He'll owe a ton of fines if he breaks contracts here. The Lizard Comet's been around forever, and the people in the Elektra system would be really mad if he did anything to it."

"He's blowing bits of it away. I'd call that doing something to it." Tara was an environmental activist. She got it from her mom, who was always putting up petitions to save this tree or that animal. Hap's parents really liked that aspect of Tara's mom. Hap's mom had said that a woman with fight in her is capable of surviving anything. She'd said that when Hap's dad had questioned whether or not Tara's mom would survive the divorce. She seemed to be taking it really hard, but when Tara linked to her mom, Mrs. Jordan seemed a lot better— stronger—more like the woman who saved trees and animals.

Confucian either missed Tara's contempt for the band blowing away hunks of the comet, or he chose to ignore it on purpose. "Actually, Bo's knocked out a few comets in his past. He pays the fines for destruction of celestial property if there's any inhabited planets in the system it happens in. They knocked one comet out so far that it eventually passed too close to the sun and was melted entirely. Poof. Gone. That's how the band came into their name . . . the Sungrazers. Seemed fitting. They had to evacuate that whole dome."

"What happens to the dome when the comet melts?"

Confucian smiled. "Well, as my ancestor would say, 'the cautious seldom err.'"

Hap and Tara exchanged looks. "And that means . . . ?"

"It means they melted a lot more than just a comet. There's nothing cautious about these guys."

"Who's your ancestor?" Tara asked.

"Confucius."

"Your ancestor is *the* Confucius?" Tara stopped short. Her mouth practically dropped down to her collarbone. "No way! That is so cool!"

It was Confucian's turn to snort. "Oh, yeah? Try living in that shadow. Try not to shame your ancestors and bring honor to your family name, when your family is filled with people like the wise and great Confucius."

They'd left the stage and were heading down a brightly lit hallway filled with Bo Shocks posters. Each one was framed in sparkling gold.

"Oh, I bet you're just like your ancestor," Tara said.

"That's nice of you to say, but it's why I had to leave Earth. I'm nothing like him."

"Well it's not like he's your dad or anything. He was just an ancestor. People don't have to be like all their ancestors," Hap said. "If they did, I'd be getting beheaded by some French peasant."

Confucian straightened and said, "Man who forgets his past has no future."

"Did Confucius really say that?" Hap eyed Confucian skeptically.

Confucian laughed. "Doubt it. I have trouble getting the quotes right . . . gave some people in my village advice, and because of my advice, the daughter of the head of the village council married a dung shoveler from the stables. I brought dishonor to my family."

"Seriously? Dude, that's . . ." Hap was going to say hilarious but caught a look from Tara. ". . . Terrible."

The door on the right hung open, out of which bright light poured.

"Hey, Fusion!" a voice called out.

"Fusion?" Hap said.

Confucian whispered. "Bo doesn't like my name. He can't spell it. He hates things he can't do. So he changed it. He thinks it sounds cooler this way, more like I'm really a part of the band or something."

"Hey, Bo." Confucian stepped inside the doorway. "You did great, man. Amazing. Zanest thing ever."

Hap peeked around Confucian's shoulder to get a peek of Bo up close. The guy lounged back against the poofiest couch Hap had ever seen. His blinding white concert costume made Hap squint. Bo held a glass with golden liquid as though it were a scepter. The guy looked downright depressed in spite of dressing up like royalty.

"It was awful," Bo complained. "Awful! Awful! Awful! It'll be the ruin of my career. There was no pop. No sizzle. It lacked *everything*!" He snapped his fingers on the words *pop, sizzle,* and *everything*.

Other people in the room who Hap couldn't see from the doorway immediately gushed over how wrong Bo was—how everything popped. Everything sizzled. Nothing lacked. "Zane!" they all cooed lovingly. "So totally zane!" A couple of people came into view—one of them a girl band member with feather hair. From up close the feathers definitely looked naturally attached.

Bo snapped them away and pointed at Confucian. "Tell me the truth, Fusion."

Confucian smiled and gave Bo a thumbs-up. "You are a universe of zane."

Bo accepted this praise, crooking his finger and saying, "You're right. Of course I rocked out this rock. Don't just hover in the doorway. You're letting out my light."

"I'll just go. I have friends with me." Confucian backed off to leave.

"What? Friends? Bring them in! Bring them in! They went to my concert, of course . . ." He jabbed a finger directly at Hap. "You *did* go to my concert, didn't you?"

The words had an edge to them so Hap answered quickly. "Absolutely. So zane. Never seen anything like it. You are a prince of music—"

"Just a prince?" Bo demanded to know.

"King!" Hap amended. "An emperor. You are the master of the Jedi, the Sith, and the clones!"

Tara let out a guffaw at the joke but hurried to cover it.

"Who's the girl?" Bo asked. "Girl, come in here!"

"Oh, please," Tara muttered. "You've got enough kiss-ups in there already."

She said it low enough that only Hap heard. He breathed a sigh of relief when she did as instructed and entered the room. She squinted in all the light.

"What did you think of my concert?" Bo asked.

"It was great!" she said enthusiastically. Hap breathed another sigh of relief. He never knew what Tara might actually say to someone when she determined they had a flaw that needed fixing. "But I can't believe—"

Hap pinched her arm, hard.

"Ow! Hap!" She glared and rubbed her arm.

"But what, girl? What are you *butting* about?"

Hap glared at Tara as if to say, *Be nice.*

She shrugged as if to say, *I'll be whatever I want.* "Nothing. It was just great—*zane,* even. Thanks for providing the tenuous ecosystem in which you now reside with such stellar performances that are sure to *knock* things out of their orbits while blasting away any sense of structure or responsibility. Nothing's as impressive as a cavalier attitude toward nature and the environment."

Oh great.

Everyone—the humans, the bird people, *everyone*—fell silent. Mouths hung open. Eyes went wide. And then everyone looked to Bo to see what he'd do.

Well, everyone but Hap.

Hap covered his eyes, waiting for armed guards to escort them out.

Bo stood, which sent his little entourage scurrying to adjust his fur cape and to getting him anything he needed. He strode up to Tara, wagging his finger in her face. "No one . . . absolutely *no* one has ever said such things to me."

Hap tensed, hoping the guards didn't hurt them much.

"Why don't any of you say such things to me?" he asked, now pointing at the others in the room. They all looked startled and unsure how to respond. "Best compliment I've ever been given! Have a seat, girl. You're welcome to stay, eat a bite, tell me about yourselves."

Tara smiled incredulously while furrowing her brow in disbelief. The guy really had no idea he'd been insulted.

Hap would have laughed if he hadn't spent some time on the receiving end of Tara's bashing. He hated it when he knew she was insulting him but had to really think about it to figure out exactly *how.* And he figured laughing at Bo *would* get them kicked out. Now that he was in the room, he wanted to stay. He was hanging out with an intergalactic rock star! How many people could say that?

Besides, the food spread out over the table against the wall made his stomach growl. They'd eaten before the concert, but dancing around and screaming out loud had burned a ton of calories. Hap could definitely use another meal that wasn't the nutty paste that served as breakfast, lunch, and dinner on board Nana.

Food and celebrities.

Super zane.

He headed over to the table, swept up a plate, and began filling it.

"So what's the word out on the links? People talking about me?" Bo asked Tara.

Confucian joined Hap and smiled. "He isn't that smart," he whispered, almost affectionately.

"Yeah. Caught that." Hap shot a look in the direction of the little group surrounding Bo. "But what about them? Are they not that smart too?" Hap almost made a bird-brain joke but managed to keep it to himself. And Tara said he could never keep his mouth shut.

"Oh, they're very smart. Smart enough to never explain what she really meant."

Hap laughed and bit into a doughy donut-sorta-thing. It was sweet and perfect. Like pure sugar. Hap had really missed sugar over their time away from Earth. He felt immense gratitude to find it elsewhere in the universe.

Yep. This was a great day. Kicking back with a rock star, eating food he didn't have to pay Amar back for.

Exactly perfect.

And then his link beeped.

He pulled it from his pocket and watched the text scroll over the screen.

Book not in caves as hoped.
Nova attacked ship.
Gygak escaped.
Do not return to ship.
Hide.
Nova is searching the comet for us
and the other two books we have.

It amazed Hap how fast "exactly perfect" had managed to disappear.

3. Paper Zoo

Hap leaned over to Confucian. "We've um . . . got some troubles."

Tara caught Hap's eye from across the room, where Bo had tried to command her attention.

From the way her entire face had gone pale, and her hazel eyes widened in fear, she must have received the same message on her link key.

"Troubles?" Confucian asked. "What troubles?"

"We need somewhere to hide for a bit."

Confucian's smile faded. "Hide?"

Hap really wished the guy would stop repeating everything he said. "Yeah, you know, lie low or something."

Tara had managed to scrape off Bo and his little band of brown-nosers and joined Hap at the food table. "Bo invited us to spend the night here, in the band's quarters, rather than letting us get hotel rooms. I think it's very generous and we should take him up on it." She gave Hap a look that let him know she'd worked this plan out. Hotel rooms were a terrible idea. Nova would be able to hack into any hotel roster and find out what room they were in and come blast them into teensy bits.

And Hap had no doubt Nova *would* come looking for them. The guy had serious revenge issues. Hap and Tara had betrayed him entirely. He'd want to get them back.

Hap really wished he hadn't mentioned a need to hide, not when they were being invited to stay, because now Confucian watched them both suspiciously.

"Awesome." Hap tried to ignore the looks from Confucian.

"What trouble? What are you hiding from?" Confucian demanded to know. "When a man hides from trouble in a bear's den, he's likely to get bit in the butt."

Hap grunted. "You just made that up."

Confucian smiled. "I make all of them up. It's in the blood."

Hap seriously doubted Confucius would have ever said the words "bit in the butt," but he had to admit there was a kind of wisdom in the words.

"So what are you hiding from?" Confucian asked again, less patiently.

Tara growled at Hap. "You have a big mouth, Hap Hazzard." Then she turned to Confucian and dropped her voice. "Don Nova. He took something of ours—something valuable. And he's crazy. He wants to kill us and pretty much every human who comes from earth. That means if he were to find out where you're from, you wouldn't have a long conversation before you found yourself no longer breathing. Seriously, the guy's a psychopath! Please don't tell Bo and the band. We really need to be able to stay here. If he finds us . . ."

Her eyes swam with tears. If Confucian said no to her, he would be the biggest creep in the universe—next to Nova, of course. Nobody with any shred of goodness in them could say no to Tara when she looked like that.

Confucian's smile and shrug came quickly. "Okay, I won't tell. Not like they'd care. Even if your nemesis came in here shooting drubbers, Bo would think it was a rehearsal for something to add to the show. He really does think everything's all about him. It isn't an act. It's just who he is."

As if to prove Confucian right, Bo clapped his hands and called everyone's attention to him. Hap took the opportunity to chow down a couple of desserts on his plate and something like a finger sandwich.

"Everybody! I have an amazing idea! Fusion's new girlfriend is pretty zane!"

Tara blushed, either from the compliment or from being called Confucian's girlfriend.

"We could have her onstage with us for the next performance!" Bo finished, as if somehow this idea was the most original thing ever.

Hap couldn't see how having Tara onstage would make anything better for the performance, but whatever. Crazy, egocentric rock stars didn't have to make sense.

Confucian shrugged and smiled, but his smile seemed wrong, like he didn't really mean it. He somehow seemed disappointed, which was weird. Why would he be disappointed to have Tara on the show?

Everyone clapped their approval of Bo's improvements to the concert. Everyone but Hap. He was busy eating.

And Tara. She was busy being irritated.

Tara whispered to Hap and Confucian. "I am *not* going onstage with that guy."

Confucian put down his plate. "What? Why not?"

"I would just rather not."

Hap guessed her "just rather not" was polite talk for *Bo's an idiot* and *I am not going to play the part of some fan girl just so he can feed his ego*. Over the short period of time Hap had spent with Tara, he'd become really good at interpreting her looks.

Confucian grabbed her hands in his own. "But you must! Bo is counting on you now. If you don't, it will be very bad for me. It will dishonor me to Bo and the band. Please, Tara! You must!"

Tara melted a little with her hands cupped in Confucian's. Hap groaned a little at that. But she relented and quietly agreed to go onstage if Bo insisted. Such a pushover.

"I don't know what I could do for you there. I don't sing or anything . . ." she said out loud so that everyone could hear. The bird-people band members cocked their heads to the side and stared at her through their feather-surrounded eyes.

Bo laughed. "Oh, girlie, we don't need you to sing. That's what we've got me for. We just need you to be pretty and to look adoringly at me while *I* sing.

Tara coughed out a noise of indignity, but Hap kicked her soundly in the shin. She scowled at him, but he smiled and pointed to the link key in his hand. She understood the message. *Upsetting the guy who's giving us a place to hide is really stupid.*

She pressed her lips together and faked a smile at Bo.

Everyone clapped and looked pleased.

Everyone but Tara and Hap, because he knew Tara would get him back for kicking her.

"Man who wishes to stay in audience always ends up on stage," Confucian said.

Apparently, no matter how good-looking Tara thought Confucian might be, good looks didn't get him out of her glares. "Why is she looking at me like that?" Confucian asked.

"Dude, you just called her a man." Hap ate another one of the sugary doughnuts and sighed with contentment. Was there anything better than good, old-fashioned sugar?

"Are you really going to sit there and stuff your face?" Tara asked.

"That was my plan. What else are we supposed to be doing while in hiding?"

"Don't you care at all about Mosh? We left him alone there with Gygak. If they got into the ship, then he might be hurt."

Hap frowned and put down the doughnut thing. "Of course I care. But we can't go back to the ship, and we're supposed to be staying out of sight. There isn't anything we can do."

"We have to help somehow . . ." Tara clicked her nails.

"We should leave this to the adults."

"What adults?" Confucian asked.

"The ones Tara keeps telling me to leave stuff to—just other people we're with," Hap answered.

"But you said you wanted to be involved!" Tara whispered loudly enough that some of Bo's band people looked over. After a moment they looked away again, realizing that the three teens weren't all that interesting.

Hap added a few things to his plate. They looked like fruit—star-fish shaped peaches. The sweet, grainy fruit didn't taste like a peach but more like a lemony pear.

"Watch out for the spines." Confucian said, taking a couple for himself.

Hap was about to ask "What spines?" when something jabbed into the roof of his mouth. "Ahhh!" Hap dropped his food plate to the table and yanked a sharp, bony sort of needle out of his mouth.

"Those spines," Confucian noted. "Chefs never pull the bones out of them because Bo uses them for toothpicks when he's done eating."

"Bones?" Hap eyed the food suspiciously. "I thought it was fruit."

"Are you even listening to me, Hap?" Tara demanded his attention back from the bony fruit.

"Yes, I'm listening. You want to go back and save Mosh, which you should know from experience will only get us in trouble."

"I don't want to go back. I'm not stupid . . . and don't look at me like that, Hap. I'm not! I just think we should link to Nana and ask her if everything's okay."

Hap's tongue rubbed against the place where the spine had poked him. It really hurt. And he hated the coppery taste of blood in his mouth. It reminded him of being a kid and eating dirty pennies. "So link, then. You have a link key."

"Do you think it's a bad idea?" Her face was pinched in worry. She tucked a blonde strand behind her ear.

"Yes, I think it's a bad idea."

"Why?" She went from worried to annoyed.

Honestly, that girl was going to be his ticket to insanity. "If they can trace the link back to Bo's quarters, you'll likely get us *and* his whole band killed."

She nodded, finally fixing herself a plate of food, though she stayed away from the fruity starfish. "Right. You're right." She glanced up. "And stop grinning. This one occasion doesn't change all the times you're wrong. And the fact that you were going to let me do it makes you a bonehead."

"I wasn't going to let you link. I knew if I gave you long enough on your own, you'd figure it out by yourself."

She smiled at that.

They both ate in silence for a while, watching Bo make big plans for his next concert. Their worry must have shown, because Confucian finally said, "I could check your ship."

Hap forgot he still had food in his mouth when his jaw dropped in surprise. Tara shook her head. "No. We couldn't put you in danger like that. You've done a lot for us, and we haven't really done anything to deserve all your kindness."

Confucian nodded in the direction of Bo. "It's been a while since I've had someone to hang out with. And Bo likes you—likes you enough he wants you showcased in his concert. He's never put *me* in a concert."

Ah, so that was the look of disappointment in Confucian's face when Bo made his big announcement. Hap thought it very forgiving of Confucian to be okay with Tara doing a concert that he'd never gotten to do. Confucian was a decent kind of guy.

Confucian became more animated, his almond-shaped eyes bright with excitement. "And since I brought you to Bo, that's bound to make me look good. You guys are helping me out too. You could put in a good word for me."

"Dude, Tara can put in a good word for you anyway, but she's right. Going back to the ship is a super bad idea. But . . ." He smacked his lips together. "But you don't have to *exactly* go to our ship. You could pretend to be going to a different one and just kind of check ours out on the way past. Yes! That's a brilliant plan! I should be a spy."

"A spy? Really?" She rolled her eyes at him, but he and Confucian were already whispering details. Confucian acted thrilled to be involved in something like this. Tara didn't stop them from making plans but clicked her nails together furiously and chewed on her lip. She was definitely worried about her big friend Mosh.

When Hap and Tara were first abducted and hauled into outer space, Hap never would've imagined her worrying about Mosh. The guy was huge and terrifying, like a monstrous bullfrog. But after a few days, Hap realized Mosh was harmless. Someone needed to worry about him, because he was too trusting sometimes. And though Mosh maintained watch over Gygak because he still called Gygak his friend, the little four-armed creep wouldn't hesitate to hurt Mosh if it meant escaping.

They finished eating and spent a few minutes talking to Bo and the band. Bo tightened an arm around Tara, almost unwilling to let her leave, but a bird-guy band member sidetracked him with some new lyrics, and Bo released Tara—practically with a shove—grabbed his guitar, and started strumming along.

Confucian led them to his sleeping quarters, just down the hall from where Bo's entertaining room was. The lights flickered on as soon as he entered. He hurried to pick up some scraps of paper from the floor and tossed them into a recycler. "Sorry about the mess. I don't usually have anyone come into my quarters."

Mess? Yes, it could be considered a mess, in an organized kind of way. He had shelves everywhere, and on those shelves he had various things made up of folded paper. He had dogs, cats, butterflies, dragons, elephants, horses, and all sorts of animals on one section of shelving. On another, he had a huge collection of spaceships, as if he'd spent time in the docking area studying ships. On another shelf were weird things like paper shirts and dresses and stuff, as though he were a clothing designer.

All that stuff was pretty cool and revealed that Confucian spent a lot of time alone in his room with no typical entertainment. The guy seriously needed to get a hobby—one that actually involved people.

But what commanded all the attention in the room was the corner where his bed sat. A life-sized tree made up entirely of folded paper stood in the corner, the branches hanging over the top half of his bed like some sort of canopy. Folded-up paper birds perched on the paper branches. It was an origami masterpiece.

"Now that's just freaking awesome," Hap said at the same time Tara exclaimed the beauty of such delicate workmanship or some such garbage. Who described stuff as *delicate beauty* when they could say *freaking awesome*?

"Did you make all this?" Tara asked.

Confucian looked very pleased with himself and nodded with a slight bow. "Man who friends the paper bird will never find himself alone."

"Is that one of your ancestor's sayings, or is that an original?" Hap wondered.

"Totally original." Confucian looked pleased by that, too.

"I thought origami was Japanese, not Chinese."

"The art of *Zhe Zhi* is Chinese. My grandmother taught me. The falcon was her favorite bird." He pointed to the tree, where Hap realized the birds did look like miniature falcons. Confucian then started rummaging through a closet. He pulled out a black-and-white piece of hard plastic. Hap bit his lip to keep from laughing when Confucian placed the thing on his head. The plastic thing was a hat. It went down to just over his eyebrows and down over his ears a bit. It was domed on the top with black-and-white colors swirled together so it looked like a funky plastic dessert. Maybe it was just that Hap still felt a little hungry.

Confucian shrugged into a long black jacket with a high collar that grazed across his cheeks. He closed it together using three large snaps that glowed red as they were fastened. The glow faded to a dull burgundy after a few moments. Confucian looked very cool—like a Chinese gangster.

Tara sighed again. That sigh was really starting to bug Hap.

"What are you dressing up for? It wasn't cold in the docking area," Tara asked.

Confucian shrugged. "Just trying to keep from being too noticeable."

That made sense to Hap—though the outfit seemed a little over the top for someone trying to stay hidden. But he wasn't about to complain. Confucian was helping them out in a huge way. Hap worried about what might have happened to Mosh. He'd feel better if he had some information.

"What station are you docked in?" Confucian asked.

"I . . ." Hap looked at Tara and winced. "Didn't look for a number or anything. We had the link-key maps and . . ."

Tara took charge and started giving instructions. "It's docked in the middle, on the left as you head toward the far end of the docking area. Our ship is the one shaped like this . . ." She pulled out her link key and blew over the top of it to power it up. She keyed in the holo tablet function and, with her finger, drew a rough sketch of the ship in the air above the link key. The lines she traced with her finger glowed faint green over her link key.

It was a crude drawing, but a zillion times better than anything Hap could've done. Especially with a finger. Hap couldn't even make a pencil do the right sorts of lines on paper. Art was not his thing. Tara was full of little surprises like that.

Confucian nodded. "You are a very good artist. My mother was as well. No one painted as she did. Her work always seemed like it could come to life right from the paper she drew on." He glanced toward his big paper tree. "She would have loved the things the universe could have taught her. I wanted to go home and show her. But no one explained going home was not an option once I left."

Hap furrowed his brow. "Just because of how you traveled though . . . right? Going home for us is different because of how we traveled, right?" He hated the suspicion in his voice. Amar and Laney had talked him through this a dozen times—each time losing a little more patience with him. They said that the way Nana traveled through the wormholes made all the difference.

"I don't know how you traveled," Confucian said.

"Wormholes and spiral drops." Hap's heart rate went up while he waited for Confucian to answer.

"You should be fine," he said finally.

Hap scowled but tried to take the comment as good news. The comment agreed with Laney and Amar's explanation, in a way.

Hap didn't want to get home and find that a century had passed and everyone he'd known and loved were already dead.

"How long have you been gone from home?" Tara asked.

"Five years." Confucian's voice cracked slightly, and he looked away. "Five years at light speed changes a lot of things at home."

It almost sounded like one of his Confucius sayings—profound and meaningful and a little bit sad. Hap had enough sad things going on in his life and didn't feel like adding any new ones. So he smiled brightly. "It's awesome you're willing to help us. How can we stay in contact with you while you go look?" When a conversation dropped into overly sentimental messiness, it was time to change the subject.

"We'll sync our link keys. It's the easiest way." Confucian pulled out a link key that resembled Tara's in shape and size but was different in every other way. The thing looked like Hap's kid sister, Alison, had gotten a hold of it. It sparkled with little jewels in the shapes of a comet and sun circling each other in an elaborate elliptical. The other side had a really tacky jeweled rendition of Bo Shocks's face. Hap didn't laugh. Confucian couldn't be blamed for the psycho ego of a rock star.

He *wanted* to laugh, though. Nana would have been so proud of his restraint.

Confucian punched his thumb against the sensor to bring his link key to life. When it turned on, it sang out, "Put your hands together for Bo Shocks and the Sungrazers!"

"Wow," Tara said. "You're a big fan, huh?"

"Of Bo? Who isn't? He's taken care of me for a long time now. He's kind of like a really icy big brother."

A brother who never lets you onstage with him, Hap thought, but he kept it to himself. Nana would be rewarding him with extra tubes of nutty paste if he kept this good behavior up.

The link keys glowed when brought together close enough they touched. Confucian held them like this until they beeped.

"Okay. We're synced. I'll link you when I'm close to the ship." He put the link key in his pocket and loped out of the room with his jacket swishing around his knees.

"So what do we do in the meantime?" Hap said, looking around the room.

Tara's eyes were slits. "We don't touch things, that's what."

"You say that like I was planning on running around ripping up his paper collection."

Tara lifted an eyebrow. Hap wished he knew how to do that. It bugged him that Tara could do it when he'd practiced and practiced and still couldn't make that muscle above his eye do anything more than twitch slightly. "You might not plan on ripping up his stuff, but that's what's likely to happen if you don't just keep your hands to yourself."

Hap made a pshaw sound and did a walk around the room. He purposely kept his arms folded to prove to Tara that he wasn't going to mess with anything. Several minutes later, Tara's link key beeped.

A little holo of Confucian showed above her link key. It was from the point of view of his hands so they were looking up into Confucian's nose. Wet nose hairs were really gross. Hap smirked at Tara. *Let's see her sigh over that.*

Tara, as if taking a lesson from his strange viewpoint, held her link key high enough that Confucian would see her face. She sniffed self-consciously. Hap snickered.

"There's the ship," Confucian whispered, and he shifted the link key so they could see for themselves.

"Yes," Hap and Tara both said at once. "That's it."

Hap couldn't see anyone standing guard over it like he'd expected. Confucian walked slowly—his pace almost ridiculous. Hap decided Confucian hadn't seen enough spy movies. The guy practically stood still, he moved so slowly. That kind of action would get him caught immediately.

"You gotta keep moving, man. You can't hang out there and not get noticed," Hap said.

"I am not hanging out. I am walking."

"Walking *slowly*. Zombies move faster than that. Keep going!" Hap didn't mean it to sound rude, but it made him really nervous to think that Nova's guys could pop out from anywhere. Things around the ship appeared quiet in the hazy fuzz of the hologram. Nothing moved. Nothing breathed. It seemed like the quiet before something bad happened.

Hap shook his head. "I don't like this," he whispered.

"Me either." Tara's fingernails hovered over each other in midclick as if she held her breath waiting for something.

Confucian rounded the side of the ship, moving on to the next dock. His pace changed slightly, so he moved faster, but not a lot faster. Confucian must've held his link key a bit behind him because it gave a side view of the ship. On seeing that viewpoint, Hap hissed softly.

"What?" Confucian whispered. "What did you see?"

Tara must not have seen, because she turned to Hap. "What?"

"Nova," Hap's voice shook as his eyes met Tara's.

"Where?" she demanded to know.

They'd stopped paying attention to Confucian but jerked their focus back to the holo floating above Tara's link key when Confucian yelled, "Help!"

They heard a loud thump and then another as the view from the link key in Confucian's hand fell to the ground and blurred into the snow of static and a lost communication.

Confucian had been ambushed.

4. Time Out for Tara

At the sound of Confucian crying out, Hap heard another noise that he couldn't quite place. A fluttering, like a breeze through trees.

"Oh, no!" Tara yelled as Hap whispered, "Holy Houdini . . ."

"They've got Confucian now!" Tara wailed, throwing her hands over her face and pacing in tight circles where she stood. "We got him captured! This is *our* fault."

"Holy Houdini," Hap repeated, following her in her crazy little pacing.

"Stop saying that and think of something!" she yelled at him. "What did you see? Did you see Nova? Did you see anyone else? What did you see?"

Hap hadn't seen Nova. Not exactly—even if he *had* said Nova's name. What he'd seen was the catlike thing that Amar had called semi-intelligent—Nova's pet. Hap had seen its tail flash around one of the arms of Nana's landing gear. If Nova's pet was there, then Nova himself would be around too.

Hap knew what he had to do. He had to go and rescue Confucian. Hazzards were men of honor, and men of honor didn't leave people behind.

"Holy Houdini," Hap whispered again.

"I said stop saying that!" As she yelled, the other noise, the strange fluttering sound, intensified and Tara jerked her head up in time to yell, "Look out!"

Hap turned while instinctively ducking—it seemed the natural thing to do when someone screamed to look out. The paper tree by Confucian's bed wriggled to life and sprang out at them.

No. Not the tree—the *birds*. The paper birds that had been perched on the paper branches were in attack mode. A sharp paper beak poked Hap's arm as he swung it over his head to keep the birds away from his face before they pecked his eyes out.

"Ow!" Hap howled as dozens more sharp pokes collided into his arm and the back of his head. Tara screamed and yelled and swatted with her hands to make them stop dive-bombing her.

"Why are they attacking?" she yelled to Hap.

"How the heck should I know?" Hap yelled back. It wasn't like he'd done anything aggressive. He hadn't ripped off any paper wings or caught any of them on fire with a magnifying glass. And who knew what ticked off bits of folded-up paper anyway?

Tara squeaked and squealed as little paper wings beat against her head and sharp paper beaks speared her skin. They moved to the door as one, trying to evade the assault.

The birds moved along with them, pecking, diving, and flapping. The door wouldn't open for them the way it had opened for Confucian. Tara beat on it with her fists. Hap kicked at it.

"It won't open!"

"Yeah! Noticed that!" Hap yelled back. He tried to glance around the wall of white fluttering to see if there was any other exit, while trying to cover his eyes to keep them from being pecked out of their sockets.

"A door!" Tara grabbed his arm. "Hap! A door!" She pulled him along toward what he hoped would be a swift escape.

And then he saw it—a door, just as Tara said. Hap reached for the handle, which was made out of rough stone and shaped like a comet, with sparkly rhinestones embedded in it. Hap pushed the handle down, and the door swung open. He had to hold it to keep from opening all the way and letting all of the birds in. Tara squeezed through first, and Hap followed immediately after.

They slammed the door, catching several paper wings in the doorjamb. The wings still moved helplessly and lamely against the wood like the arms of mutant zombies not quite fully dead. A few actually made it into the bathroom with them, but Hap turned on the faucet and cupped his hands to make bowls so he could hurl water at the little paper demons.

Tara joined in on the counterattack. In a few minutes the paper birds were soggy messes of pulp on the floor. They kept throwing around the water for several minutes after the last bird went down. Tara stomped her foot on it. Both of them heaved great gulping breaths and inspected the tiny bathroom to make sure their assailants really were all gone.

Tara slumped against the door and slid to the ground, her foot dragging a mass of soggy pulp across the floor. "We're stuck here."

"Maybe not . . ." Hap said, though he knew she was right. They were completely, in every way, stuck. It's not like they could exit through the toilets or anything, and they couldn't go back out into the room without the birds attacking again. And what would be the point of moving into the other room? That door was locked or broken or something. It wasn't about to open for them.

Tara glared her typical glare at him before dragging her hand over her face.

"You know, my mom says if you keep making faces all the time, your face will freeze like that. Do you want your face to be frozen looking like you're going to kill someone?"

She didn't stop glaring. "If that person is you, it might not bother me so much."

Hap laughed as though she were joking. She didn't laugh, but her lip curved up in a smile. Little drops of blood speckled her forehead. And her forearms. And her cheeks. And the backs of her hands. Hap looked down at his own arms and hands, which weren't any better.

Hap searched around the bathroom to find a towel or something they could use to clean up with. He found a basket of rolled-up hand towels under the sink and ran one under warm water before stooping down to Tara on the floor. He pressed the warm cloth onto her cheeks, dabbing until it seemed the blood had stopped, then he moved to her arms, but Tara took it from his hands. "I can clean myself up, Hap." Her voice trembled slightly, and she bit into her lip a little.

He shrugged. "I know. Just trying to help."

The glares and scowls and general displeasure seemed to have left her face, replaced by one of dread. "I know you are. I'm sorry. I just . . . What happened to Confucian?"

Hap shook his head as he ran a towel under the warm water for himself and dabbed at blood on his own face. "I don't know."

"What are we going to do?"

"Go help him." He stopped her glare with one of his own. "Don't look at me like that. We got him into this mess, and he's been nice to us. He deserves our help."

"Of course we need to help him—you're right. But what bright ideas do you have to get us out of here so we *can* help? Anything? Because honestly, Hap, I got nothing."

"Too bad we don't have any water guns."

Tara lifted her chin up and twisted her head to the side just a little so she could see into the shower area. "Shampoo bottles!"

She jumped to her feet and shoved aside the curtain designed to look like Bo Shocks's concert costume. She swiped the bottles from the ledge and turned back to Hap. The triumphant gleam in her eye made him take a step back as though she were aiming a weapon at him.

"You're finally losing it, aren't you?" he asked when she twisted off the caps and dumped the contents out onto the shower's tiled floor.

"This is your idea, so if I'm losing it, so are you."

Hap peeked over her shoulder. "How is wasting Confucian's shampoo my idea?"

"We'll fill these up with water. Then we can use them like water guns. We can spray the paper birds and get to the door."

"Brilliant. How would you think up something like that?"

She grinned. "Lots of water fights with my mom. I had to get inventive or she'd always win."

Hap nodded, feeling the lump that formed in his throat whenever either of them talked about home. Tara's mom would be proud to know that a few hours of playtime with her daughter had turned into useful tactical information.

"Great. How are you getting out the door?"

He hated deflating her excitement, because the shampoo bottles idea was a really good one, but they needed to think everything through before he was willing to let those demon paper birds get to him again.

She searched the bathroom, opening the cabinet and rummaging through things. "His link key was biocoded to his fingers . . . maybe . . . no . . . I have no idea . . ."

Hap grabbed one of the bottles and filled it with water. "Maybe the door isn't really locked. Maybe we just couldn't see how to open it because we were a little busy with the pigeon attack. Let's get rid of them. We can always retreat back here if we have to."

She nodded her agreement and filled her own bottle.

"Ready?" Hap's hand rested on the door handle, waiting for her to nod her approval before he swung it open and held their bottles at the ready. They caught the first attack wave full on, spraying down the pieces of possessed paper easily. They had to retreat back to the bathroom several times to refill before they finally finished off the last of Confucian's personal assault team.

Hap had been right about the door. They only needed to lift a latch near the top that automatically fell into its locked position when the door closed. Hap suspected Confucian's biocode would have lifted it automatically.

"Well, I feel stupid," Tara muttered about the lock as she peered around the corner to see if anyone was coming down the hall.

They cleaned up a little before venturing out. They didn't want to get delayed by security simply because they looked like bleeding war refugees.

Hap blew a warm breath over his link key to activate the map and hurried to follow it back to the docking area. Tara stayed at his heels until he stepped onto the stone floor of the docking station. There she tugged on his arm. "Careful," she cautioned.

He nodded. "Careful," he agreed.

They crept around ships, trying to spot any sign of Nova or his lousy cat or his lousy guards. They'd ducked behind the landing gear of a ship that looked like a giant hairdryer. It was parked right next to Nana. It took all of Hap's energy not to run to his own ship and take down anyone who dared mess with Mosh, but he didn't have a weapon. Shampoo bottles only went so far.

He peeked around the corner and then turned back to Tara. "I don't see anything."

"Confucian didn't see anything either before we lost him."

Hap did not like the way she said that. They hadn't lost him. He would be fine. Confucian would be fine. Mosh would be fine. *Everyone* would be fine!

Tara slipped around him and peeked around the corner herself. She drew back sharply.

"What?" Hap breathed the word more than said it.

"Gygak."

"You saw him? Where is he?" Hap was surprised she'd heard his whispered words. His heart pounded so loudly, he couldn't hear himself over the noise.

"He's in the control room."

He nodded and peeked for himself. Sure enough, Gygak stood in front of the large window in the control room. He wasn't looking out the window, though. He appeared to be talking to someone. No. Not talking. He was arguing, from the way all four of his arms waved wildly like they did when he was angry and trying to make a point. Hap couldn't see anyone else in the control room because whoever Gygak argued with stood too deep inside. If he went around the back of the ship, no one in the control room would see him.

"Stay here." He ducked around the back corner before Tara could stop him.

He thought he heard the beginnings of a hiss from her, but she cut off whatever she might have said, understanding the need for absolute silence.

He made it to Nana and leaned against the ship, the scratched and dented metal feeling comforting to him somehow. He ran his hand over Nana as though she were a loyal dog or pet that needed soothing after having been in the care of a dog catcher. "You're okay, girl," he said.

At his words, a compartment opened up in Nana's underside, and a black stick dropped out. Hap looked around to see if anyone noticed the clatter as the stick hit the stone floor. The few people four ships down were busy dealing with crettles. The blowers they used to burn the little space hitchhikers off weren't anywhere near as effective as the box of scourab beetles that cleaned Nana.

He took a deep breath and chanced diving out of the shadow where he hid to the underside where the stick lay.

He snatched it up and raced back to his previous hiding place. *Laney's going to kill us,* he thought. And she would. She'd be furious that they were going directly against her orders to stay hidden and to stay away from the ship. But they didn't have a choice. They couldn't have just left Confucian to face Nova on his own! They had to find out what happened. It was the right thing to do.

Which was why Tara hadn't argued about Hap's directly disobeying Laney's message. Under normal circumstances, Tara never would've agreed to doing anything that went against Laney's and Amar's wishes. Since the last time they'd disobeyed, they ended up endangering the lives of pretty much everyone—including themselves.

Hap turned the cold black rod over in his hand, trying to see what it was and how it worked. It looked like a magician's wand—long and tapered. Holding it tickled a memory in his mind. He'd seen it before . . . where?

And then it hit him.

Svarta had used this when Tremble had given in to Googool and started blasting holes into the ship. Tremble was a twin soul from the planet Delat. Tremble was nice when she was Tremble, but when Googool took over, bad things happened.

That was why Svarta had knocked Googool out with the stick. How had Svarta done that?

Svarta had aimed it and yelled something about a blackout. Then Tremble/Googool had collapsed. Was the word *blackout* like *abracadabra*? Was it a spell of some sort?

No. That was dumb. Magic was about tricks and knowing how things worked—not using spells. Real magic came from knowledge and practice and believing in yourself. Grandpa Hazzard had spent years teaching that concept to Hap when Hap was learning basic tricks that seemed too hard to master.

Hap had no idea how this black wand worked, but he did know that Nana had given it to him on purpose. She'd known he was near and had handed him a tool that would help. As he further examined it, he noticed a slight depression at the base of the stick. He pushed his finger into the depression at the same time he heard footfalls behind him. Startled by the noise, and fairly certain the noise meant he'd been caught, he turned the stick on whoever stood behind him.

Tara crumpled to the ground like a puppet with its strings cut.

"Holy Houdini," he whispered. "Tara!" Hap rushed to her side and put a finger at her neck to check for a pulse. He'd never been able to check for a heartbeat on someone's wrist, no matter how many times his health teacher made him try it.

"Stupid. Stupid. Stupid!" Hap hissed.

She had a pulse and was still breathing, which meant he hadn't likely done any real damage to her, but knocking her out was definitely not something she'd thank him for—especially if it ended up with them as Nova's prisoners again.

Hap glanced around. No one had noticed still. He dragged Tara back to the ship that looked like a hair dryer and hid her in the shadows by the landing gear. She blended pretty well in those shadows, and he felt pretty sure she'd be okay there until she woke up. He hoped the ship didn't leave before then. Tara was going to be mad enough as it was.

He went back to Nana and crept to the hatch. It seemed suspicious that the hatch was open—like someone knew Hap couldn't resist entering simply because it *was* open.

But what if Nana had been the one to leave it open? What if she was trying to give him access to the ship so he could take it back? She had, after all, handed him the blackout stick. He held the stick firmly in his hands and took a deep breath before stepping out onto the ramp leading into who knew what mess.

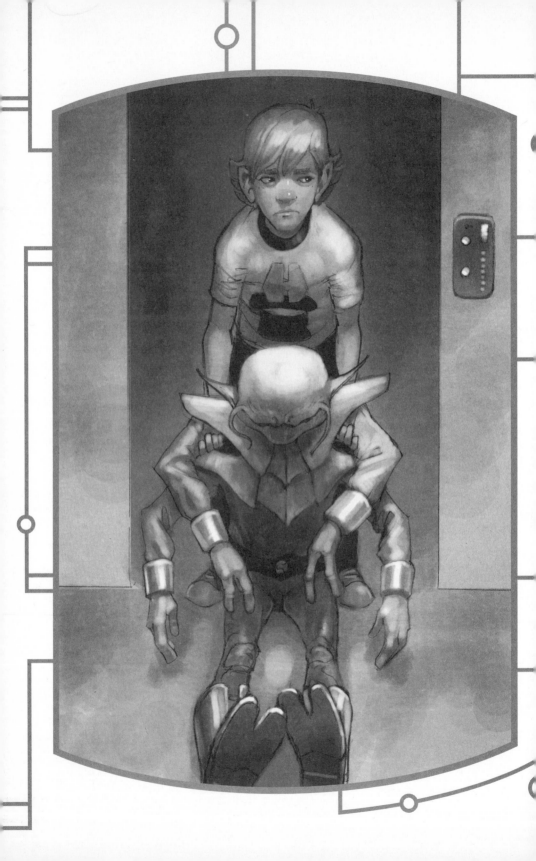

5. Missing Persons

Hap's erratic breathing sounded loud in his ears as he made his way up the ramp and into the belly of the ship he'd come to call home. He peeked around the corner of the ship's entryway and down the hall. Empty.

He tiptoed down the hall and into the airlift tube. Nana hadn't spoken to him since he'd boarded the ship, but he'd been given access to pretty much everything, which had to mean she was leading him to the control room, where he'd seen Gygak. She meant for him to do this. She wouldn't let him walk into a trap. Nana's programming wouldn't allow her to endanger one of her charges. Telling himself this kept him from scooting on back down the ramp and over to where Tara lay hidden in the shadows.

He let his thumb hover over the depression in the black stick as he glided up in the airlift tube. He floated to the top, where a platform pushed out of the wall and settled underneath him. Hap felt a tugging at his feet as they reconnected with the solid surface. He hesitated at the door, knowing that it made a swishing noise when it opened, which meant he had to act fast as soon as it did open. Gygak was inside and someone else—someone Hap hadn't already identified.

Gygak alone didn't really scare Hap. Gygak was a coward, and he was pretty dumb besides. When Hap first met them, he thought Mosh to be the dumb one and Gygak to be the brains of the pair. He'd thought this because Mosh talked slow and Gygak's voice was always on superspeed.

Hap soon found that the speed of speaking had nothing to do with the speed of thinking. Mosh was actually really smart. Gygak . . . not so much.

What scared Hap now wasn't Gygak but the unknown person with Gygak. Most of Nova's people had weapons bigger than Hap's leg.

"Well . . . staying out here won't solve anything," Hap whispered. "I'm ready, Nana."

And with that declaration, the door swished open, revealing the control room.

Hap had the stick aimed at the door and pressed his thumb hard into the indentation, figuring he didn't care who was on the other end of the blackout stick. If they had control over the ship, and they weren't Laney, Amar, Svarta, or Tremble, then they deserved whatever they got.

It surprised Hap to see Confucian crumple to the floor.

"Oh, no!" Hap groaned. How could he knock out two of his friends in a row?

"Nice move," Gygak said.

He looked smug and satisfied to see Hap make such a dumb mistake, which made Hap furious. Hap turned the blackout stick on Gygak and pressed the indentation again. "Shut up, Gygak," Hap said as Gygak fell into a heap on the floor.

Hap scrubbed his hand through his hair. "Holy Houdini!" he said as he looked at the two unconscious bodies in the control room. "Now what do I do?"

"You should tie up the Gygan before he wakes up," Nana suggested.

Hap jumped and threw his arms up as she spoke, surprised yet grateful to hear the ship's voice. If she was talking, no one else was on board.

At least, he *hoped* that was the case. "Where is everyone else?" he asked while he tried to figure out what he could use to tie Gygak up. He couldn't see anything useful in the control room. "Where's Mosh?"

"They've taken Mosh," Nana said.

"Do you know where?" He couldn't believe he'd accidentally knocked out both Tara *and* Confucian. He left the control room to find something with which to tie up Gygak. He continued his conversation with Nana as he went.

"Gygak informed Mosh's captors of my recording capabilities. They never said or did anything that would leave clues as to their plans. They marched Mosh off the ship and left Gygak and the lemsk here to await the return of everyone else."

"Lemsk?" Hap interrupted Nana, worried that someone else was hidden on the ship. Hap didn't want to be ambushed.

"Don Nova's pet. It's a lemsk." Nana didn't seem annoyed that Hap had interrupted. "Of course, I communicated with Laney over the link key, warning her *not* to return to the ship. It surprised me when they brought an unknown prisoner aboard. The lemsk had felt the boy to be dangerous to them."

"How would a dumb cat know if Confucian was dangerous or not?" Hap entered the supply room.

"A lemsk is slightly more than a cat—smarter, capable in ways an earth cat would never be."

"Cats are smart," Hap said as he dug around the supply room and found some sort of stuff that looked suspiciously like duct tape. He hurried back to the control room.

"Cats are smart. Lemsks are much smarter. And since you actually know the boy in the control room, it proves the lemsk accurate. The boy was a danger to Nova's plans."

"Did they hurt him?" Hap felt absolutely awful that he'd gotten Confucian mixed up in the whole mess.

"Gygak and the lemsk hardly had resources to cause harm to the boy. *You* were the one who blacked him out." Nana's tone sounded less than approving.

"Hey! You were the one who gave me the blackout stick in the first place!" The control room door swished open for Hap.

"Yes. To use on the Gygan. Certainly not to use on Tara or the boy."

Hap cringed. So Nana knew he'd knocked out Tara too. There would be no getting over the stupidity of such a move. Svarta, who never missed a chance to tease, was definitely going to tease him about it. But dang it all! Tara had sneaked up on him. He'd told her to stay put. If she'd done what he'd told her, she'd have been fine.

"When will they wake up?" he asked instead of getting defensive the way he'd wanted to.

"Your focus was off. It shouldn't last long on any of them."

"What does my focus have to do with your magic wand?" He crouched down next to Gygak and taped his four arms together. The tape made a ripping sound as he wound it around the Gygan's hands. He moved to Gygak's feet—likely using more tape than was really needed, but he wasn't taking chances. Gygak had a way of getting out of trouble he deserved to be in.

"It isn't a wand, and isn't magic. It runs off of energy—like when you link home. The pulse of your brain powers the blackout stick. You weren't using that much mental energy when you made your attack."

Getting a lecture about not using enough mental energy from a computer who had no real mental energy of her own was salt in the wound for Hap.

"So what should I do now?" he asked, surveying his handiwork with the duct tape. Svarta would be proud of him. No way would Gygak ever get out of those wrappings. *Houdini* himself wouldn't have been able to escape.

"You should drag the Gygan into the cargo hold," Nana suggested. "It's not comfortable there like it was in his own cabin, but he's not really deserving comfort right now, is he?"

"No. He isn't. How did he get out?"

"Mosh is far too trusting. He gave the Gygan a little freedom. The Gygan did the rest. I tried to warn Mosh, but no one ever listens to me." She sighed.

Whoever programmed Nana with motherly nurturing tendencies got it one hundred percent right. She sounded very motherly. Hap reached around and grabbed Gygak under the arms to drag him out.

"How do we keep Nova's guys from getting back in?" Hap wondered. He was glad the airlock held Gygak's weight without Hap having to do anything. It made moving the little four-armed creep a lot easier.

"I've already locked the hatch, but you need to get Tara in here. Leaving her out and exposed as you have is not a good idea. They do not need more hostages than they have."

Hap halted. "Hostages? As in plural? They have more than one?"

"Laney returned in spite of my warning to stay away."

Hap's stomach dropped into his toes. They had Mosh *and* Laney.

"What the heck was she doing coming back after you told her not to?" His mind raced over the ramifications of this new turn of events. *Laney.* The closest thing he had to a mom out in the wild of the universe. And now she was captured.

"The same thing as you, verifying Mosh's safety. *You* were also told to stay away."

The cargo hold door swished open and Hap dragged the Gygan inside. "Yeah, but I didn't get myself captured!" Hap dropped Gygak's weight once he got him far enough into the cargo hold that the door could still close.

"You only had the Gygan to contend with. Laney was outnumbered by quite a few, and she came alone."

Hap heard the reproach in her voice. "Well, why didn't you shoot at the guys taking her?"

"All firearms are banned under the dome—for safety reasons. No pulse or plasma weapons work in the docking area. Lizard Comet management has successfully rendered the use of such weapons useless. And are you getting Tara or not?"

"Of course I am," he muttered, hurrying to the hatch, which Nana had to unlock for him. He dragged Tara on board the ship.

It bothered him that no one working in the docking area seemed to care that he was dragging bodies all over the place. Tremble had said that these casino resorts were pretty weird, with people having an anything-goes attitude, but not worrying about a teenager moving bodies? That was way beyond weird.

He accidentally slammed Tara's shoulder into the side of the door. He apologized even though she wasn't awake to hear it.

Once Hap had Tara and Confucian in the control room, he sat down to wait. He wasn't sure what he waited for exactly, but he didn't know what else to do. Sitting down increased the odds that no one would see him from the windows the way he had seen Gygak. He worried about Mosh and Laney and the whole mission of getting books, which felt like nothing but failure at the moment.

"Do Svarta and Amar know about Laney?"

"Yes."

"And they aren't back here searching for her and Mosh?"

"Of course they are searching for her. But searching here would do no good since she was taken *away* from here."

He hated it when Nana got snippy with him.

And then it occurred to him that he hadn't asked the question that really mattered now that Gygak was taken care of. He'd been so worried and busy, it hadn't seemed relevant.

"Nana? Where's the lemsk?"

Nana tsked. "The lemsk is locked in the pantry. I opened it on purpose to hopefully lure her inside and then shut it when she did go inside."

"I thought you said that lemsks were smart."

Nana tsked again. She tsked a lot when Hap was around. "I said they were smart. I never said they were brilliant."

"Do you think it's messing up our food?"

"That is not your most pressing concern," Nana said.

Hap scowled, distracted a little from their conversation by the fact that Tara's head jiggled a little. He really hoped that meant she'd wake up soon. "Laney and Mosh . . . I should be worrying about them," he said.

"While Laney and Mosh are a pressing concern, they are not *your* most pressing concern."

"What is *my* most pressing concern, then?" He rolled his eyes as he repeated her words.

"The lemsk is wearing a tracking collar, which also has recording capabilities. I would imagine this is a new accessory for Don Nova's pet because she scratches at it all the time. It would appear she isn't used to the device yet."

"Why is a flea collar *my* pressing concern?"

"The collar would inform Nova that the lemsk has been captured. Chances are high that he has his people coming to our location to determine the nature of the lemsk's misfortune."

Hap leaped to his feet. "And you were going to tell me this when?" Hap yelled, as he quickly checked on Confucian and Tara. *Wake up! Wake up, please!*

"I told you just a moment ago." Nana sounded baffled by his question. One would think that after dealing with Tremble and Svarta, Nana would be more used to sarcasm.

Hap crouched down by Tara and patted at her cheeks. "Tara! Tara, you gotta get up. Nap time's over. Tara!" Her eyelid twitched, but other than that, she didn't move at all. He ran back to the supply room, where the pantry and the locked-up lemsk were. He heard noises in the pantry as the lemsk thrashed around inside. They'd definitely need new food supplies. The catlike lemsk had probably shredded everything in there. Hap grabbed a hydration packet.

He ripped it open as soon as he reentered the control room and dumped the water on Tara's face. She awoke immediately, sputtering and spitting water away from her mouth. "What in the world do you think you're doing?" she yelled.

"Waking you up."

"Drowning me is how you wake me up?"

"It's important!" he insisted.

"What's important? What's going on? Is Confucian okay?"

Hap worked to keep the tremor out of his voice. "He's fine. But they've got Mosh and . . . and Laney."

6. Confusing Confucian

"Laney?" Her eyes glossed over with tears.

"Yeah. The others are looking for her, which means they aren't looking for the book anymore. We don't have time to mess around." He used what little water was left in the pouch on Confucian, who mumbled and rolled over in his sleep.

"Help me get him up too!" Hap demanded.

"Where are we?" Tara might have come to consciousness yelling at him, but her mind must have still been pretty fuzzy, because she moved slowly like she was still dreaming.

"On board Nana. I've gotten Gygak locked in the cargo area, and Nova's lemsk is locked in the pantry. They had Confucian, and I accidentally knocked him out."

"You knocked him out? How? He's bigger than you." Tara folded her arms in the way she did whenever she challenged Hap on anything. She did that as often as Nana tsked.

"He's not that much bigger . . ." Hap said defensively. The blackout wand was stuffed down his sock for safekeeping. She didn't seem to remember he'd knocked her out too, so he figured he'd keep that information to himself. "And if you could see past that lame little crush you've got on him, you'd realize that I just saved him. Gygak's tied up in the cargo hold." He huffed and crossed his own arms. *So there!* he wanted to add but didn't. He didn't want her to think he was sulking.

Her ears turned bright pink, and little spots of red stained her cheeks. "I do not have a crush on him!"

"Oh yeah, then why do you sigh like a girl all the time when you're around him?"

"I am a girl . . . and if you think I'm gonna—"

"Children?" Nana interrupted again.

"What?" they both snapped. At the same time.

"You're friend is now awake. Probability predicts that Don Nova is returning to collect his pet. He should not be able to breach my walls, as he would have to attack me directly with weaponry that is not allowed in docking stations throughout Elektra's galaxy. But perhaps you can argue over Tara's feelings for your new friend somewhere more appropriate—somewhere in hiding . . ."

Tara's face went even redder, which Hap didn't think was possible. She looked at the floor instead of turning to see where Confucian blinked in confusion.

"Man who sleeps without pillow is man with huge headache." Confucian held his head in his hands, not seeming to notice Tara's embarrassment or even what Nana had said to make Tara embarrassed.

"Can you walk?" Hap looked hopefully at Tara and Confucian.

They both nodded, though Tara still refused to look up.

"Then let's get going." Hap tried helping Tara to her feet, but she swatted his hands away.

"Ow! My shoulder hurts like crazy!" She rolled her shoulder back and gently probed the place where Hap had slammed her into the door.

He busied himself with helping Confucian up so she wouldn't see his guilty expression.

"I think you should tell me more of what's going on here," Confucian said as they moved toward the hatch and the ramp that led to the docking bay. "That little Gygan ranted about a lot of things. He said you had him as a prisoner, and he was only trying to get free. *Were* you keeping him prisoner?"

It was Hap's turn to blush. Confucian's voice sounded so accusing. "Well, yeah, but it isn't like it sounds. We had to. He tried to shoot Tara. And he nearly got the scientist killed. And he's helping a guy who wants to destroy Earth. He's one of the bad guys!"

Confucian leveled a look at Hap that made Hap stop short.

"That is what the Gygan said about you."

"Well, he's lying!" Tara interjected before Hap could respond. "Gy-geek is a weasel, a snake, a rat, and a . . ." She floundered for another insult and finally settled on, "creep! He's totally not trustworthy. He's the kind of guy who would backstab his own mother if he thought he'd get something out of it. He has the moral integrity of an ax murderer!"

"So I'm guessing you don't like him?" Confucian said.

"Of course I don't!" Tara sputtered, but Hap had caught the brief smile on Confucian's face. He'd sent out that last jab to tease Tara. Hap couldn't help it. He liked Confucian—and not just because the guy gave him free tickets to a concert.

"We'll explain on the way to somewhere else—somewhere that isn't here. We'll tell you everything you want to know. We'll even give you Tara's link key code so you guys can be link friends or whatever."

Tara leveled her very best of glares at Hap, but Hap didn't mind at all. She deserved a little teasing. She must have had a bigger crush on Confucian than Hap thought for her to be getting so ticked off about the jokes.

"You'll tell me everything?" Confucian confirmed.

"Everything," Hap promised. "As long as we get out of here first. And if you know of any way to get us out without being noticed, that would be best."

Confucian led them down the ramp and out of the docking area by using an employee's access Hap hadn't seen when he and Tara had gone to find the causeway.

And while they walked, Hap told Confucian about Earth and the nine unknown scientists of Emperor Ashoka. He told how they had books of power hidden throughout the universe and how somehow these things called Dark Ones discovered the existence of the books.

"And they . . . *hired*, I guess, is the right word . . . this guy Don Nova to get the books for them. Nova wants them because he's looking to get revenge and to restore his family honor. He wants Earth gone. The Dark Ones . . . I don't know what they want. But whatever it is, it's bad—so we don't want them to get the books. We have one of the actual scientists with us. He's from India . . . originally. He's pretty cool most of the time—he's smart too. Gygak works for Nova. Nova works for the Dark Ones—and any people calling themselves the Dark Ones *can't* be up to anything good, right?"

Confucian listened intently as he led them back through some kitchens, where sweaty chefs yelled at each other and raced around their pots and fires while tossing food from pans to plates and sending the plates off to the dining area. A few of the chefs said hello to Confucian and offered him little bits of whatever they were cooking. Confucian accepted the samples and shared with Hap and Tara. They followed a maze of back rooms filled with laundering facilities, supply rooms, and more kitchens until they were back to the hallway where they had first met Bo Shocks.

"So, you seek the books . . . what will you do with them when you have them?" Confucian asked.

"Destroy them," Tara said resolutely, looking up from where she continually, and unsuccessfully, tried to contact the others on her link key. She'd gotten over her embarrassment sometime between the docking area and the kitchens.

"Yes." Confucian nodded in agreement. "That would be the only way to keep such mischief from recurring. Man who keeps dragon for pet cannot feel angry when dragon burns down his house. Do you agree, Hap?"

Hap didn't answer the question. The little moral or whatever it was Confucian was trying to convey made sense. Destroying the books seemed like the right thing to do. They couldn't keep people like the Dark Ones and Nova from that knowledge forever. As long as the books existed, someone, somewhere, could do bad things with the knowledge inside those books. But Amar hadn't ever mentioned destroying the books, and Hap had no intention of destroying one book in particular.

One of those books taught how to heal people—to cure people of *anything,* even scary things that no one could heal. Even cancer.

Hap intended on using that book. Just one book—just one time.

Amar had said the knowledge inside the books was dangerous for people to have. *Too much information can corrupt a soul,* Amar had said.

But Hap didn't believe that. That was as dumb as when people said that the root of all evil was money. Grandpa Hazzard had always scoffed at such stupidity. Grandpa Hazzard had said that the root of all evil was greed and pride. He'd said that money just revealed people for who they already were.

Hap believed information was the same thing as money. Too much couldn't corrupt a soul that wasn't already corrupted. It could only reveal what was already there.

Hap liked to think his soul wasn't corrupted. He liked to think he was at least mostly as good as his own dad—who was the best man Hap knew.

And that was why Hap had to use the book—no matter what Amar said. He had to save the best man he knew.

He thought of the dream he'd had after he'd linked home the first time. He'd witnessed the explosion of Earth. That was what someone like Nova would do with the books.

That was what a corrupted soul's actions looked like.

Hap didn't want the books for power or wealth or revenge. He wanted to heal his dad so they could go hiking together and wrestle around the house while his mom rolled her eyes.

"What's the matter, Hap?" Tara asked.

Hap shook his head, trying to rid his mind of the sound of glass crunching under his feet and the vision of people running for their lives as Earth exploded with light and fire. "Nothing's wrong." His voice cracked, and he looked away. "Just worried because no one on our side is looking for the books now."

"They will be, though. They just have to help Laney and Mosh first. I wish we had an idea of how to help them with that . . ."

"Or even help them with finding the book. We're totally useless right now," Hap said.

"You say the book is here?"

"Yes." Tara answered. "One of the scientists liked it here, I guess. He hid it in the caves underneath the dome."

"I can go to the caves and can help you look," Confucian offered.

Tara's face lit up. "Would you? Then we could at least be doing something. Going out to search for Laney and Mosh might just end up with us getting caught too. But this . . . this is something we can do. Confucian, that would be *wonderful*." She said it with the same breathy sigh she'd used before.

Hap *did* roll his eyes at that.

Tara must've seen because she jabbed an elbow into his arm.

He ignored her. "Do you have suits for us to wear?" Outside the dome, the atmosphere on the comet was pretty much nonexistent. There was nothing to breathe, and he'd never survive it without a suit, not even down in the caves.

"Bo has suits," Confucian said.

Hap didn't get into the logistics of whether Bo would care if they used his suits. Too much depended on this. And Hap really wanted to go down into the comet's caves.

"Have you ever been in them before?" Hap tried hard not to look too excited.

"Yeah, several times. Bo likes to collect the rock formations and stuff and use them for photo ops."

"And he lets you go with him into the caves?" Hap couldn't keep the longing out of his voice this time. Amar and Laney really were overprotective.

"It's more like he has me go *for* him. Bo really doesn't like hanging out in the caves. He's afraid he'll hurt his voice or something." Confucian lifted his chin. "It's a very important job. He doesn't trust just anybody to do that sort of stuff for him. It's totally zane being Bo's most trusted person."

Hap felt a little sorry for Confucian. The guy spent a lot of time restating that things were "zane" between him and Bo, but Hap hadn't seen actual evidence to support the theory. It appeared to Hap that Bo used Confucian as an errand boy.

"Oh, yeah. Totally zane, man," Hap agreed, because he felt that Confucian really wanted him to agree. Confucian was growing on Hap.

Confucian smiled, and Tara sighed her girlish sigh.

Hap rolled his eyes again, which earned him another dig from Tara's elbow.

They'd made it to Confucian's room, also where Bo stored the space suits for his glorified errand boy. Confucian opened the door just as Hap realized the mess he and Tara had left when they'd been attacked by the birds.

"Wait!" Tara said at the same time Hap said, "Hang on a second!"

The door fell open exactly one second before Confucian's mouth fell open.

They had some explaining to do.

7. A Paper Bird Named Lily

"WHAT HAPPENED?" CONFUCIAN WHISPERED UNDER his breath—his eyes wide with horror and his voice shaky. His face was twisted in devastation. He shook his head and fell to his knees to scoop up the soggy pulp remnants.

"I can explain," Tara said at the same time Hap said, "It wasn't our fault!"

"They attacked us!" Tara lifted her hands to show where tiny red puncture marks spotted the insides of her arms and the backs of her hands. The red marks looked angry and a little swollen, as though they were infected.

Hap looked at his own arms and frowned. His were also swollen and each pin-sized hole was surrounded with a ring of red under the skin. Stupid birds.

"They wouldn't have attacked you unless you'd done something to me! They'd only attack if I was in danger." Confucian's clipped words demanded a response.

"We were watching you on the link. And then you went down, and we lost connection with you. We were just trying to leave the room to get to where you were. We just wanted to help you. We were so worried something bad had happened to you—"

"Yeah, totally worried, man." Hap knew Tara was better at this sort of thing—better at explaining things that made sense to logic and emotions, but he had to add in his bit too. He felt really bad that Confucian rocked those little bits of mush in his hands as though rocking a baby. He felt bad that he'd ruined something that obviously meant a lot to the guy. He wanted to let Confucian know that he cared.

"They must have heard you cry out for help on the holo link," Tara continued. "They must have thought we'd done something to you, because they went crazy. We couldn't think of anything else to do. We knew we had to get to you, because Nova's guys are *really* bad guys. They could've really hurt you."

"And we never would have been able to live with ourselves if anything had happened to you. It would've been all our fault for letting you go out there to help us," Hap added.

"So we had to get out of the room, but they wouldn't let us anywhere near the door. The bathroom was our escape, and . . ." Confucian knew the rest just by looking at the damage in the room. Tears filled Tara's eyes. "We're really sorry. Tell us how to fix this for you."

Confucian seemed affected by Tara's gentle voice and didn't shake her hand off his shoulder like Hap might've if the roles had been switched.

"We'll pay you back for them," Hap offered. "Buy you new ones."

Confucian sniffed and wiped his eyes with the sleeve of his coat.

"You can't buy paper birds." He sniffed again. "They have to be planned, considered, folded, and pressed before they can fly."

Tara shot Hap a look that said, *What is he talking about?*

Hap shrugged in the reply of, *I don't know, but let's roll with it.*

"If we can't buy them, then we'll help get you materials and help you plan and consider and all that other stuff too. We're really sorry. We would've never damaged your stuff if we'd had any other choice."

Confucian sighed and moved heavily to his feet as though his body were made of lead. "I know you didn't mean to do this to me. I can re-create them, and I still have one falcon . . . Lily. But we need to find your books. You did say the matter was urgent, didn't you?"

He smiled, but his red eyes and the slight tremor in his lip were like a neon sign showing how devastated he was. Hap felt like a class-act creep, but he couldn't really fix things beyond what he'd already offered, and the fact remained that they did have an urgency to find the book while the others looked for Laney and Mosh. Nova could not be allowed to win.

So Hap and Tara followed Confucian to the closet, ready to do the best with the situation they'd been given.

Confucian pulled out three shiny suits from the dozens that were stuffed in there. The closet went pretty deep and was lined with costumes and weird stuff that Hap couldn't begin to guess a purpose for. Confucian handed the smaller suit to Tara. "Try it on. See if it fits."

She wriggled it over her clothes and zippered up all the zippers and fasteners. It fit perfectly. It was created with a form-fitting material with a hard plastic layer everywhere except at the joints, to keep those spots flexible. The metallic blue-and-silver material glinted in the light of the room. Confucian handed her a helmet and helped her into it. The helmet's face was see-through—like the dome that protected the people on the comet from the elements of deep space.

"Do we need to learn how to use it or anything?" Hap wondered aloud, thinking of how long Laney said it would take to teach him to use her space suits so he didn't accidentally cut off his own oxygen.

"Oh, no. Bo . . . has a hard time with things that require instructions. Even though he hasn't ever used any of these, he wanted to make sure they were all user-friendly—in case he ever had to." He handed Hap one of the other suits. It was a rusted color, somewhere between the color red and pink.

Hap shook his head. "Do you have a different one . . . a different color maybe?"

"This is the only one that'll fit you."

"Stop whining and put it on, Hap. We don't have time to be picky." A faint echo chased Tara's words as she spoke through the helmet.

"That's easy for you to say! You got the cool blue one!"

He took the suit from Confucian and wondered if this was payback for what happened to the paper falcons.

He stuffed his feet into the legs and slithered his hands through the arms of the suit, the hard plastic clacking as Hap fastened the zippers and buttons. It surprised him with how the fibrous gloves allowed him to use his fingers completely. His snow gloves back at home didn't do that.

Once Confucian had fastened Hap's helmet over the suit and digital readouts scrolled in his peripheral vision, Tara grinned.

"What?"

"You look cute in pink, Hap."

He felt his face heat up to sun surface temperatures. "It's not pink. It's just . . . watered-down red." He noted that Confucian's suit was black and tried not to feel jealous. It wasn't like anyone was taking pictures of him or anything. Tara would be the only witness to this when they got back to Earth.

Confucian looked to be shaking off his grief over the paper bird incident and bounced on his feet as though excited to be going out with them. "You guys ready?" he asked.

When they acknowledged that they were, he went to the side of his bed and removed a cloth draped over something large and bulky.

It was a huge wooden bird cage. The bird screeched as it blinked in the light. "Let's get some exercise, Lily. These are my friends. Be nice to them."

It was another paper falcon. But instead of being small, she was life-size. Her head bobbed as she stepped out of her cage and then opened her wings in a slow stretch. Her wings were massive, and Hap felt immediate gratitude that she'd been ordered to be nice. If the little ones could peck them, he had no doubt that this bird could shred them.

"She's beautiful," Tara said.

And Hap couldn't argue that. Every feather looked like it had been individually designed. Her sharp hooked beak and talons were tipped with silver metal, and her eyes were made of little mirror insets.

Confucian was a genius.

Hap didn't know one person back on earth who could pull off such a creation. Confucian had folded paper and then made it *alive* somehow.

"Dude, that's totally zane," Hap said with approval.

Confucian grinned. "She is my best friend."

Hap paused at that. A paper bird for your best friend? He sneaked a look at Tara, who'd become *his* best friend over their adventures. Poor Confucian—living in a world he'd had to fold into existence.

"I have to keep her caged because she liked to peck at the little ones," Confucian continued.

Hap was grateful Confucian didn't mention anything about the little ones not being a problem anymore since they no longer existed thanks to Hap, Tara, and the shampoo bottles.

"Wait." Tara stopped at the door. "What if we run into Nova's guys?"

"Lily will take care of us."

Hap didn't share Confucian's confidence. A paper bird hardly felt like protection.

"Trust me. We're fine. I know ways into the tunnels that no one else has access to. Bo likes things his way, and since he brings in a lot of business to the casinos, they pretty much let him do whatever he wants. He can move around this entire rock and not run into one person, because he has all the access. And because he needs me to help him so much, I have all that same access." Confucian straightened with pride in his responsibility, but Hap couldn't shake the feeling that Confucian was more a glorified manservant than a right-hand man.

But he wasn't about to argue—not after being so swiftly forgiven for drowning Confucian's birds.

They left the room and wound through a maze of rooms that led to hallways that led to other rooms and hallways until they came to one huge door made of metal and stone. "This was here before Bo ever claimed this comet for his tour through the Elektra system. Bo really liked it and asked for total ownership of it and the caves it led to while he stays on the comet. It's a good place to start."

"Aren't the caves all connected?" Tara asked.

"Oh, no. This is the only entrance to this set of caves. Bo doesn't want anyone stumbling into his rooms while they're out exploring, so he made sure he was the only one with access to these. He's very private."

"A private public figure . . ." Hap laughed.

Confucian didn't laugh and went on as if Hap hadn't said anything. "The historical society had made a few brochures for these caves to increase tourism and had marked off several landmarks and petroglyphs. They didn't want people to feel cheated, so they had to re-create them in the other caves. People have no idea they're seeing fakes, but Bo doesn't care if they get the originals or not as long as he gets his privacy."

"What?" Tara exclaimed, her hazel eyes widening as she tugged at Confucian's shoulder to look at him directly.

"Are you serious?" Hap demanded to know.

Laney, Amar, Svarta, and Tremble had all gone off to the caves to find the box. Did they know they were going to the tourist caves? Or did they have access to the real ones?

Hap looked up at the door, now able to see it entirely, because Tara had moved Confucian out of his way. He stopped short when he realized what he was seeing.

The rock-and-metal door had symbols on it. They matched the ones on the wall in the control room on board Nana.

Laney had told them that the symbols on the wall matched the ones written in the deserts of Peru—the Nazca lines.

The symbol in the middle of the door was the lizard—meaning the Lizard Comet. And inside the lizard's belly was a square box.

Inside the square box was a picture of the lotus flower, just like Amar had described it.

They'd found the tunnel to the stone box that held one of the books of the nine unknown scientists.

8. Comet Caves

"Tara?" Hap tugged on her arm and pointed. She glanced over from Confucian to the door, and her mouth fell open in an O shape as she quickly sucked in air.

"Do you think this is the same place the others were searching?" she asked.

Hap didn't answer, because he was hoping it wasn't the same place. The others hadn't found anything. Hap hoped they hadn't found anything because they'd been in the wrong cave system.

And he hoped Nova and his hirelings had gone to the wrong caves too.

"What's wrong?" Confucian asked. His bird had flapped around their heads for a few minutes before realizing they weren't moving to open the door. It must have grown bored, because it landed on Confucian's shoulder and ruffled its papery feathers at them.

"Nothing's wrong!" Tara reached out and hugged Confucian, her helmet banging against his. She was too excited to even blush, although Hap thought he saw a slight pink creep up Confucian's neck. "Nothing's wrong at all! This is probably it! You've probably saved the universe from the Dark Ones ever getting their hands on this book. You're brilliant!"

If she hadn't been wearing a helmet, Hap suspected she might have kissed Confucian. He rolled his eyes again in irritation and gave her a teensy shove. "All right, all right, let's save the celebration dance for when we actually find something."

Confucian opened the door and Lily the falcon swooped into the darkness of the tunnel before them. The headlight on his suit only reached ten or so feet ahead of him, making it feel like the darkness swallowed the bird whole. For the briefest moment Hap almost called the falcon back because he was afraid it would die in the caves without the proper gear on, but then he remembered it was paper.

Confucian had created something so lifelike that Hap had forgotten it was paper. This was a guy who would definitely win the ninth grade science fair.

Tara tensed as they went into the oxygen chamber and Confucian shut the door behind them. A hissing sound filled the room as the oxygen drained from the room to be recycled elsewhere so it wasn't lost when they actually entered the caves through the secondary door—also made of stone and metal and filled with symbols that looked like the ones Hap had seen on the wall in the control room.

"Are we sure we're safe?" Tara asked, glancing nervously back at the door leading to the dome and its life support systems.

"Your suit's the finest made in any mapped and legitimate star system," Confucian confirmed.

"What if we get lost or locked out of the dome?"

"I've never been lost, so I'm sure you'll be fine. But even if you did get turned around or got stuck here, you could live for several weeks in the suits."

"Without water and food?" Tara looked doubtful, and the tips of her gloved fingers whispered together as though she were trying to click her nails. Maybe the suit could break her of that habit if she had to survive in it for several weeks.

"The suit monitors your life energy. If you start to get low, it'll take over. The suit comes equipped with vitamins. If you get low on nutrients, you'll feel a little jab at your wrist, and the suit will feed you what you need to survive. It recycles your water, so sweating, crying, and other liquids get recycled."

"I don't want to go into details on that, AND I don't want to try that function out, so let's not get lost, okay?"

Confucian smiled and focused on the falcon that fluttered down into the darkness of the tunnel and back again like a ghost bird. "Lily won't let us get lost—that's why I always bring her. We won't have to worry about it. I only mention the survival function of the suit to ease Tara's mind. She looks sick."

"Nah. She always looks like that. Let's get going."

Tara punched Hap's shoulder. Even through the suit, and even with her fingers and those sharp little knuckles padded in cloth, she still threw the meanest punch in the universe.

"Ow! You've got to stop hitting people!" Hap said.

"Stop deserving it."

He scowled and stomped behind them into the caves. Stomping was really hard when gravity was so limited. Even with the density shoes of the suit, gravity had a hard time pulling them to the ground. He hadn't noticed it so much under the dome, where artificial gravity made up the difference. But out here in the caves, things were not the same. The lack of genuine gravity made it more fun because he bounded a little with every step. "We're in a cave . . . in a *comet*!"

By the fifth time he'd said this, Tara spun on a heel, kicking up dust that floated around her ankles. She put her gloved hands on the hips of her suit. "I am *not* glad to be here, so you know. I don't like that this is the second time I've ended up in a hole in the ground with you. This isn't a game, Hap. Please take it seriously."

He made a pshaw noise and blew a raspberry at her, which resulted in flecks of spit inside of his helmet. "A positive attitude doesn't mean I'm not serious. It means I am pleasant to be around, unlike some peop—"

"Don't even go there." She spun back around. "I *am* pleasant to be around," she muttered.

"Do you two ever stop arguing?" Confucian asked.

"Oh, heck no. This is our primary mode of entertainment." Hap grinned. Tara laughed at that.

Lily swooped in over their heads, spun around, let out a screech, and disappeared again.

"So we're looking for a book . . ." Confucian said.

"Yep. An old book, with metal and leather bindings." Hap described the book while keeping his eyes on Tara.

She looked from side to side, examining the walls, and stayed in front of them. She chose the first couple of turns—totally ignoring Hap's rule of always turning to the right when they weren't sure where they were headed.

"What are you doing?" he finally asked her.

"Following the map." She pointed at the walls of the cave.

And sure enough, more symbols like the Nazca lines in Peru pointed the way.

"Oh. Yeah. I knew that." Of course, he *hadn't* known that. He'd been so excited about being in a space suit, even if it was watered-down red, and exploring caves on a comet, that he'd forgotten to focus on the mission.

Confucian took an interest in the walls. "Those symbols are pretty icy."

Hap wondered if Confucian knew he'd just made a little pun since the entire comet was made of ice, and the symbols were carved into the comet.

"Haven't you seen them before?" Tara asked Confucian. When she turned back to look at them, her face glowed in the weird light of her headlamp. She looked a little scary like that. Hap wondered if he looked scary too and wished he had a mirror to see.

"Oh, I've seen them, just never really paid attention. We're not allowed to touch them, and Bo only ever wanted me to bother with the rocks that weren't protected by the historical society."

"How do you know you're following them correctly?" Hap got up close to the wall so his helmet nearly touched it. The icy rock glittered with the light shining on it.

"You're not the only one who studies that wall in the control room," Tara said.

Which was true enough. Tara had spent as much time as Hap in the control room. Her goal was to find the books and get home so she could have her own life back. Hap's goal was to find the books and get home to make sure that *everyone* could have their own lives. He'd studied the wall until he'd felt like his eyes were going to fall out of his head.

He had to.

Because of the dream.

The crunching glass.

The explosion of white.

Hap shook his head to clear it of the memory. No. They *would* find all of the books. The dream would stay just that—a dream. It wouldn't come true.

Tara was right. He needed to get serious.

He watched the walls and tried to help Tara interpret the symbols and the directions they seemed to indicate.

When they'd marched over the same ground for the third time, he hollered for everyone to stop. They'd been in the caves for what felt like several hours, and his stomach was rumbling. They had continued trying to link to others from the crew but with no luck. For all they knew, everyone had been captured or killed, and they were the only ones left to find the books. They'd covered all the ground at least twice. There wasn't an inch of this particular cave system that they hadn't seen.

"Time to go back." Confucian sounded tired, like Hap felt. They were all frustrated. Every turn led to a dead end. And what didn't dead-end simply led to nothing interesting or connected to places they'd already been.

Lily screeched happily as she flew around Confucian's head. She looked anything but tired, and flying in circles over them while they walked in circles hadn't bothered her a bit. *Must be nice to be paper,* Hap thought.

"We can't go back!" Tara insisted. "It's here. I know it is! We can't fail the others. We've got to be close!"

Hap sighed, feeling exactly like he'd failed everyone. "We've searched everywhere. It isn't here."

"It might be here," Confucian interjected. "But Bo has another concert—the late showing. You said you'd join him onstage, and he'll be really mad if you aren't there." His voice went from merely tired to downright depressed at the mention of Tara joining Bo on stage. "We can try again after the concert." At least he was being optimistic, despite their misgivings.

"But I—"

"Tara, you gave your word, and we owe Confucian big time." Hap couldn't believe he had to be the voice of reason here. Tara was all about keeping her promises.

"But we've got to be close . . ." She trailed off, the disappointment in her face illuminated by the bright headlamp.

Hap knew how she felt. They'd really expected to find the book in these caves. They'd really expected to emerge victorious, to be able to link to the others and tell them the book was safe. Hopefully, they would receive good news about Laney and Mosh.

"You're right," Tara said, *not* sounding happy about it. "We'll search after the concert."

She trudged back toward where the door to the dome was located then whirled around, her eyes wide. "We're supposed to stay hidden! I can't go onstage with Bo!"

Confucian laughed. "That's why we need to get back. Wardrobe and makeup will want to fix you up. Your own mother won't recognize you when they're done."

"Are you sure?"

"Trust me."

They'd made it back through the door and into the hallways and rooms that led back to Confucian's room when Tara stopped all of a sudden. They'd already passed the stage and Bo's rooms. Tara's breathing was raspy and echoed through her helmet. They'd decided to keep their helmets on for the sake of hiding. No one would recognize them unless facing them directly.

"Hap?" Her urgent whisper made him look back. She pointed behind her in the direction of Bo's resting chambers—the one with all of the food. Hap had fully intended on heading there while Tara got all fixed up for the concert. He planned on dropping off the suit, filling up on food, and then napping in Confucian's room until Tara was done. He was exhausted.

"What?"

"I just saw Nova."

He jerked his head up, now paying full attention, and squinted in the direction of the hall. "Where?"

"He just went into Bo Shocks's reception room."

"Are you sure? It could've been anybody. Nova isn't the kind of guy looking for a backstage tour."

She hissed out a breath slowly between her teeth. "But he is the kind of guy who would be searching *everywhere* for a book! Bo has more access on this hunk of ice than anyone. Of course Nova's going to use Bo to get to the book. He has to!"

Hap grabbed Tara's arm and Confucian's shoulder to pull them back with him to Confucian's room. Laney had said to hide. To find somewhere safe. In a hallway, with the only exit passing the place where Tara had seen Nova, they definitely weren't somewhere safe. They were trapped.

9. Cosmic Cosmetics

"Do you think Bo's in danger?" Confucian had already tried rushing out of his room back to save Bo from Nova, but Hap had blocked the door. He eyed Lily suspiciously, and she eyed him right back. He wasn't certain she'd behave and not just peck his eyes out because he was arguing with her master. Who knew what a paper bird would do to the people who massacred his friends with shampoo bottles?

Tara peeled herself out of her space suit. "They seemed to be laughing together. Nova patted Bo on the back before they went into his resting chambers."

"This is *not* zane." Confucian raked his fingers through his hair and then kind of left his hands on his head as if they'd been glued there. He looked manic. "Bo's all I got. He's my only friend in this universe."

Lily screeched at that and, in what appeared to be a tantrum, flew back to her cage, where she fluffed up her papery feathers and marched in. She pulled the door closed and turned her back on Confucian.

Touchy bird, Hap thought. But he didn't say that. He said, "Nova's probably lying to Bo, trying to get access to the caves."

"I knew we should've kept searching!" Tara wailed. "He'll beat us to the book, Hap. We can't allow that to happen!"

"What we can't allow is anything bad to happen to Bo!" Confucian's yell matched Tara's in pitch and volume.

Hap briefly wondered if Tara would still sigh over how cute she thought Confucian was when he had no problem yelling like that.

A knock came at the door.

No one moved.

No one even breathed.

Another knock. "Fusion? Fusion, you in there?"

Confucian exhaled in a loud gust of air. "It's just Cameron. He's the tech guy." Confucian kept his voice low so only Hap and Tara heard him. Then he called out, "Yeah? What's up?"

"It's Shocks time!" The voice on the other side of the door announced. "Is that girl with you?"

All eyes went to Tara, who shook her head as Confucian yelled back, "Yeah, she's here!"

"Zane. Bring her to the resting chambers. Bo wants to introduce her to his new friend before she gets ready for the show. And Bo needs his star cloak cleaned. Pronto, Fusion. You know how he hates waiting."

Cameron walked back down the hall.

Tara still shook her head. "No way! I can't go in there! Nova's in there!"

"You're right," Confucian agreed. "You can't go in like that. Let's get you to wardrobe and makeup first. Bo'll be mad to have to wait, but he'll be even madder if you get shot before you ever join him onstage." Confucian took off his coat and wrapped it over Tara's head. "Let's go."

"Go?" Hap put up his hands to stop them. "Out there? With a guy who shoots people for fun? You don't know who you're dealing with. The guy's insane. And what about me?"

"You stay here."

Hap looked around to all the other shelves filled with various creatures made of paper. "No way. The last time you left me here, things didn't turn out so well."

Confucian grunted. "I don't have a disguise for you."

Hap looked doubtfully in Tara's direction. "And a jacket over the head is a good disguise for her, you think?"

"Well, I'm not taking her to the resting chambers like this. I'm just getting her down the hall—the opposite way of the resting chambers."

Hap put his helmet from his space suit back on. "I'm going with you."

"I can still see your face." Confucian reminded him.

"Not if I'm looking at the floor, and anyone in the reception room will only see my back." Hap went to the door. "Well c'mon!" he said after a second, when no one followed him.

Confucian finally shrugged and led Tara to the door. He put out his hand to open the door but stopped and said, "We're going left. Wardrobe and makeup are at the end of the hall."

Hap nodded and they exited the room. Lily slipped through the narrowing gap as the door closed. She must have let herself out of her cage.

"Lily! You cannot come with!" Confucian ordered and moved to open the door and make her go back.

Hap tapped his shoulder and whispered. "People are in the hall down there. They look like they're joining the little party. Let's just get out of here. Lily can come with."

Confucian didn't seem happy about it but agreed. They hurried away, hoping not to catch anyone's attention. Lily screeched happily, seeming to think the whole dodging down the hallway was a game.

Just as Confucian opened the door at the end of the hall, Hap thought he heard someone call out, but they tumbled into the room anyway and made a point of closing the door behind them—hoping that whoever had called out was looking for someone else.

"Confucian! Zane to see you, man!" A red-faced woman looked up from where she sat on a cushy metallic-gold beanbag. A feathery blue scarf wrapped around her head, and she wore pants that looked like the ones Hap had on. Her shirt matched her pants—a shiny sort of plastic material. The woman didn't have any link key that Hap could see, but a hologram glowed in front of her. The hologram was of a person teaching how to give a cleansing treatment on something called Mobisks. The Mobisk getting treated in the hologram looked human, but instead of normal hair, hers looked like thick spaghetti noodles. It wasn't *hair* exactly, not like soft strands of fuzz from the head like Hap or Tara had, but more like . . . *noodles*—like thick ropes of skin.

The long thick strands were ringed by a spiral of bright lime green against the pale parts.

"Handle each strand delicately," the hair stylist on the hologram said. "Many different nerves are located at the tips of each strand. A careless stylist could end up inducing extreme emotions in a Mobisk. Those emotions can range from anger to deep sorrow to giggling. Mobisks are extremely ticklish."

The woman on the beanbag wasn't watching the hologram anymore, though, now that Confucian was in the room. She turned her head and with one of her hands she swept the scarf from her head, revealing a gold-plated cone—no . . . not gold plating, but gold-colored bone. Instead of hair she had a knob of golden bone.

"Hey, Artell." Confucian waved a hand. Lily let out a squawk that sounded like a greeting as well. She landed on the table near where Artell sat.

She stood up from the beanbag and patted Lily on the head before she waved one of her four hands through the hologram— cutting off the stylist explaining what to do with a giggling Mobisk. The image dispersed like a cloud until it was gone completely.

She looked human enough aside from the red face, extra set of arms and the golden-boned head. Hap wanted to whisper the word bonehead to Tara since she called people that all the time, but he didn't want to be rude—at least not out loud. He was sure Tara would laugh at the joke.

"Don't tell me he doesn't like his new pants. Do you have any idea how many Rotillian cycles those took me to make?" Artell had her hands on her hips.

"Rotillian cycles?" Hap repeated the words, trying to make sense of them.

"Rotill is the biggest planet of all the known inhabited star systems. One rotation on that planet gives new meaning to the words, *I've had a long day.*" Confucian settled himself in the beanbag Artell had just vacated. "And no, we're not here about the pants. He loved the pants. He insists he's never looked better."

"Wow," Artell said. "That's quite a compliment coming from the guy who's madly in love with his mirror."

And with that, Hap decided he liked her.

"We do need some work done, though. Bo wants Tara here onstage with him." Confucian pointed at Tara, whose hair had suffered from a static attack after having been under Confucian's coat. It stood straight out as if she'd put her finger in a light socket.

Artell's smile dropped, and her face showed her sympathy. "But not *you* onstage?"

Confucian smiled and shrugged. "No, not yet, but he will. He promised."

Artell brightened again. "Of course he will, kid. Have you shown him your idea about the birds?"

Confucian shot a glance at Hap. "That idea isn't exactly ready anymore. It needs some . . . work."

Oh great, Hap thought. *Those birds were for a concert idea to get Confucian onstage with Bo.* If Hap hadn't felt guilty before, he felt outright miserable now. "I'm sorry, man. Really—"

Confucian interrupted. "Don't worry, Hap. Man who wastes all time worrying over what cannot be changed fails to actually change anything."

Confucian was right. If given the chance to do it again, Hap would make the same choices. It was between the paper army of birds or rescuing Confucian. Hap would have never forgiven himself if Nova had hurt Confucian. He felt bad enough that Nova had Mosh and Laney, and that wasn't even his fault.

Artell raised her eyebrows at the interchange but didn't pry for details. Instead she turned her attention on Tara. "He wants you onstage, huh?"

"Yes," Confucian said. "But he said she isn't zane enough the way she looks now. He said she needs lots of work."

Tara looked like she might protest, but Hap beat her to it. "Yeah. He said he doesn't want her looking *anything* like herself."

Tara must have realized they weren't insulting her but working to disguise her. She closed her mouth and nodded in agreement.

Artell circled Tara. "Should be easy enough. She's got stuff to work with . . . nice hair, good nose. Her chin's a little pointy and sharp, but we can fix it."

Tara covered her chin with her hand as her eyes widened. "What's wrong with my chin?"

No one answered her. Personally, Hap thought Tara's chin was just fine. If anything, it was the girl's knuckles that were too pointy and sharp.

"Yeah, we can fix her up. No problem. But what about you, Fusion? You going to be all right?" Artell rested one of her hands on Confucian's arm.

Confucian shook it off, insisting he was fine. Artell became all business again. She scooted Tara over to a chair and sat her down.

"Hey, Artell?" Confucian asked.

"Hmmm?" She'd filled her mouth and three of her hands with pins, while the last one pulled Tara's hair back.

"We probably ought to prep Hap too. Bo mentioned he might want to use him. And if he decides he does, he'll be mad if he isn't ready."

She grunted and spit the pins out of her mouth into her top left hand so she could glare at Hap. Her red face made her look really ticked off. "I can't do both of them! There isn't time!"

"I could help . . ." Confucian offered.

"Fine. You get him ready while I work with her. Be careful with the makeup. Just put it all back where you found it, and don't spill stuff. Half of it cost more than his life is worth." She pointed to Hap with a hairpin.

Hap looked at all the little jars filled with glittery and shiny goo and seriously doubted any of it was worth anything at all.

Confucian pushed Hap into a chair. "Time to make you invisible."

10. Hiding in Plain Sight

Confucian meant what he'd said about making Hap blend in. He slimed a bunch of icky-smelling makeup all over Hap's face then he topped it off by tapping a feather duster everywhere he'd placed slimy goop. "Just a little stardust to complete the effect . . ." he said.

Hap wished he had a mirror so he could see what the heck Confucian had done to his face. The makeup felt so thick, it was like a mask. Hap had done various makeup things—fake scars and bloodied bits of fake skin hanging off his face at Halloween time, but he'd never done anything that covered his whole face before.

After Hap's facial, Confucian went to work on Hap's hair. More slime, more powder, lots of pulling and twisting. Hap yelped a few times and then felt stupid because he noticed that Tara didn't even wince as her hair was being stretched and twisted around these crazy wire things.

How could she not wince when someone was tugging her hair out by their roots?

Hap finally yelled, "I give!" and ended up having to explain that he wasn't actually giving anything except for giving *up,* to which Confucian tried to explain that the direction *up* wasn't Hap's to give.

"Never mind," Hap grumbled. Lily made a noise that sounded like a falcon version of laughter.

"All done!" Artell said, stepping back to admire her handiwork on Tara. With four hands doing that handiwork, she had moved fast. Hap couldn't see Tara because his chair was turned to face Confucian, but he could see Artell, and she looked very pleased with herself.

"Now for wardrobe . . ." Artell said, tapping her finger against her lips as though thinking very hard. "Flash!" she said at last. "She'll look icy zane in a flash gown."

"We could put him in a flash suit, too." Confucian pointed to Hap. "Bo might like them as a pair if they matched."

Artell gave Confucian a look of exasperation. "And what about you? What do we do to get *you* on stage?"

"We don't. Bo will invite me when he thinks I'm ready." Confucian straightened his shoulders.

Artell wasn't having any of it. "We could just do a little stage makeup. Maybe Bo will see you if you try standing out a little."

"Let's just get them costumed." He walked away and opened up a closet big enough to make a princess sigh with jealousy.

Tara *did* sigh.

Artell followed him to the closet and helped him sift through the bright and overly sparkly clothes until she said, "Here!" and pulled out a couple of outfits. One looked like a dress from the 1920s, which Hap recognized from his five-page report about the Great Depression. The dress was a light blue gauzy sort of material with little ruffles at the bottom. It was total *girl*. He knew it the moment Tara stood up from her chair and crept up to the dress like it was an animal she didn't want to scare away.

Hap could only see the back of her head.

Her hair was no longer blonde, but a freakish pale blue color— like snow in the shade on a cold day. Little braids had been twisted into a knot on top of her head. From that knot a bunch of miniature braids flowed outward like a fan—like the scary lady in the shop where Hap bought his pants. Only Tara's hair didn't look scary. It looked awesome—even if it was blue.

Tara's fingers slowly stretched forward to touch the dress and Hap smirked. Yep. Total girl. She cooed, "Do I really get to wear this?"

Artell cooed right along with Tara and they both started speaking in the girl language that was a little bit actual words and a whole lot squeal. Apparently, Artell didn't get the chance to dress up someone who appreciated fashion as much as Tara did.

Confucian held the suit, and though it looked decent enough, Hap didn't want to touch it reverently or gush about how it was super cute, super zane, or super icy. It was just *clothes,* for crying out loud, and it was not pink—thankfully. And it didn't have sparkles on it like the outfits the rest of the band wore.

Hap drew the line at wearing anything with sparkles. Once he'd gone to a magician's camp, and the camp shirt had a wand with an explosion at the tip of it.

The little diamond-looking gem at the center of the explosion at the tip of the wand seemed cool enough—at least until he started school that fall. Nathan Davenport had made that one of the most miserable days of his middle-school life. That was where Hap learned that guys shouldn't wear sparkles.

"Dressing room's there."

Tara hauled her dress to one of the doors and disappeared behind it faster than Confucian handed the suit off to Hap. "You'll have to forgive her. She's been stuck in the same clothes for a while," Hap said, taking his clothes to the dressing room and putting them on. His outfit was a darker blue than Tara's—a midnight blue. They fit a little loosely, but not so bad—at least he didn't think so. Without a mirror it was hard to tell. When he did the button just under his Adam's apple, the suit flashed like lightning. He jumped and blinked. Had he imagined that? Then the suit flashed again, and a brilliant blue-white light forked its way down the lapels of the suit jacket and down the sides of his pants.

Zane. Awesome. Icy.

No matter what word he picked, they all meant the same thing. He'd never worn anything so cool in his life. He almost forgot to be unhappy that he hadn't been able to find a new pair of jeans. He exited the dressing room at the same time as Tara.

He couldn't help himself. His jaw dropped when he saw her. Her dress flashed in forks of lightning that trailed over the ruffles and edges in a way that made her look like a super hero out of a comic book. She had on light blue leggings that Hap would've laughed at if he saw them on a shelf since they looked like something you'd put on a baby, but they didn't look bad on Tara, so what did he know?

He almost told her she looked pretty, but that would've been weird, so he gave her the best compliment he could think up. "You look awesome! Totally not like you at all!" he said.

"Oh, thanks a lot. Are you trying to say that I can't look *awesome* if I look like myself?"

"No! That's not what I meant at all! I just meant, well . . . you're all blue!"

She took a deep breath and let it out slowly. "All blue? That's really all you have to say to me?"

She was mad at his reaction, but Hap didn't really understand why. It wasn't like he'd said she looked stupid or anything. He'd been trying to compliment her. He hadn't insulted her at all, yet she acted as though he'd kicked her,

"And you're blue too!" she said, pointing a glittery blue nail at him.

"I am?"

Confucian laughed and tugged Hap over to the mirrors in the closet of clothes.

Hap gasped when he saw himself. His red hair was now a dark blue color with light blue highlights that forked in the same way the suit did. It was styled up to look like blue flames. His face was a pale yellow color with a blue glittery sheen over it. It really did look like he'd been powdered in stardust. He leaned closer to the mirror. "It's just like you said. My own mother wouldn't recognize me!" He turned to Confucian. "You totally did it! No one will notice us like this at all! Tara could go anywhere. She could spend hours with Nova, and he'd have no clue it was her. This is absolutely brilliant!"

Tara had also been given a mirror. But she didn't say anything except for whispering, "I really wish I had a camera."

"Now for you!" Artell grabbed Confucian and shoved him back into a chair. He pled with her that there wasn't enough time, but she wouldn't let him get up, and Lily seemed to be in agreement because each time Confucian tried to stand, she nipped at his ear.

"Traitor," he muttered to the bird, who only cocked her head to the side in response and nipped his ear again.

Artell fluffed up Confucian's hair but didn't add any color. She styled it then dusted a bit of black glitter through it. She put a little stage makeup on him but only in a way that enhanced his natural features. His almond eyes looked darker and more intense, and his cheekbones deepened and more defined.

"There. Now you're ready to be a rock star." She smiled and stepped away so he could get up. "Hey, mind if I scan the three of you in? You all look great—some of my best work, and I could really use the scans of something that isn't Bo and the Sungrazers in my résumé."

"What do you mean by scan?" Tara asked.

"Record your image."

"A picture!" And Tara was back to gushing.

A light flashed at them, but it didn't look like Artell held anything in her hands, and she wasn't even really paying attention. Artell had focused all of her attention on Confucian and had put a hand on his arm, upsetting Lily enough that she flew off to perch on the back of one of the chairs. "I wish I could help Bo notice you. If you need help preparing the birds for his act, let me know. I'll do anything I can to help."

Tara finally stopped gawking at herself in the mirror long enough to notice the interchange.

Hap felt a bit of relief and even victory over Tara's crush seeming to belong to Artell, but the victory felt hollow when Tara's face fell in disappointment with the suspicion that Confucian might *like* the four-armed hair stylist.

What had she expected? Confucian was at least three years older than she was in normal human years, but in "space years"? He was hundreds of years older. And it wasn't like Laney would let them take on one more passenger. Nana was pretty cramped already. To get depressed because she found out that the guy had a girlfriend already was lame. He'd have teased her, but it seemed she felt bad enough without him making it worse.

Someone burst into the room, interrupting the quiet moment between Confucian and Artell, as well as interrupting Tara's disappointment.

The newcomer with orange dreadlocks and an orange goatee locked eyes on Confucian. "Bo's looking for that girl! He's really mad. Where is she?"

Confucian stepped out of the way, revealing Tara, who'd been behind him at the mirror. "She's right here. Stage ready."

"Well, don't just stand there! Come on! Everyone's waiting at the stage already. The girl was supposed to be at the reception room forever ago. This won't look good for you, Fusion."

"Keeping him waiting so you can give me a lecture won't look good for you either," Confucian said, while wrapping a hand around Tara's wrist and gently tugging her toward the door. Artell threw a long black duster jacket over Confucian's shoulders as he strode out of the room. "Just in case!" she called.

Hap followed along behind him even though no one had told him to. The orange guy hadn't even looked in his direction. Hap didn't care. He wasn't about to let Tara out of his sight—not with Nova lurking around.

Lily took to the air and fluttered along with them.

They hurried through the network of halls, with the orange goatee guy barking at them to move faster, when they finally reached the staging area with its glass pillars and perpetual sunset making the pillars and stage glow like they were on fire.

Bo Shocks and all of the band members stood onstage while Bo explained to the few people in the audience how the concert worked.

"And when the concert starts, I'll be under the stage. I sit on my throne and wait for introductions, then my throne comes up out of the floor and we detonate a bit off the comet so the pieces can explode into the space behind me. The detonation's really important because it creates a sort of natural fireworks. We strive to work with nature rather than against it. And—"

Nova sat next to Meg, who looked bored. She pulled out knives from under the black cuff at her wrist and moved to dig into the chair's armrest, but Nova stopped her with a glance. She sighed and inserted the dagger back under her cuff. There were a couple of others Hap didn't recognize, but none of them were paying attention to Bo blabber on and on about how great he was.

Tara groaned when she heard Bo's comment about working with nature, but her step faltered when Nova and Meg came into view.

"They won't recognize you," Hap whispered to her, taking her hand and leading her along so she didn't draw attention to herself. He hoped he was right. He hoped they were disguised well enough that Nova and Meg would think they were just part of the weird assortment of Bo's band members. But he couldn't keep himself from straining to see if Mosh or Laney were with them.

They weren't—not that Hap could see.

Nova let his gaze linger over them, and Hap's heart felt like it stopped, paralyzed under the inspection of Don Nova. Confucian drew in a sharp breath but managed to smile and wave up at Bo. "Sorry we're late, Bo."

"Fusion! Fusion, my man!" Bo crouched down on the stage so he was closer to them. "I waited and waited. Not zane, man. Not zane. Where's the girl?"

Confucian pointed at Tara, and Hap cringed, hoping Bo wouldn't complain that she didn't have her blonde hair and pale skin anymore. That kind of description would definitely alert Nova that something was wrong.

Bo seemed to be chewing on his own front teeth as he pursed his lips and mumbled to himself. He finally brightened, his wide, unnaturally white smile almost hurting Hap's eyes.

Nova turned his attention from Hap, focusing on Bo.

Everyone relaxed.

Bo finally said, "I get it! You wouldn't want me on stage with a bit of shabby rubbish, so you fixed her up. Good thinking, Fusion! Don't want my brand to be cheapened."

Tara growled low in her throat at having been classified as *a bit of shabby rubbish*.

"The box . . ." Nova said, clearly impatient about being side-tracked by Bo's ego.

"Box?" Bo echoed.

"You said you would allow me access to your private caves to locate the box."

"Yes, yes. Of course, of course. I'll lead the expedition myself once I'm through with this concert. It's important I don't disappoint my fans."

"It's really a matter of some urgency." Nova was obviously hanging onto his patience by a fingernail. Hap didn't exactly blame him. Bo could try the patience of a nun.

"Oh, fans are always a matter of urgency. Have to take my bread and butter seriously." Bo laughed as though finding such an idea ridiculous.

Nova's tone held a warning in it. "No, the *box* is a matter of urgency. The box in the caves, the one you are going to help me find."

Confucian had herded Hap and Tara over toward where the stairs leading under the stage were located. But Hap still strained to hear Bo's response.

"I'm sure that's a matter of importance to you, but I must warn you—there isn't any box in the caves. I've been in there hundreds of times and the only thing that looked like it didn't belong was that stone altar I use as my stage throne. It looks really great against all the glass and shines really nice in the right light."

"A stone altar, you say?" Nova had perked right up and had a dead-determined look on his face.

Confucian stopped trying to hurry Hap and Tara down the stairs, seeming to sense the change in the mood of the room. The tension thickened.

Bo shrugged. "Yeah. It was the only thing of value, and really, it's only valuable as a prop. It's horridly uncomfortable as an actual chair."

"I'd like to look at that," Nova said with as calm a face as he could manage given his psychotic nature.

Hap tried not to look at him directly, tried not to give him any reason to think Hap looked familiar, but he couldn't help it. The hunger in Nova's eyes confirmed what Hap feared.

The stone altar was the box that housed one of the books of power. Bo Shocks had been *sitting* on it the whole time.

11. Confessions

Nova, as if sensing being watched, turned toward Hap and locked gazes with him. Hap hurried to look away, hoping Nova's flicker of recognition remained just that—a passing flicker, not *actual* recognition. Hap felt paralyzed, afraid to move or call attention to himself any more than he already had.

Voices filtered down from the entrance to the concert, where people who'd bought tickets had finally been allowed to take their seats.

He heard Bo laugh and say, "Sure, you can see my throne, but you'll have to wait. It's show time!"

With a shove, Confucian moved Tara and Hap down the stairs under the stage. "Keep moving . . . all the way to the bottom. He can't come down here. And he can't do anything while you're onstage." Confucian pressed his hand into a space at the bottom of the stairs, and a red light glowed over the passageway. Lily screeched at the light and swept as far away from it as she could get in the area under the stage.

"A light lock?" Hap guessed.

"Yeah. Can't have rabid fans finding their way under the stage. It's always on when the ticket holders are being seated and all through the concert. It's extra sensitive so that even getting too close will melt your skin right off. Bo likes his privacy."

The stagnant air under the stage smelled like oil and machinery and dust. In spite of the high ceiling, the place felt stifling.

"You didn't mention that you'd found the stone altar in the caves." Tara's bright blue eyelashes fluttered as she blinked to try to adjust her vision to the darkness under the stage.

Every few seconds, the room lit up from the lightning flashes in their clothes, making their eyes continually need to readjust.

"You said you guys were looking for a book, not a block of stone. Man who wants chicken for dinner should not go fishing."

"This isn't about dinner!" Hap had a hard time controlling his temper. He felt out of control—like Tremble. Their enemy was just up a flight of stairs, *and* that enemy knew where the book was. "It's about saving the universe!" He inhaled sharply, nearly coughing on the dust.

"Have you ever tried to open the altar?" Tara asked more gently. She was better at gentle. It was Hap's favorite thing about her.

Hap squinted in the dark and could make out the shape of a square bulk in the center of the room. When his and Tara's suits simultaneously flashed blue white light, he saw it perfectly. The lotus flower carved into the top and carved leaves with smaller blossoms banding around the middle of it—exactly as Amar had described it.

"It's not a box; it's a big brick. There isn't anything to open." Confucian led them to it to inspect it. Sure enough, Hap couldn't see any way to get inside the thing. It didn't even look like it had anything inside. It was a massive solid brick.

"We could take a hammer to it or something . . ." Hap muttered to himself. He almost ran his hand down his face in frustration but remembered the makeup. "We're in way over our heads. Contact Svarta," Hap told Tara.

"Me? Svarta's probably panicked as she's looking for Laney. Or maybe she's in the middle of a rescue. She's not even answering any contact, so why do *I* have to tell her we're in trouble?"

"Because she likes you better. It's a girl thing."

"Honestly, Hap. You're a coward!"

"We need help. Nova's up there. And we're outnumbered. This is getting out of control. Svarta, Amar, Tremble—*someone* needs to come get us. You need to do it, because I can't get the words right without a real keyboard. I'm not good at typing in the air."

Tara huffed, mumbling something about how typing in a pretend environment should be easy for a guy who lived in the world of make-believe. But she still pulled out her link key and moved her fingers as though she were typing on a keyboard in the air. The link key registered her movements and formed them into a message to Svarta.

"Send the message to everyone's link keys. We don't know that they're together. We're going to need everyone."

Tara added more to her message and then flicked her fingers out as though throwing something invisible. The link key registered that motion as "send," and Hap knew the others would be getting the messages immediately. He felt better about that.

"What about Bo?" Tara asked. "We can't just leave him up there with Nova. How do we get Bo down here?"

"Through the shaft," Bo declared, making Hap jump and search to see if Nova had come with. "It's the way I always go. Stairs are so tedious, don't you think?"

Nova hadn't followed Bo under stage.

"Where's Don Nova?" Hap felt a little stupid demanding answers from a rock star who could not care less about anything Hap had to say.

"That old guy with the unibrow? He really rocks out, you know? The guy's super intense. He's a genius but needs to relax. I told him to sit back and take it easy while he watches the concert. He can wait until after the show and then come on down. Can't have my fans seeing me before the concert. If they see me before my grand entrance, then it takes the *grand* out of the entrance, you know?"

Three sets of eyes blinked at him.

"He's a madman," Tara finally said to Bo. "You can't let him anywhere near you or your stuff. You definitely can't let him take anything from this comet. I promise he'll use anything he gets from here to hurt people. The guy is totally insane."

Confucian laughed nervously and tried scooting Tara away from Bo. "She doesn't mean that. All geniuses are a little mad, aren't they?"

Lily the falcon screeched, but it didn't seem like she actually agreed. She'd settled on top of the box.

Tara must have worked through her crush on Confucian, because she turned her best angry face on him. "He's working for some people called the Dark Ones. Doesn't that sound a little, I don't know, *bad* to you? Not genius but *bad*."

Bo finally, for the first time, had the decency to look worried. Hap almost sighed in relief; they'd have help. But then Bo said, "Are they a new band? The Dark Ones? Is he a spy coming to steal my concert ideas?"

Tara threw her hands up in the air. "Is this guy joking, Confucian?"

Bo put his hands up as though protecting himself from attack. "Whoa, little girl. My man's name is Fusion—not that other thing you just said. I know some words are hard so I'll help you. Say it with me: Fyoo-jzun."

Tara opened her mouth to argue, but Confucian was finally able to move her aside. "She's joking, Bo. No one could steal your concert ideas. Even if they tried, it wouldn't work for them, because no one has your moves."

Bo nodded. "I *am* pretty zane. Totally true, Fusion."

Hap wanted to tear his blue hair out. Bo was the most useless adult Hap had ever seen in his life. And he'd met some seriously useless adults. Why Confucian just went with it made no sense at all. They were *trapped* down in this hole under the stage. Even if they could get the book out of the box, which Hap hadn't even begun to figure out, they'd never get it out of the auditorium. Meg, with all her guns and knives, would make short work of them.

"We gotta get out of here," Hap whispered.

"Oh, no!" Bo interrupted before Tara could argue the details of the point, which she would, because she *always* argued. "The little lady and I need to rehearse." He tugged Tara aside as the other members of the band had found their way down the shaft. "And may I say, your gown is very zane. Icy choice."

Tara glanced back pleadingly at Hap and Confucian, but Confucian waved her on and mouthed the word *please* to her.

"Why do you care if she does this?" Hap whispered once Bo and the band were strapping Tara up to wires. Hap thought he heard a low wail of distress from Tara but wasn't sure if it was her or the machinery that started humming and whining as the band members turned everything on.

"I know he doesn't seem like much, but Bo is all I got. If he takes off with his band and crew and leaves me behind because I didn't prove myself helpful enough, I'm just a guy on a rock with nothing to do. I need to make myself part of the band."

"You have more than just Bo. You have Artell," Hap said. He

couldn't be sure, because the light was so dim under the stage, but it seemed that Confucian's face darkened into some shade of pink.

"Yeah, there's Artell too. But she works for Bo. If he leaves, so does she."

"We have to get the box open before Bo goes onstage. Do you have a sledgehammer? Or some kind of pry bar?" Hap picked up a metal guitar that looked heavy, and he staggered with the weight of it.

Confucian swiped it out of his hands. "We can't break the altar! Bo would go supernova on us if we messed up his prop."

"I'm not as worried about a supernova as I am about *Don Nova*. The guy wants Tara and me and everybody on our ship *dead*. He already has two of our friends, just like they had you. Bo can pay to have a new chair built. But we've got to get the book out now while we have a chance!"

Hap made a grab for the guitar.

Confucian danced back a couple of steps with it. "Wait! Wait until Bo gets onstage. The altar comes back under the stage while he does his routine and then goes back up toward the end so it can take Bo offstage without having to deal with the fans. Got it?" he asked carefully.

Hap shifted his weight and scrubbed a hand through his hair, ending up with a handful of blue goop that he had to wipe on a nearby instrument case. "Got it."

As it turned out, Bo really wanted nothing more from Tara than to stare at him while he performed. Well . . . that and to hang from some wires while they flew her over the stage. From the looks of things, she wasn't all that happy with the arrangement.

Confucian had hurried over to Tara to coach her and smooth out the things she'd said to Bo. She must've come to the same conclusion Hap had.

Yes, they were desperate.

Yes, Nova really was sitting just up the stairs from them, and he had his own personal assassin with him.

Yes, the book was in the box sitting right in front of them, begging to be smashed open.

Yes, they had to wait until the concert started to get the book.

Yes, Bo was an idiot who'd likely get them all killed.

But . . . yes, they owed Confucian for all he'd done for them since they'd arrived on the Lizard Comet. Confucian had risked a lot in going to check on the ship. He hadn't freaked out on them when he found out they'd wiped out his army of paper birds. And he'd taken them into the caves, and he'd disguised them.

Tara and Hap owed Confucian and needed to keep their promises to him. Tara had promised she would go onstage with Bo, and Hap had promised he'd leave the altar alone until the show had started. Hap *really* didn't feel like keeping his promise.

But he took some satisfaction in knowing Tara didn't want to keep her promise either. She fumed at the small crowd surrounding her.

The band fussed over Tara like she was a new pet: they loved her dress, loved her hair, loved her blue eyelashes. Loved her because Bo wanted her onstage with him.

Those sorts of people bugged Hap. His grandpa had called people like that *coattail voters*—the kind of people who waited until the last minute to go to the polls so they could be sure to cast their vote for the winning guy instead of voting for the person they actually wanted to win. During every election, Hap had to listen to Grandpa Hazzard rant about followers and the lack of real leaders in the world.

Grandpa would have hated the band. And he'd likely have given them all lectures on how to be okay being themselves with their own thoughts and opinions.

Hap really missed Grandpa Hazzard and wished with all his heart that Grandpa would just magically show up and have a solution to getting all the books and escaping from Nova and saving Laney, Mosh, and Hap's dad—along with the rest of the world.

Above them, the sounds of a frenzied crowd heightened into a dull roar.

"Time to go!" one of the band members shouted.

The band members moved into place on little platforms.

"Who runs everything? You know, makes sure the ropes and stuff all work? Doesn't he have stage hands?" Hap worried workers lurked somewhere in the dark and would stop him from getting the book out of the altar when it came back down.

"Bo only uses me. He doesn't like a lot of people around. He's not big on trust." Confucian had positioned himself near the altar, where a greasy blackened panel of buttons hung from cables. It looked old fashioned and less than reliable—which was saying something considering Hap had come from Earth, where technology was still infantile by universal standards.

Tara had been positioned on the back of the altar with her arms stretched to the sky like she was calling down the lightning forking through her dress. They had wires strapped to her that would connect with other wires once she got onstage. Bo sat in front of her, looking regal and smug. The band people crouched low on their platforms as if preparing to jump, and then the announcer shouted above, "Bo Shocks and the Sungrazers!"

The band members' platforms shot up like bullets exploding from guns.

Then Hap remembered how it had seemed that they'd leaped inhumanly high straight from the stage. The quick little elevator platforms they stood on likely helped create that illusion.

Bo's platform moved much slower for his grand entrance. Tara's face looked terrible.

Not terrible as in ugly or messy or anything, but terrible as in scared out of her mind, furious with everyone, and likely to hit the first person who messed with her. That person would likely be Hap. It usually was.

Also terrible as in cool, with her arms outstretched and her dress forking in lightning flashes. She looked powerful. Hap smiled at her. He remembered his dad saying, "Bravery is being afraid but doing it anyway." Tara was the living definition of bravery.

Then everyone was gone except Hap and Confucian.

The crowd topside whistled, screamed, and sang along as Bo crooned out the words, "Riding a comet to the end of time . . ."

"That has got to be cool," Hap said.

"What?"

"Having all that noise up there be about *you*. It would be awesome to have people cheering your name and singing your songs. Bo is pretty lucky. It's gotta be cool."

"Yes. I'm sure it is." Confucian's jaw moved, like he was grinding his teeth or something.

"Dude, you okay?"

"Fine."

Only he didn't look fine at all. He looked miserable. But not knowing what he could do about that misery, Hap could only try to be pleasant and listen if Confucian decided to talk about whatever was bugging him. Hap wandered to where the altar had been and looked up.

"You know . . . all that screaming and *noise* up there is about *me*—in a way," Confucian said finally. He'd stood next to Hap, following Hap's gaze to the ceiling—now closed off and covered by the altar.

"How so?"

Confucian sighed. "It's a secret. Even the band doesn't know."

"Is this a secret you want to tell? Because you can tell me. I can keep secrets." And he could. Keeping confidences was as important as telling the truth.

Confucian seemed torn, as if considering all the implications of letting his secret out. "I write Bo's music." The words came out in a rush of air, and then Confucian blinked and smiled a little stupidly. "There. I said it. All those songs that people all over the universe sing in their showers—those are *my* lyrics."

Hap couldn't keep from seeing Confucian in a whole new light. "Seriously? That's awesome! You're probably the richest kid in the universe! I bet you make a ton of money."

"You'd lose that bet. You'd have better luck at the tables."

Hap felt the smile slide off his face. "What? Are you saying he doesn't pay you?"

Confucian shook his head, his fingers knuckled white around the cables. "It's like an apprenticeship. He owns anything I create until I learn everything I can learn from him. He says he'll let me onstage with him when I'm ready." Confucian's gaze trailed back toward the ceiling and the screaming fans. "There's more . . ." But Confucian never said what *more* was.

"So he's *really* not paying you?"

"No. He really is not."

"That is totally whacked. And don't give me that look! It *is* whacked. I know you say the guy is like a brother to you, but I'm a brother, and I can tell you I would *never* take advantage of my sister like that. I might pull her hair every once in a while or hog the TV so she can't watch her lame girl shows, but I would *never* steal from her."

"Bo isn't—"

"Yes, he is! He's totally stealing from you! Dude, you need to man up and get a backbone. I've been thinking this all day. He's taking you for a ride. You're probably the smartest person I will ever meet and you're, like, overboard crazy nice to people. You don't owe Tara and me anything, yet you've been nothing but helpful and forgiving. Bo is taking advantage of your doormat personality. It's time you stand up for yourself."

"I don't think he's taking advantage of me. He's training me."

Hap blew a raspberry. "Whatever. You're trained enough if you're writing the guy's songs. You know what I think? I think he's afraid of the competition. If you get the chance to have your own name as a singer and start writing your own songs, then he'll be left in the black hole of his ego."

"He isn't that bad." Confucian's protests weakened as Hap's tirade grew in volume and intensity.

"Not that bad? You run his stage, get his props, clean his suits and capes, and the guy can't be bothered to learn your actual name? Don't get me wrong, I think nicknames are cool. My real name's Frederick, and I'd beat up anyone who tried calling me that because I like my nickname. But you *don't* seem to like yours!" Hap pointed a finger at Confucian. "You need to get out on that stage!"

Confucian stopped protesting altogether. He looked like he at least considered Hap's words. And while Confucian was thinking, Hap realized that a lot of time had passed, and the altar had yet to come down from the stage.

"How long until it comes back?" Hap said.

"Not long." Though Confucian looked shaken from his private thoughts. He wrinkled his brow. "It should've come by now . . ."

Hap tapped his foot—he felt like he was going to suffocate if he breathed any more of the stifling, greasy-smelling air under the stage. He needed to move, wanted to go where there was light, where the blue-white flash of his suit wouldn't blind him every few moments.

The other platforms that the band had used to burst from the stage floor were already down.

Hap tried to breathe normally. He felt light-headed and nervous and *worried*.

"What's taking it so long?" he asked after several minutes of feeling like his heart was going to leap out of his chest.

"I don't know . . . maybe Bo changed the routine because of Tara being in the act?" Confucian didn't look hopeful that this was really the case, which made Hap worry even more.

That's when Tara screamed.

12. Bo Shocks Gets Shocked

"Tara!" Hap grabbed a hold of one of the pulleys used to hoist the altar, but it was taut and unmovable.

"How do I get up there? We gotta get up there!" He yanked hard on the pulley but couldn't make it budge even a little.

"You can't go up there!" Confucian's face was wide in horror that Hap would even suggest such a thing. "They're in the middle of a concert!"

"I don't care if they're in the middle of figuring out universal peace. I'm going up!" Hap hopped onto one of the platforms and hit the red button he figured would start the thing.

He was right. It did start, but he was totally unprepared for the way it rocketed him up. The stage floor remained dark above him. He'd expected it to open automatically, but the platform hurtled him up to the ceiling. He threw his arms up, bracing himself for the inevitable crash.

At the last moment one layer of the ceiling whisked to the side, but a thinner secondary layer remained closed. He burst through, feeling the splintered wood scratch at his arms and face as he raced past.

And then he was weightless—above the audience and stage, looking down at the lights layering patterns all over the dome, and the fans throbbing and screaming in delight at this new turn of events.

Weightlessness ended way faster than Hap would have liked, and Hap began plummeting to the stage. He'd spent a lot of time in his life fantasizing about being famous and onstage. But now that he faced the impending death of crashing into the ground, fame didn't seem as cool as he'd once imagined.

And then something hit him hard in the middle of the chest, and he was no longer falling but swinging wide to the right.

He felt himself slipping and grabbed on to whatever had caught him. The *whatever* turned out to be a *whoever*.

"Tara?" he felt bewildered to have been saved by the girl he'd been trying to save. "What are you doing?"

"Catching you! Idiot!" She added the *idiot* almost as an after-thought. He held on tighter, feeling her grip on him give way entirely as they swung back over the stage. "What are you doing?"

"You screamed!" Hap felt a wave of sickness wash over him as another burst of wood heaved up from the floor followed by Confucian.

Unlike Hap, Confucian was ready to be propelled into the open air and knew how to use his legs to catch his fall so that he landed on his feet into a weird sort of crouch that looked very cool. He looked up and saw Hap and Tara hanging and immediately ran along the length of the stage to hit a button that apparently ran a pulley system that slowly lowered the swinging Hap and Tara toward the stage.

Lily glided over the stage, circling over Confucian as though keeping a protective eye on him.

Bo shot them glares in between shooting dazzling white grins at the audience. He kept singing, but Hap knew that when this was all over, Bo was going to order them dead for interrupting his show.

The fans went ballistic. They loved the new twists of the concert, clapping wildly, louder than Hap imagined possible.

"Why were you screaming?" Hap demanded to know.

And then he saw the tears in Tara's eyes. "Laney!" Her breath caught in a sob in her throat. "Laney!"

"Laney what?"

But she couldn't say any more than she had. She pointed, and from their vantage point Hap saw what could possibly be bad enough to make Tara scream.

Meg.

Standing over Laney in the aisle.

Meg's gun was trained on Laney, who was lying down on the ground, blood pooling underneath her.

Meg had shot Laney.

No one in the crowd seemed to even notice the assault that had taken place in the aisle at the center of the stadium. The crowd was so wrapped up in the concert, nothing else in the world mattered—not even the life of one really nice human who had taken care of Hap and Tara and had watched out for them ever since they'd left Earth.

Hap's foot touched down at the back of the stage. "What happened?" he asked, but before she could answer, the wires still attached to her went taut, and she was pulled into the air again. One of the band members had danced over and readjusted the settings. Hap tried to grab hold and keep her with him, but the wires had jerked her up so suddenly that he didn't have enough time to react.

He looked back over to the area where Laney lay on the floor but couldn't see her anymore now that he was lower. But he could still see Meg.

Confucian picked his way toward Hap—his mouth saying things that Hap couldn't hear or understand.

Hap had no idea what he should do—what he *could* do. He took a step forward toward Laney, then one to the side toward Confucian, then one back toward Tara, where she hung from the wires. And then, without any plan or thought, he charged forward, intent on jumping off the stage and saving Laney.

He was so blinded by rage and fear for Laney's life that it took him entirely off guard to run smack into Bo, who'd unknowingly been dancing in Hap's way.

Bo made an *umph!* noise.

Hap made an *eyah!* noise.

And then Bo was down on the ground with Hap sprawled over the top of him.

Oddly, Bo's music kept playing. More specifically Bo's voice kept singing. Without a hesitation. Without a glitch. The music and singing went on *without* Bo.

And everyone noticed the problem immediately.

And the crowd went from cheering and frenzied to silent, with nothing but the croon of the song still filling the air—with a voice that, now that Hap considered it, sounded a lot like Confucian's. Hap tried to untangle himself from Bo's ridiculous cape. He didn't care that everyone had stopped screaming. He didn't care that Bo was going to be furious. *Laney* was there and she needed him. He finally got his legs underneath him and stood, darting a quick glance behind him to locate movement from the corner of his eye. It was one of the band members who'd gone and replaced a spoon-looking thing into the bowl that they called a sonico basin, which was like a recording device.

The music cut off with a strangle. And the silence became something more. Something tangible.

Confucian lowered Tara from the wires again. Only this time, no one stopped him. Hap jumped off the stage and into the silent, startled crowd. They allowed him to pass through, moving aside to give him room.

When Hap finally arrived at the spot he was sure Laney had been, the ground was empty.

Meg was gone. Laney was gone. Nothing but the puddle of blood remained to prove he'd come to the right place. He pivoted, trying to see through the silent crowd. Where had she gone? What had happened?

Some people watched him curiously, but most were focused on the stage.

Then murmurings started. A low undercurrent of discord.

Bo's a fake!

He's not even singing!

I want my money back!

We should all get our money back!

Fake!

Fraud!

Hap whirled back to face the stage, not knowing what else to do and deciding to return to Tara and at least get her off the stage now that the crowd was going pitchfork-and-torches crazy.

The crowd didn't part for him on his way to the stage, so he had to shove and weave through bodies to get back.

Someone in the crowd whistled when Confucian picked up the microphone. Another person screamed out, "What's going on here?"

"Hi," Confucian said to the crowd.

"Get off the stage!" someone shouted.

"Hey, sorry. I know things seem a little less than zane right now, but you're here for a show, and you're going to get one."

Hap had made it to the stage when Confucian's low clear voice sang out. It was something Hap hadn't heard before. It wasn't from any of the Bo Shocks songs that Svarta had in her collection. It must have been something new.

Hap climbed up onto the stage while the crowd grumbled loud enough that Confucian could barely be heard over them. Tara was down and detaching herself from the wires. The rest of the band was hovering over Bo, who had acquired a bloody nose in his fall.

They handed him parts of their clothing to mop up the blood on his face. The guy looked miserable. Hap thought he deserved a little misery.

Confucian sang loud enough that his voice overcame the cacophony of the audience.

Hap reached out to Tara and helped her finish up with the wires. He was grateful no one stopped them. Tara reached her arms around Hap. "Meg . . . just . . . shot her!" she whimpered into his shoulder.

"How? Drubbers aren't allowed under the dome."

"It was a gun. An Earth gun. She just shot her." Tara's whispered words shook with horror.

"What happened after that? Where is she now?"

Tara's head rolled against his shoulder as she shook it. "I don't know! Some guys carried her out when you got off the stage."

Hap pulled her into a hug, patting Tara's back, feeling stupid and helpless.

Confucian's voice was now loud and filling the space inside the dome. The crowd had stopped catcalling and seemed to be listening to the music. A few people actually began cheering. They liked what they heard.

The audience clapped, swayed, and bobbed to the music.

Confucian was a hit. Lily swooped and dived over the stage in a way that delighted everyone in the audience. Hap noted that several of his Confucius-style quotes were mingled into the lyrics.

Bo stood up and scowled at Confucian. "How dare you?" he yelled. "How dare you ruin my concert!"

Confucian stopped singing, and silence filled the auditorium once again at this new turn of events. The audience didn't look upset to have the new concert disrupted by the argument. They were enthralled, like they were watching a movie.

"All of you!" Bo yelled. He pointed at Hap, Tara, and Confucian in turn. "*I'm* the star here! How dare you ruin my concert and then take it over! How dare you!" His face was full of thunderous anger. He actually looked pretty scary with the bloodied nose and the anger.

"How dare *you*?" Confucian returned, only he seemed calm, not angry, not scary, just a little bit sad. "I've written your songs *and* sung them for you. Yet you've always denied me the opportunity to join you onstage. You say you'll help me and train me, but I'm starting to think you're just using me. And I'm done being used."

"You tell him, man!" someone near the front of the stage shouted out. A few whistles and cat calls followed.

Bo's face twisted as if he felt uncertain on how to proceed when the people of the audience seemed to be on Confucian's side.

Hap had a thing or two to say to Bo and opened his mouth to be as impertinent as his mother always accused him of being. But at that moment a gun popped and a bullet hit one of the crystal guitars leaning against a pillar, creating a horrible ringing noise before the guitar exploded in a shower of crystal shards.

"I guess the concert's over!" Don Nova shouted. The six-barrel gun in his hand was now aimed directly at Bo. Two of the band members gasped and threw themselves in front of Bo like human body shields. The other two cowered where they were, likely hoping to go unnoticed by the man with the dark unibrow and gun.

People in the audience, realizing a working gun had been introduced to the concert, had decided that maybe the concert really was over. Screaming started up again, only this time it wasn't a cheering-on-a-rock-star screaming, but a run-for-your-lives-in-terror screaming.

Hap turned his body a little to shield Tara more from Nova's view.

"You said I could check out that altar of yours when the concert's over." Nova pointed his gun from Bo to the altar and back to Bo again. "Since everyone's leaving, I guess you won't mind if I have that look now."

Bo sniveled, cried, whimpered, and shook his head. "I . . . I d-don't mind," he stammered.

"Fantastic." Nova motioned someone forward, and several big guys with bulging arms hopped onto the stage and over to the altar. They hefted it, making their huge arms bulge even more under the strain of the weight, and they carried it to the edge of the stage.

Feeling angry, Hap stared at Nova. He'd failed. Again. And Nova would get yet another book beyond the one he already had.

What would Grandpa Hazzard do? Hap wondered. *What would a man of honor do?*

Nova shifted to meet Hap's stare, and then his long furry eyebrow raised up over his black eyes and his mouth twitched. With the twitch of his mouth also came a flicker in those horrible dark eyes.

Nova knew.

He had recognized Hap.

13. CONCERTS THAT END WITH A BANG

HAP SWALLOWED HARD, UNABLE TO MOVE.

"He knows!" Hap whispered. "Tara, he knows who I am!"

"Are you sure?" she whispered back. He felt her breath on the back of his neck. She'd stayed close behind him. He wished he could hide her behind something solid—something that Nova would be unlikely to shoot at, since it seemed inevitable Nova *would* be shooting soon.

"Absolutely," Hap breathed, holding Nova's stare. "Absolutely sure."

"Well, well." Nova's voice boomed, even over the roar of a rapidly departing crowd. He seemed unsure where to keep his gun aimed, whether at Bo or the altar. Or at Hap. "Looks like I've finally found the vermin on this rock."

Hap remained motionless.

"After all I did for you. I let you link home, took you in as one of my own, and what did you do to repay me? You stole my book. You freed my enemies. No loyalty from kids these days. Come on down here, kid."

"Why? So you can shoot me?" The strength of his own voice amazed Hap. It hadn't cracked or wavered at all.

"Shoot you?" Nova laughed.

Bo whimpered from where he stood bleeding and looking ridiculous. His lip trembled.

Hap felt good about the fact that his lip didn't tremble, even if his knees knocked a little. No one would notice knees like they would notice Bo's terrified face.

"I'm not going to shoot such lovely bait. The scientist will want you alive. And I want the book you stole from me. I bet he'd be willing to trade."

"He's not going to trade! My life isn't worth the problems you'd create if you had that book." Did Nova not know they had two books now? Did he not know about their stop at the Anansi planet?

"Hap, what are you doing?" Tara breathed behind him, so low that he almost felt the words more than he'd actually heard them.

He didn't answer. If he moved, he would leave Tara exposed. He couldn't do that, so he was just stalling—delaying the inevitable. But what choice did he have. It wasn't like Nova hadn't seen Tara. He knew she was there. She just didn't make an easy target with Hap in front of her.

Nova flicked his wrist to the side and shot out a pillar near Hap then trained his gun back on Hap. Crystal shards rained down on him and everyone else on the stage—including the guys who were wrestling the stone box off the stage. Those guys grunted and looked irritated, but didn't actually grumble against their boss's pelting them with shrapnel.

They finished their job and settled the stone box at Nova's feet.

The crystal shards hurt as they pelted into Hap's exposed skin. Tara screamed, but so did anyone who was left still trying to scramble out of the auditorium. Hap might have screamed too; he wasn't sure.

"I said, *come down*. I don't have time to mess around. We have all those other books to find for my employers." Nova looked genuinely angry.

Tara pressed her hands into his back, nudging him forward. She wanted him to do as he was told. It remained the only option left to them.

Hap moved forward, feeling that Tara remained with him, moving forward as he did.

"Hap . . ." Confucian started to protest, but Hap waved him back. They'd gotten Confucian into enough trouble.

"That's right. That moralistic girl, bring her too."

They picked their way over the splinters of crystal, trying not to slip. Hap hated the way the crunching under his feet reminded him of the dream, of all the glass on the streets and the panic in the faces of all the people of the world in the moments before the world exploded.

He hated anything that reminded him of that nightmare-vision. He hated knowing that handing himself over to Nova so Nova could use him as bait to get another book would take Nova one step closer to making Hap's nightmare-vision come true. He hated the worry over what had happened to Laney.

He crouched low at the edge of the stage, ready to hop off, when his arm brushed against his leg and felt something that Hap had forgotten he'd placed inside his sock.

The blackout wand.

Hap still had the blackout wand.

He reached under his pant leg cuff, pretending to scratch at his ankle, and slid the slender black rod into his sleeve.

He silently thanked Grandpa Hazzard for all those hours of sleight-of-hand practice. Hap at least had *something* with which to defend himself—if he could only move fast enough. He jumped off then turned to help Tara off the stage. The lightning forks of her costume flickered, but they seemed far less electric with her eyes swimming in tears over her grief at watching Meg shoot Laney. And she looked exhausted. They hadn't had any sleep since arriving on the comet, and Hap's internal clock told him he was up way past bedtime. If he looked anything like Tara, no wonder Nova recognized him.

He met her eye and tried to be reassuring. He offered a smile and a wink, which snapped Tara out of her resignation. She'd given up— Hap could tell. But with that smile and that wink, she knew he had a plan, and a fire seemed lit inside of her again.

Nova had gone to nearly ignoring them now that they'd moved as directed. Besides, he had the stone box in front of him. Everything else took second place to the box and the book he'd find inside. He tugged at his collar and produced a long silver chain and pendant. He unclipped the pendant from the chain, which looked like it would fit perfectly inside the carving of the lotus flower on the box.

Hap would *not* allow Nova to open that box.

Not today.

Not with Laney hurt or worse.

Not with Mosh still missing.

Not after all Hap had done to find that box first.

He put out his arms and lifted Tara off the stage, swinging her around and down so he faced Nova directly, placing Tara between them.

He motioned with his eyes and chin for her to duck.

She immediately obeyed.

As she did, he pointed the wand directly at Nova and focused all the energy he had into it. "Blackout!" he yelled, still not knowing if the words needed to be said to make the wand work as he jammed his thumb hard into the depression at the base of the wand.

Nova collapsed.

Several Earth guns belonging to Nova's guards clicked and were suddenly aimed straight at Hap's head.

This is the end, Hap thought. *Here's where I go down, but I'm going with honor.*

He closed his eyes, waiting for the bullets to start flying, and wondering what would happen when he was dead.

His family was filled with church-going people. He was a church-going kind of guy himself.

He hoped they'd all been right about heaven.

He squeezed his eyes tighter, waiting for the pain after hearing the guns fire—seemingly all at once

And waited.

And waited.

Until he finally peeked. Shouldn't getting shot hurt?

He stumbled over Tara when he took a step forward in surprise. "Holy Houdini . . ." he breathed. None of Nova's guys were left standing. They lay in heaps all around. None of them so much as twitched.

Hap ran his hand over himself to check for blood, but he really *hadn't* been shot!

"I'm alive!" he yelled.

Tara finally dared to look. She'd closed her eyes too. "You are?" she asked, looking up from her crouched position.

"He is," Amar said.

"Wow. That was good timing. I thought I was a goner for sure." Hap gave a little smile of gratitude, though he was sure the smile was as wobbly as his legs.

"Where's Laney?" Tara demanded while she checked Nova for any weapons he was carrying. She'd changed a lot since they'd left Earth. No way would she have rummaged through people's pockets back then.

"They still have her." Svarta sounded caught between rage and anguish. Those few words were like a howl of pain. "I was looking for a way to get her back when she called in saying she'd gotten away on her own and had found the box and that it was being used as a prop by that idiot moron—"

Her hair was slicked back. She looked soaked, like she'd been in a steam room. Sweat stained her clothes. And with her hair slicked back, Hap saw her threatening eyes scanning through the debris and people on the stage until they found Bo Shocks.

He yelped when he realized he'd been targeted.

In one bound she was onstage and had him by the collar, dragging him to his feet. "What do you think you're doing messing with the artifacts and history of the comet, you spineless no-talent faker?"

He made several noises in his throat, but nothing formed into actual words.

"If my sister dies, I am going to expel you into dark space with a space suit that will keep you alive long enough to be really, really sorry that you are absolutely stupid. Do you understand me?"

Bo made a few more noises and then passed out.

"Coward." Svarta grunted, letting him drop to the floor. She turned to Amar. "I need to find her." Svarta's eyes swam like Tara's had—full of tears and pain.

Amar nodded. "I'll stay with the children. Tremble is at the front, dealing with comet security, who, of course, showed up too late to be of any use. Take her with you for backup. I'll handle security on my own."

Svarta agreed and was off the stage and bounding up the stairs leading to the casinos and the causeway.

Amar swiftly removed a chain and pendant that had been hanging around his neck under his shirt. It was identical to the one Nova had. He pressed his silver flower into the one carved into the box, which made the carving deepen into the stone with a grinding noise and hiss like pressure being released.

A drawer opened along the middle, where the band of carved leaves and flowers hid its existence. It had looked like nothing more than decoration, but that decoration hid the seams of the panel within the box. Amar removed the book, tucking it into a pack he had slung over his shoulder and under one arm.

On impulse, Hap pulled the identical necklace from Nova's body and stuffed it into his pocket. No reason for Nova to have access to the other stone boxes.

"So you didn't just write his songs? You sang them too?" Hap looked at Confucian for an answer.

"Yes, I actually do the singing too." Confucian shrugged. "Bo hurt his voice when he went to Roche Limit. He screamed for too long and hard, and it permanently damaged his voice. I've been singing for him ever since."

"And he's not paying you?" Hap exclaimed. "Wait, what's Roche Limit?"

"An amusement park. Bo's apparently afraid of heights." Confucian grinned, warming up to the idea of sharing Bo's dirty secrets.

Comet security marched down the aisles and stairs to the stage. "We demand a full explanation!" one particularly beefy guard asked.

"I can explain," Confucian said before anyone else had a chance. Lily screeched in response to her master's voice, as if telling everyone to shut up and listen. "Your incompetent security has endangered the lives of Bo Shocks and the Sungrazers! Look at our stage! Ruined! Bo's career has been thwarted. I had to step in to try to salvage the show after a paying guest to our concert was fired upon at close range right there in the audience, *in the middle of a concert!* If you'd been doing your jobs, this would never have occurred. Then an entire mob of militants came in shooting up the stage, threatening the band. Where have you been during all of this?"

Confucian's fury had pretty much made everyone feel a little sheepish. Even Hap and the other band members lowered their gazes to the floor in shame.

"These pirates," Confucian continued, "very nearly killed the newest member of our band. Does your insurance cover the death of a band member? If Bo decides to take action against you in Elektra's court systems, he will *own* this muddy ice ball and he'll have you all fired so you can be replaced by competent security!"

The beefy man spoke up again. "I'm terribly sorry, Fusion. You'll put in a good word for us with Bo, won't you?"

"My name is Confucian! You will call me by *my* name. You will not dishonor my family by taking away the name they gave me."

And even with everything else that had gone wrong, even with Laney's and Mosh's safety still in question, Hap smiled. Confucian had finally stopped being a cosmic doormat.

Bo would have a lot to deal with when he finally got over his fainting spell. Hap suspected Bo had been faking it and was secretly pretending to be passed out on the floor so he didn't have to deal with the mess of the situation.

None of the band argued with Confucian's story. No one called Confucian out for taking over the concert—even if Bo had been furious. No one mentioned that Bo's career was likely in the universal toilet because he'd been discovered to be a fraud. As soon as the news broadcasters got hold of that information, it would be game-over for the comet-cruising rock star.

The guards hadn't been in the auditorium. They didn't know that Bo was a fake who'd likely get mobbed by angry ex-fans.

And Confucian didn't bother explaining any of that to them. He stared them down and made them all mumble apologies and send off for a medic to see to Bo and the members of the band who had cuts and nicks from the exploding crystal. Confucian was in control. And no one argued.

The security personnel cleaned up everything, put Nova in their detention block, and had his henchmen hauled off. Confucian remained busy, taking care of the band and the aftermath of the concert.

Hap, Tara, and Amar made their way back to Nana. She'd suffered a bit of damage because Nova *hadn't* been as rational as she'd assumed, and he *had* tried to blast away the hatch to get to his little pet.

Scars of gunfire surrounded the door, and dents testified to the places where people had tried to kick the door in at weak points.

"Can you still fly?" Amar asked as soon as she allowed him access to the ship. "Will the doors still seal out the vacuum of space?"

"We will not need repairs," she responded. "Not immediately. The life support will not be affected. We can leave as soon as the others return. They *will* return, won't they?" Nana sounded frantic at those last words, as if desperate to hear news of why everyone had not yet come back to the ship. She apparently suspected bad news.

Amar didn't respond.

"Where are they? I have not been able to connect with them on their keys." Nana was nothing if not persistent.

Amar wiped his hand down his face in general defeat. He reached into the bag hanging around him and pulled out the book they'd rescued from the stone box. He thumped the book down on the counter in the supply room and pulled the table from the wall, letting it slam down into place so he could unfold a chair and sit at the table.

Nana didn't lecture him on minding his manners and treating her with respect. She usually freaked when anyone slammed things around. She must've been worried.

"I don't know where they are," he said finally, addressing Nana. "Laney was caught under fire. They took her away. We don't know her condition."

"If she still lives, what are your plans to recover her?" Nana asked.

Tara leaned against the wall, alternating between clicking her nails and chewing her lip. Tears still flowed down her cheeks. Hap sniffed. Tears didn't flow down his cheeks because he wiped them away too fast for anyone to see them.

"We'll need a bargaining chip."

Hap glanced up at the determination in Amar's voice. "What kind of bargaining chip?" he asked.

"We need to get Nova out of the Lizard Comet detention block."

Hap shook his head. Surely he hadn't heard Amar right, but once he met Amar's serious dark eyes, he realized it was true.

Nova was the most dangerous man Hap had met in the universe, and Amar planned to break him out of jail.

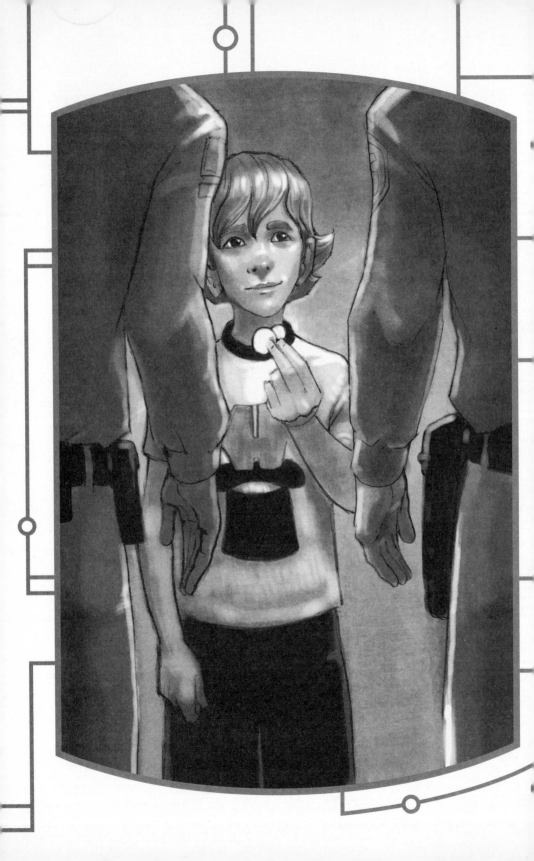

14. MAGICAL MISCONDUCT

AMAR CALLED SVARTA AND TREMBLE back to the ship to make plans for the jailbreak. The debate over how to get him out of prison had been fiery, but they'd calmed down once they got the basics down.

Tremble spoke up. "What are we doing about docking security? Like you said, they're more alert now than they were before. How do we keep them from noticing we're rolling a fugitive onto our ship?" Tremble looked grim, not angry like she was going to break off into Googool or anything, but determined. Her antennae stood straight and firm, not quivering, and her hands opened a holo projection of the docking bay, security check points, the doors to the causeway, and all exits. They had a job, and she'd do her part. When she wasn't fighting Googool for control of her body, she was a huge asset. When she was fighting with Googool? Well, the best thing anyone could do was run for cover and hide until Tremble got control back.

Svarta and Amar joined Tremble at the holo projection. Schematics ran in glowing computerized lines down the side of the projection. "Security guards are always on duty here and here." Svarta said as she pointed.

"And the monitoring system has hookups here, here, and here," Tremble added. Every time the holo area was touched, it lit up red and flashed.

It worried Hap to see so many flashing red spots. Those were all trouble areas—places where the plan could go wrong. He kept telling himself that the adults would handle everything, that Laney and Mosh would be safe soon enough. But it felt *tricky*.

"We need to distract the guards. They're gamblers—everyone on this snowball is. Does anyone have cards? Anything they can make bets on?" Svarta looked wild with desperation. Laney was the last bit of family Svarta had. They needed each other.

"I have a few scotch and soda coins," Hap offered, thinking of the few magic tricks he had in his jacket pocket. He'd left the jacket on the ship while roaming around the comet because he didn't want to lose it. The jacket and those few little things in his pockets were his only physical links to Earth.

"It's a thought, but I doubt they're going to take a kid up on buying them drinks when they're on duty, but thanks for trying." Svarta turned her back on Hap to focus on the holo projection.

"No. I'm not offering to get them drunk. It's a trick. A magic trick. Scotch and soda coins . . . I can get them to place bets on whether or not I can make the centavo disappear. Here, let me show you." Hap hurried to his room, grabbed his jacket, and hurried back.

He fished around for the coins until he found what he was looking for. "See . . . It's a trick." He handed the copper centavo and the silver half dollar to Tremble and told her to hold them in her hands while he worked the magic. He waved his hands over hers and then told her to give him back the copper coin.

Tremble gasped when she opened her palm to find there was no copper coin, only the silver half dollar and a silver quarter. The copper coin had disappeared.

"Where did it go?" She looked at the floor. "You've got it, don't you?" She made him open his own hands and turn out his pockets to prove he didn't have anything.

"I promise. I don't have the copper centavo." It made him laugh to find an alien from a planet that had space travel, and who had seen so much of the universe, could still be fooled by a little scotch-and-soda trick.

"We're wasting time!" Svarta said. "The trick is good, kid. Keep the guards busy with that. We only need a few minutes to get Nova on our ship. Tremble, I need you to—" Svarta blew her hair out of her eyes and turned a stern gaze on Tremble, who still stared at the coins in her hand. "Can you pay attention? This is important."

Tremble's body shook like she was in the startup mode of an earthquake. Her face pinked and then paled again. "Yes, I can pay attention."

"Very good, Tremble!" Nana encouraged. Nana always praised Tremble when she managed to keep control of herself.

Tremble smiled but immediately turned her focus on Svarta.

"I'll need you to wipe out the monitors. We certainly don't need them sending even more security down here."

While Svarta gave orders, the ship underneath them vibrated. Someone was either landing or taking off on the comet. Hap looked out the windows to get a look as to who it was. He worried maybe Nova's guys had changed their minds and were taking off without Nova.

It was someone landing. A flashy red spaceship. Hap looked away since it wasn't anything to worry about. If Svarta caught him daydreaming, she'd be really mad.

No one wanted to make Svarta mad right now.

The plan was simple enough. At least simple for Hap and Tara, who only had to distract the docking guards while the rest maneuvered Nova onto the ship. It was pretty complicated for everyone else. When everything was settled, everyone left to do the tasks assigned to them. Hap felt like they should have had a pep talk or something for courage before they left, but Svarta had merely grunted, "Don't anyone mess up. My sister's life is on the line."

"This is a bad idea." Tara had said this four times already as they hovered near the place Amar instructed them to wait.

Confucian had been a big part of the plan, giving them access to places they'd never been able to go otherwise. Hap, Tara, and Confucian had made hasty good-byes. Confucian had finally demanded some respect from Bo and was granted quite a number of things, like back pay, costumes, and a couple of space suits. He gave Hap and Tara the suits they'd worn in the cave system and the costumes they'd had onstage as parting gifts. He'd also given Hap a little paper dragon and taught him how to wake it up and put it to rest. He'd given Tara a new falcon he'd barely put together to begin replacing his little army of birds. He explained that with training, their paper pets would be as obedient as Lily the falcon. Hap hated not having anything to give in return and tried to hand over one of his pocket tricks, but Confucian had cast a doubtful look over the lot of Hap's pocket contents and insisted nothing was necessary.

"You've given me courage, which will help me restore honor in time. There is nothing greater you could give me," Confucian had said. Tara seemed over her crush on the guy, which was good, because that had been annoying.

Hap was glad to get the chance to thank Confucian for everything and to say good-bye. After they busted Nova out of detention, they were all going to be in tons of trouble, and there wouldn't be time for good-bye then. He hoped Confucian wouldn't get involved in the investigation that was sure to follow. He kept insisting he wouldn't, but Hap wasn't so certain.

"I mean it—this is a bad idea," Tara said a fifth time.

"Do you want to get Laney and Mosh back?" Hap kept watch on the intersecting hallways as he'd been instructed.

"Of course I do, but we've finally got the bad guy in jail. Shouldn't we leave him there?"

Hap spared his watch on the hallways a few seconds so he could shoot her a look of disbelief. They'd washed off all of the makeup and had changed into their own clothes again, but Tara still had bits of gold and blue glitter in her eyelashes. "You're such a girl."

"Yes, I am. It's one of my better qualities. It means I don't pass gas on small spaceships when other people like to breathe clean air, and I try hard to keep my body odor pleasant. Those are obviously girl traits since *you* don't seem to care about those sorts of things at all. And my being a girl has nothing to do with breaking Nova out of jail!"

"Tara, honestly! Can you shout that a little louder? I don't think they heard in the next solar system."

"Well, it's true." She lowered her voice, but speaking softer didn't mean the words weren't sharp.

"You're forgetting the Dark Ones." Hap still wasn't sure what the Dark Ones were exactly, but even Amar shuddered when anyone mentioned them. That had to be bad. "Do you think they'll let him sit in a jail run by people with less intelligence than Gygak? He'll be out with or without our help. And if he breaks out without our help, then we lose Laney and Mosh too."

She harrumphed.

"What if it doesn't work?" she said after several minutes of grumbling to herself.

"You don't have to worry about that."

"Why not?"

Hap pointed at the miniature holo. "Because they've already got Nova, and it's our turn to do our job."

Tara groaned but followed Hap.

He tried to walk casually toward the causeway doors where the guards stood, looking ominous and unpleasant. One was bald, and one had hair like Bo Shocks. He must've been a fan.

"Loosen up," he whispered to Tara.

"I am loose," she whispered back.

"A robot who's never been oiled is looser than you. Seriously, Tara." But her legs remained stiff as she moved them forward. It would've been funny if it didn't look so suspicious.

"Hey," Hap said when he was within a few feet of them.

One of the guards looked up and then looked away. The other acted like Hap hadn't said anything at all.

These guys weren't like the stupid guards back at Stupak's Circle. Hap realized tricking them wouldn't be anywhere near as easy. So he switched tactics.

"Hey, mister." Hap coughed pathetically as though he was sick. "Can you spare some credits?" Starting out as a panhandler made more sense than starting out as some kid just messing around. He needed to look *needy*.

Tara, who'd stood so stiffly next to him that she could have passed for a concrete pillar, finally moved naturally. Unfortunately, her natural move was one that showed her surprise at his question and only made them look more suspicious than they already had appeared.

The guards were, at least, both looking at him now. "No," the balding one said.

"Look, I'm really low on funds. We need to eat. We're starving. And we need to refuel, and if I could get a little seed money, have a go at the tables . . . I could get enough to get off this rock and back home. I'd pay you back out of my winnings."

"If I give you money and you go to the tables, you'll just lose it and then neither of us has any money," the bald guard said.

"I bet you're wrong."

"How can you bet I'm wrong? You got nothing to bet with."

Hap foraged in his pockets for a bit, taking his time and making a big show of it. He coughed a little more. He finally pulled out his coins, one silver American half dollar and one copper Mexican centavo. "I've got a little money to bet with." Hap held out the two coins.

"Those little bits of metal aren't going to buy you nothing on the comet, kid. I don't know what kind of money that is where you're from, but it isn't money on the comet."

"It's valuable where we're from." Tara finally found her voice. She threw in a cough too. It was about time, since Hap really didn't like being the one doing all the talking. It looked weird for him to be all pathetic and sickly when she stood there looking fine. Her cough didn't look too convincing since she rolled her eyes when she did it.

"If it's valuable, the money changers will handle it for you," Hairy Guard said.

"Oh, right." Tara coughed again. "Like we can trust them. Money changers are always taking advantage of kids like us. What do you think happened to all of our funds in the first place? The money changers took everything and handed us some sort of . . . *beans* and told us they'd given us a good deal."

"Beans?" Hairy Guard said.

"Beans?" Hap said at the same time.

"The magic beans."

Tara was apparently *not* good at improvisation.

Both guards laughed. Hairy Guard said, "Magic beans. You two are dumber than you look if you took magic beans in place of actual currency."

"Not me," Tara said. She lowered her voice like she was telling a secret. "I didn't believe it at all. At least not . . ." She paused and looked around.

The guards couldn't help it: they both leaned in as she continued speaking in her low, mysterious voice.

"I told him not to take the beans. I told him he was being stupid. I was like you guys. I didn't believe any of it. But then, I found . . . well, he can do things now. It's like the magic rubbed off on him a little."

The guards both groaned, rolled their eyes, and started shaking their heads. "You kids better scram before we haul you to detention. We should do it anyway. That way, you'd at least get a meal, since you're so *starving* and all." Bald Guard gave a look that said Hap looked anything but starving. Which was totally unfair. Hap hadn't lied. He was *always* starving.

"Okay, fine." Hap dropped the pretenses. These guys weren't stupid, and Hap didn't look sick. "But I *can* do a little magic."

"Magic is for underdeveloped star systems who haven't figured out weather yet," Bald Guard said.

"Sometimes, but I bet I *can* do magic. I *bet*." Hap itched to glance back at Nana to see if anything had happened yet. But if he looked, the guards would too, and that would totally defeat the purpose of diverting their attention on the trick.

"So what are you betting? You don't look like you got anything I want," Hairy Guard said.

"You can keep the coins if I lose. They really are valuable. They're from Earth. You ever been there?"

"Never heard of there," Bald Guard said.

"It's a pretty cool place. We're trying to get back to Earth, but these things take money. We need a little more. The universe is an expensive place."

"So my wife keeps reminding me," Bald Guard said. "All right, all right. Show us your all-powerful magic so we can take your worthless coins and then beat it. We're working here."

Hap thought he heard some scuffling on the stone tiles back toward the ships, but he kept his attention purposefully and dutifully on the coins in his hands. He opened his palm to display the two coins then picked them up with his other hand and slid the copper centavo behind the silver half dollar. "Hold out your hand," Hap directed Bald Guard. He seemed nicer than the other guy.

Bald Guard put out his hand, and Hap placed the coins into his palm. "Close your hand. Squeeze it tight into a fist then hold it out."

Bald Guard's lips quirked as if not believing he was actually doing what a kid told him to do, but he *did* do it. Hap wondered if the guy had kids of his own. He seemed like the sort of person to want kids, to be a good dad, to be patient even when the kids were being stupid.

Hap waved his hands slowly over Bald Guard's closed fist and chanted, "Abracadabra, bippity boppity . . ." He then blew lightly over the closed fist and held out his own hand again.

"I need you to hand me the copper coin back."

When the guard opened his fist and flipped the half dollar over to get the copper coin, only to find a silver quarter instead, he started laughing. "Hey! That was pretty good! You got me. How'd you do it?"

"Magic. Pure and simple magic." Hap smiled and bowed with a flourish.

Hairy Guard didn't laugh. He frowned and stamped a bit, insisting Hap had cheated and was hiding the copper coin in his pockets. Like Tremble, Hairy Guard made Hap show both of his hands and then turn out his pockets and roll up his sleeves.

"My kids would love that!" Bald Guard said.

So Hap had been right. Bald Guard was a family guy. It was nice to know that out in the universe, other people had dads. It made him miss his own dad a whole lot more, but he smiled.

"Not done . . ." Tara whispered between her teeth.

Hap took her words to mean that Nova was still out in the open. If the guards saw him, they'd all get put in detention for breaking him out. He eyed the guards for a moment before deciding what he had to do. "I could show you how to do it . . . if you want. I could give you the coins, and you could show your kids. They'd love it."

Tara inhaled sharply. She started to protest Hap's offer to give the coins away. She knew what they meant to him, but Hap smiled and shrugged and acted like she hadn't protested at all.

Hap's dad had shown him the scotch and soda trick when he was very little. The fuzzy memory gave comfort to Hap. He'd loved the trick and had spent several years begging his dad to teach how it was done.

It was a little disappointing to learn the trick behind the magic when he was eight years old. He remembered feeling let down that it wasn't really *real* magic, just a trick—an illusion. But he learned how to perform the illusion himself and learned all sorts of variations of it.

As he looked at Bald Guard, he thought about the kids who would learn the trick. Would they love those memories with their dad the way Hap did? He thought they might.

Besides, teaching the trick would require several minutes of training. It would buy time.

"Okay, let me do it again, but you hold the coins this time," Hap told Hairy Guard. "You just watch, so you can get a feel for how it's done."

He did the trick again, throwing a few other words into the magic spell he chanted—*Open sesame. Alakazam! May the force be with you . . .*

He figured if he was giving kids in the universe an earthling magic trick, he might as well throw in some earthling sayings to go along with it.

Then he slowly and carefully taught the mechanics of the trick. He almost laughed at Hairy Guard when the look of disappointment that it wasn't really magic spread over his face. Hap decided not to rub it in, though. No reason to make anyone angry.

He made Bald Guard do it several times until he had the hang of it. Tara nudged him as people began approaching the causeway entrance. They were the people from the flashy red ship that had landed earlier. It was time to wrap things up and get back to the ship.

"Your kids will love it," Hap said with a smile. "They'll think you're a superhero."

"I can't just take this," Bald Guard protested.

"Sure you can. I'm giving it to you. No strings attached." Grandpa Hazzard had liked that phrase, since some magic tricks *did* have strings attached.

The guard put the coins in his pocket and pulled out a thin bag with designs burned into the material. "You said you needed money. How much do you want for the magic beans?"

Hap laughed outright. Tara smiled.

"It's a gift." Hap shook his head, turning down the offer of payment.

"Well, okay. Then this is a gift too." He pushed the bag into Hap's hand then stiffened.

Hap heard it too.

A shout. A slam. A scream. And the engines of a ship firing up.

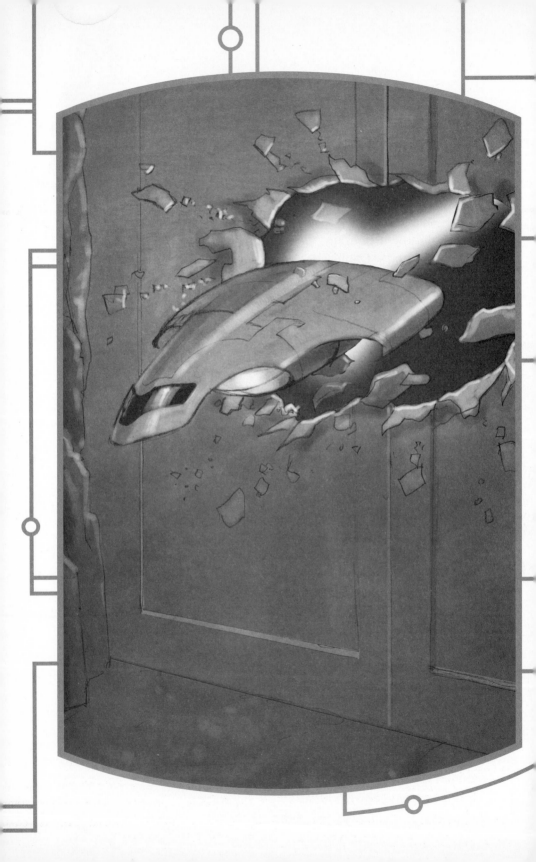

15. Don't Color on Bad Guys

The guards immediately abandoned Hap and Tara and ran toward the commotion. Hap and Tara followed close on their heels. At the hatch to another ship, Hap saw Mosh.

"Mosh!" Hap yelled. He was relieved to see his friend but terrified for his friend's safety as the big guy fought his way down the ship's ramp. Several of Nova's thugs were hanging off both of Mosh's arms and straining to pull him back on board as the ramp began lifting.

"Mosh!" Hap yelled again. He passed up the guards in his rush to get to Mosh.

"Hap!" Mosh roared, managing to throw off a couple of the guys pulling on his arms. Meg showed up in the hatchway and pointed her earth-made gun at Hap. Then she called out to Mosh and nodded toward Hap so that Mosh could see who was in her line of fire.

The ramp was halfway up. Mosh could still make it if he jumped. But he met Hap's gaze and stopped struggling.

"No! Mosh!" Hap took a step forward, but Meg tightened her grip on her gun. Hap was certain that if he'd taken a second step, Meg would have fired.

The guards moved to apprehend Meg, but Meg shook her head and said, "Don't be stupid."

They stopped, unsure how to proceed.

"It's okay. I'll be okay." Mosh nodded—his big bullfrog-pouched chin wobbling with the motion. "Good-bye, Hap," Mosh called, keeping eye contact with Hap until the ramp closed and sealed shut.

Hap closed his eyes against the image of Mosh making such a choice. By staying on board that ship with Meg, he'd prevented Meg from shooting Hap. *My fault. This is my fault.*

The ship jolted forward. Hap, Tara, and the guards jumped to get out of its way as it raced to the doors leading out to space.

Other clusters of people jumped to avoid being run over.

The docking area had a dual-chamber system. When a ship left the comet, it exited through the first set of doors. Then the oxygen drained out and the ship would be cleared to leave.

But the ship barreling toward the doors now had no intention of waiting for the proper protocol of allowing the first set to open, allow them in, and then to close so the docking bay wouldn't be exposed to the void of space. The ship fully intended on blasting its way out.

Someone screamed. It might have been Hap, but he wasn't sure. Bald Guard waved his hand over his chest, which activated a holo projection. He tapped furiously into the schematics floating in the air then slammed his hands together over the holo projection.

The ship made it to the doors, shattering through them, but a blue plasma shield went up at the same time, protecting the docking bay from the vacuum of space before the ship blasted through the second set of doors. Another wall of blue went up where the last set of doors had been shattered.

Hap released the breath he'd assumed would be his last.

"I am *so* going to get her," Tara hissed as she looked toward where the ship had blasted out.

"I'll help," Hap said.

Bald Guard put a hand on Hap's shoulder. "You kids okay?"

They nodded. Then Hap cocked his head and stared at the guard. "That was you who put up the plasma shields, wasn't it?"

Bald Guard shrugged but he smiled too.

"Wow. That was brilliant. You saved everybody. That ship was like all—bam! And then you come in all saving the day and everything. We owe you one, man."

Hairy Guard was sprawled flat on the paving stones. He'd apparently slipped while running or something.

Several people were in varying states of recovery from the incident. A little alien was spinning around on the ground, trying to get back onto its spindly four legs. It looked like a short, pudgy totem pole with several mouths and eyes running down the length of it until it reached the creature's clothing. Hap wondered if the faces ended at the clothes or if the clothes just covered the rest of them up. On the face toward the top, one of the eyes had a monocle lens over it. The top face was the angriest—probably because it had the farthest to fall.

Tremble helped the totem-pole alien back to its feet, which were covered by silky bright red booties. The totem's several faces were in varying degrees of flustered, upset, and angry. Svarta was nowhere to be seen. Neither was Amar.

They must have made it to the ship with Nova.

The totem alien grunted. "Such behavior!" All of the mouths moved, but it didn't sound like multiple people talking. Hap heard only one voice. "I wish to file a complaint with the comet security. That ship made an attempt on my life! First, someone shoves me over then smashes the only thing protecting any of us. It could have killed me!" One of the eyes had a spasm in the muscle underneath it. The totem man reached out a hand that had *feelers* rather than fingers. Hairlike tentacles massaged at the spasm under the totem's eye. His other hand with feeler-fingers pulled a handkerchief from his pocket and dabbed at two of the mouths and wiped at several of the eyes.

"File a complaint?" Tara said. "It was comet security who saved your life! I'd think you'd want to praise this man for a job well done." Tara pointed at Bald Guard.

Bald Guard looked guiltily at Hap, who'd been distracting the guards from their jobs. But Hap didn't feel bad. Whether the guard had been distracted or not, he never could have stopped that ship from slamming its way out of the docking bay. He'd probably done the only thing he could have in such a situation. He saved every single person in the docking bay and possibly the comet from certain death.

As far as Hap was concerned, that made Bald Guard a hero. So he immediately agreed with Tara and thanked the man for saving his life.

Totem Pole blustered and grunted but finally followed Hap's example and thanked the guards as well, promising to put in a good word for a job well executed.

Totem Pole tickled the top of Bald Guard's hand with the feeler-fingers. It looked to be a handshake of some sort. "I'm here to speak with a young man named Confucian? He's part of the Bo Shocks band. I heard the most recent concert. Disaster from the sounds of it.

But I'm very interested in the young boy. Quite a talent. Bo Shocks might never work in the profession again, but that *boy*! That boy with the perfect pitch! What a career I have planned for him! 'Course he'll need to change his name to something easier . . . Fusion, maybe? Where can I find him? And I want to file a complaint against the owner of that ship. Take me immediately to the head of your security. Now!"

The security guards were left with no choice but to escort the demanding little Totem Pole to the causeway entrance, where they were met by a contingency of security filing in to check on the smashed doors.

Nothing like coming to the party late.

Tremble grabbed at Hap and Tara and dragged them up the ramp. "Let's get inside."

The ramp folded in, even before Hap had stepped inside the ship. The hatch closed but made a horrible grating metal sort of noise when it did. Hap covered his ears until the door was fully closed. He looked at it suspiciously. "Are you sure that's going to hold?" he asked, but Tara and Tremble were already down the hall to the control room.

"It will need repaired soon but will hold for the time being. Please join the others in the control room." Nana used the word *please,* but Hap knew an order when he heard one.

He went to the control room.

Nova was strapped into one of the chairs but still managed to look smug when Hap entered. "Ah good, you brought the children. Now I know my chances at escape are absolutely nullified. As cunning and dangerous as they are, I'm trembling with fear over my new captors."

Nothing was more irritating than a sarcastic mob boss—especially when Mosh had been so close to escaping and yet still remained a captive. "Shut up," Hap said, wanting to punch the guy and to also run and hide from him at the same time. He sure hoped the adults knew what they were doing.

Amar leaned over Nova's chair and then took Nova's head in his hands.

Nova flinched at the physical contact—flinched and looked fascinated all at the same time. "You going to kill me with the knowledge from your book? That's very unprincipled of you."

"No. I will not be killing you today. We are the same in that we both thirst for knowledge. We are different in how we feel that knowledge should be used. I'm allowing you to rest so that you will be more comfortable while with us." Amar then mumbled something under his breath while focusing on Nova's face.

Nova's eyes shut, and his head lolled to the side. A great phlegm-snore rose from him almost immediately.

Svarta left to make arrangements for a trade.

Tara pressed her lips tightly together for several moments before she finally said, "Are you sure we shouldn't just kill him?"

Hap felt his face go slack with the shock of her words. "Tara!" She was supposed to be the nice one. Hap was the one who said things that made people upset.

Amar turned to consider Tara for a moment. "What are your reasons for such a suggestion?"

Tremble snorted and said in a voice a little too low to be completely Tremble, "Because it would make us feel better."

Tara ignored that. "If we give him back, he'll keep coming after us. He's got more money or credits or whatever than we do, and he's angry and mean, and he's as determined as we are."

"If we kill him, we have nothing with which to bargain. Are you willing to sacrifice Elaine Sanchez and Mosh for the greater good?"

Everyone stared at Tara. Hap was glad Svarta had already left, because she'd likely punch Tara out for suggesting anything that would put Laney at risk.

Tara shook her head. "I wouldn't ever put anyone at risk. He's just . . . he just scares me." She turned and left the control room.

"I'll check on our other guests," Tremble said and also left.

"What book did we get?" Hap spoke up as soon as everyone had gone.

"It is not the one you seek," Amar answered softly. "This book will teach us nothing on how to heal your father."

Hap sucked in air hard with the intent to dry out the despair stuck in his throat. "Right. Okay. Just wondering."

"We now have in our possession three books. The first is the book of gravity. The second is on propaganda. And now this one . . ."

Hap held his breath while waiting to hear what this one was.

"This is the book on sociology. This teaches you to understand the evolution of society and, by understanding, predict how to lift it to the fullest potential or trample it into the dust."

Hap blew out a breath. "So it's worthless."

Amar smiled. Hap liked that Amar was so patient when Hap felt grumpy about stuff. It reminded him a lot of his dad. "It is most certainly not worthless."

"Yeah, well . . . Nova still has the book on how to turn everything in the universe into gold. He has his own personal banking system. And, thanks to me, he has the crystal pyramid, so he can actually read the book." Hap picked up the old leather- and iron-bound book from where Amar had placed it on the table. "What you're saying is that we have a basic history book on society, *and* we have no way to read it, so it's the same as having a blank ream of paper."

"But we also have the man who can read it very nicely wrapped up and unconscious. So he won't be reading or implementing what he might read. And he'll never, *ever,* see its pages open. Does that make you feel better?"

"Not really." Hap grinned. "But it might make me feel better if you let me draw on Nova's face with a permanent marker while he's sleeping . . ."

Amar laughed and steered Hap toward the door. "That is a monumentally bad idea."

"Oh, c'mon!" Hap protested as Amar pushed him out of the room. "Just a mustache! Maybe a few freckles! It would be funny."

Amar smiled and shook his head. "Oh yes, very humorous, until Don Nova discovers you've used him for a canvas and decides to get even. Truly, Hap, where do you come up with such ideas?"

Hap shrugged. "So this no means no for real?" Amar almost always meant what he said. Svarta would've let him draw on Nova's face if she wasn't busy. She'd probably help . . .

"It means absolutely no." The door swished closed between Amar and Hap.

Dang. A villainous mustache and maybe a couple of horns on his forehead above those horrible black fuzzy eyebrows would really improve Nova's looks.

Hap went back to his room, passing through Tara's room to get to his. She was on her little coffin bed leaning back against the wall flipping through holographic pages in the air above her link key.

"What are you reading? Studying up on the junk man before we go?" he asked. He'd started calling it the junk man when he'd learned that an entire civilization had disappeared and left all their stuff behind there. The place was really called Koda.

"No. Just reading." She snapped her fingers over the holo, and the glowing pages melted into the air. "I couldn't do anything to help her," Tara said after a few moments of silence. She rolled to her side to face Hap directly. "I thought Meg was a nice person."

"Are you kidding? Meg carries more weaponry on her person than most small countries will ever have access to. She's definitely not nice."

"It's just . . ." Tara growled in frustration, "disappointing to find out how many rotten people there are in the world."

"You mean universe. Technically we're not just in the world anymore."

Her eyes became slits.

He sat next to her, making her scoot a little to give him room. "Laney's going to be fine. Svarta and Amar won't let her—" He was going to say die but couldn't make the word come out. "Everyone's going to be fine. We're going to get the books, get home, and eat pizza—a lot of pizza."

Tara laughed and bumped her arm into his. "Do you ever think about anything besides food?"

"Sure, I do. I think about things exploding, which, let's face it, is always fun."

"Unless, of course, it's *us* exploding?"

Hap imitated Tara when she put her hands on her hips to explain things. "Well, naturally. Us exploding isn't cool at all." He shook his head to clear his thoughts. *I'm not going to think about that anymore. I will save my family. I will not let the world explode.*

"I also think about gaming and comic books and thinking about how cool it is to not have to go to school. I had a test a few weeks ago, or whenever that was back on Earth, on the war of 1812. I'd already failed the essay part because Mrs. North said I wasn't taking it seriously enough. I would've bombed the test."

Hap was glad to see the smirk on Tara's face. It was a zillion times better than seeing her look sad and worried.

"What was in your essay that made her think you weren't taking it seriously?" she asked.

Hap stood up and threw his hands in the air for dramatic effect. "I don't know! It was the coolest essay ever! I called it the "Return of the Brits." It compared all the similarities of the War of 1812 to Star Wars. It's the best paper I ever wrote."

Tara laughed.

They'd been talking for quite a while when Nana interrupted them. "The deal with Meg has been made, and the trade has been set. Laney is still alive." Nana sounded relieved.

Tara hopped off her bed and practically knocked Hap off his feet with a hug. "She's alive! Hap! She's alive!"

Tara released him with a shove of impatience as if *he'd* been the one to stall her by initiating hugs.

"That girl is so weird sometimes," Hap said to Nana.

When Hap made it to the control room, Tara was hugging Svarta like crazy. Svarta shook her head and finally had to pry Tara off. Tara bounced on her feet lightly with her hands together as though she'd been clapping. Her face was split by a smile.

"Everybody's okay, then?" Hap said as the door swished shut behind him.

"Mosh is perfectly unharmed. Laney's injured but stable enough that they were able to let me talk to her. I made them prove it. I'm not handing over the unibrow without proof that she's okay. I talked to Mosh too. Meg agreed to trade Mosh for Gygak and the lemsk . . . well, really for the lemsk. I threw Gy-geek in as a bonus, but she didn't seem too worried about getting him back. She just wanted the lemsk, but I don't want him either. He's a waste of skin, tying up oxygen, water, and food. I'm not wasting resources on that little insect. If Nova's people won't take him, then we'll leave him at the trade-off place."

"When's the trade-off?" Tara asked.

"When we get there." Tremble was already seated and strapped in her seat as if she was ready to leave the comet altogether, which was weird . . . they certainly weren't planning on leaving without making the trade first, were they?

"Get where?" Hap glanced at Svarta.

Svarta rubbed her chin absently and looked at the floor when she said, "To the planet Koda—where the next book is located. Meg won't do the trade-off here. She's actually already gone. She was commanding the ship that crashed out of here a bit ago. I had to tell her where one of the books was located—one she didn't already know of."

Amar sucked in a breath and closed his eyes.

No one else said anything, because there was nothing to say. Svarta hadn't exactly handed over one of the books, but she might as well have.

"Well," Amar said, "that certainly makes things more complicated. I'd hoped to do the exchange here—in civilization—where laws and rules kept Nova's thugs from taking advantage of the situation where they already have the upper hand, because they aren't ruled by morals. We won't have that luxury at Koda. And she now has a head start . . ."

Svarta nodded but didn't turn her eyes up to see his face. "That means we're in a hurry. We should get going."

No one moved at first. They were all stunned by what felt like betrayal to Hap. But Amar clapped his hands, which startled everyone into motion. "Get ready! We leave immediately." Hap put his hand on Svarta's shoulder as he passed her. He didn't know why he did it, but it seemed good to let her know she wasn't alone. If it had been his family . . . he'd have done the same thing, betrayal to the universe or not.

He glanced at the still-snoring Nova.

Everything was falling apart.

16. Flight Lessons

Since all of them apparently planned on taking off whether Hap was strapped in or not, he hurried to his chair. The straps zipped over him, sucking his body tightly into place as the ship taxied out of its parking place.

"Will the plasma doors open for us?" Tara asked.

"They work just like the others, only they're more effective." Tremble answered as her eyes roved over the schematics in her holo to keep Nana's nose in proper alignment for takeoff.

"Maybe they'll stop being cheap and pay to keep the plasma hangars operating all the time like everyone else," Svarta mumbled as she manipulated her holo projections. She spoke louder into the link key—communicating with whoever coordinated landings and take-offs.

And without further delay, Nana burst into space. Hap wanted to love takeoffs, but the intensity of the forces pulling and pushing on him all at once made it really hard to enjoy.

The forces settled after a moment, making it easier to think. After they'd achieved distance from the comet, they headed to the familiar outline of what looked like the mouth of a huge coiled snake made out of light, which was really just the spiral drop.

No one talked as they traveled to the drop, and no one talked as they entered it. The ship spun around and around in the freefall. Hap kept thinking he'd get used to the way his brain felt like it was sloshing against his skull when they went through these things, but from the looks on everyone else's faces, it seemed no matter how many times a person did the drop, no one ever got used to it.

Outside the porthole windows, lights flashed, zigged, then zagged, over and over again. The drop ended instantaneously, even though it felt like it had lasted an eternity.

A cold blast of air from the little wall blew straight at him, drying off the beads of sweat pouring off his skin. Hap was grateful for the cold blast of air. It kept him from passing out.

"How long until the next drop?" Amar asked.

Tremble checked coordinates. "Fourteen standard hours."

Amar unbuckled himself, slid out of his chair, and wandered to the Multi-D display. His gaze slipped over to where Svarta still sat strapped in her chair. Svarta's head hung low.

"We'll get her. We'll get them both," Amar said gently. "Let's focus on what we need to do, as well as the things we've managed to accomplish. We have another book—thanks to Hap and Tara."

Svarta looked up, though with her hair covering her expression, it was hard to read her mood. "Yeah. We have another book. You guys did good things on that snowball. I'm proud of both of you." Her voice sounded flat, though Hap could tell she meant what she said.

Hap felt good that he had done something right—something that gave everyone a little hope. They'd found another book. Amar and the others wouldn't have beat Nova to it if Hap and Tara hadn't gone against instructions and gotten involved. Some of it was dumb luck, of course. Who knew that lunatic Bo would use the ancient stone box as a concert prop?

"We'll find the rest of the books too," Hap said, "and get Laney and Mosh back. Of course we will." No one else said anything. No one else wanted to pretend to keep their spirits up when things felt less than hopeful.

Hap looked out the front windows. A planet with a murky gray sort of coloring was off in the distance but approaching rapidly. Two moons orbited the cloudy gray planet—at least only two that Hap could see. There might have been more on the other side.

"Koda?" Hap looked at the lines and shapes on the wall and then back out to the planet with its moons. "Where is that on the map?"

Amar pointed to the shape of what looked to be a lumpy person with huge hands reaching out to grab something. "I wasn't sure at first, but my brother on the Lizard Comet left me a clue. The writings on the stone box made mention of Koda. It's a well-known planet—mostly because of the temptation it provides to mining corporations. As I told you before, Koda is the home to a rare blue gemstone that can fuel the electricity of one planet for years. But the risks of mining the stones are too great. No one dares to go there anymore except salvagers who gather the equipment left orbiting the planet. And even many of those salvagers never make it home . . . their ships join the other wreckage in orbit."

Amar took a deep breath. "Anyway, everyone's tired." He didn't look up from the wall with the symbol of the large reaching hands. "I suggest we all sleep for a bit—catch up on our cycles, especially you, Svarta. You need to rest." He finally settled his gaze on her and gently took her hands in his to lift her out of her chair as Nana released the straps.

She didn't argue but flashed a tired smile at Hap. "You guys really did do good. Though, going out onstage during a huge concert wasn't exactly what we meant when we told you guys to keep low and stay hidden."

Hap let out a guilty sort of chuckle. "Yeah, probably not what you meant."

"I'll come up with a punishment later. Go get rest, you two monsters."

"Punishment?" Hap said when they were in the hall leading to their rooms. "We get the book *they* were supposed to get, and we get punished. Typical."

Tara must have been tired, because she didn't argue with him. She fell into her little coffin bed, pulled the sheet over her, and said in a barely intelligible voice, "Warmer, Nana." Hap figured she meant she wanted the blanket to be warmer, but he didn't ask because he didn't care. He wanted his own bed with his own warm blanket.

The bands zipped out and around him to keep him in place in case the ship needed to make sudden moves. He also mumbled, "Warmer, Nana," but was asleep before he could tell if Nana had made the blanket warmer or not.

* * *

They'd been through the second spiral drop, and Hap had managed to get back to sleep when he felt a light knock on his forehead. He popped open one eye.

Svarta leaned over him, a mischievous grin on her face. "Hey, kid. Wake up."

Hap groaned and propped himself up on an elbow while he rubbed the sleep out of his eyes. "You're giving me homework as my punishment, aren't you?"

"While that scenario is entirely possible, no. Everyone's still sleeping—including your little girlfriend, so I figured we had some extra time to get things done."

Hap felt the red crawl out of his collar and up his neck. "She's not my—"

"I know, Happenstance. Just teasing you." Svarta had a way of incorporating other words into people's names. She called Amar *Amarvelous*, Gygak *Gygeek*, Laney *Shady-Laney*. And she'd just started calling him Happenstance. She only did it when she felt good, or in Gygak's case, when she felt mean. Hap figured her waking him and using his nickname must mean she was feeling better about the way things went down with Laney. "Anyway, I was your age when Laney let me drive Nana for the first time. It was pretty cool. I thought you might want to give it a try."

Hap had to stamp down his excitement. There was no way she meant what he thought she meant. "I thought Nana was biocoded so she could only be flown by you or Laney."

"Who's the engineer here?" She pointed at herself and straightened. She still kept her voice low so she didn't wake up Tara. "I keep up Nana's programming. I'm the one who fixes her wires and makes her wires do what they're told."

"Is she going to tell on us?"

Svarta blew her hair out of her eyes. "Do you want to learn or not?"

Without another word, he leapt out of bed and silently padded along after Svarta to the engineering room. He figured he'd have to be in the control room to fly the ship, and so he thought it was weird to be heading into the belly of the ship, but he didn't say anything in case Svarta changed her mind.

He'd only been to the engineering room a couple of times. Svarta called it her territory, always using the word *territory* with a growl, like a wolf guarding a den. Svarta was fun to joke around with but not so much fun when she didn't feel like joking.

But now, she invited Hap into the engineering room and didn't growl at all. "Come over here, Hap. I need you to breathe on this."

"You want me to breathe into a tube?"

"Nana needs to decode your biometric information. If she doesn't get that information, I can't alter the programming to allow you access to the steering wheel."

"Nana doesn't have a steering wheel."

Svarta laughed.

"I don't have a steering wheel," Nana confirmed.

"So you're okay with this?" Hap stood next to Svarta and breathed into the tube.

"Svarta makes an excellent argument for why I should allow you access to the ship," Nana answered.

"Oh yeah? There's a good argument for us doing something Laney would give me a mountain of homework for and something Amar would call bad judgment?"

"It didn't read. Breathe into it again." Svarta shook the tube. "A big breath this time."

Hap filled his lungs and then expelled the air into the tube.

"We are on a mission that may damage some of my charges," Nana said. By "charges" she meant anyone on board her ship. "While I can make choices that seem logical for flight, I am not allowed complete decision-making programming. I require a human guide to direct our departure, travel, and arrival into new systems. Tremble has limited access to navigation. But only Svarta and Laney have full access. If Laney or Svarta are rendered incapable of directing me, we will need a substitute."

Hap understood. Svarta hadn't brought him down here because she wanted to lighten the mood on the ship but because she felt vulnerable with Laney missing. Svarta wanted a backup plan.

"But why me? I'm just a—"

"You're just a kid," Svarta interrupted him and finished his sentence. "That's why I chose you. Amar is an old guy. A seriously old guy. In a way, you could call him a time traveler. He isn't like us. He has a different value system, a different method of achieving his results. And it isn't that I don't trust him, I just—"

"Don't trust him." Hap finished her sentence like she'd done to him. He didn't bother telling her that he wasn't all that sure Amar trusted her methods either. Not that he needed to. The way Svarta shifted uncomfortably told him she already knew Amar was disappointed in the way she'd given away the location of a book to get Laney back.

She pushed her hair back, revealing eyes that showed she *did* trust Hap, which made him question her motives even more.

"But me?"

"Look, Happenstance. As we've seen, anything can happen. Laney really liked you two kids. If things don't go down right somewhere along the way, she'd skin me if I didn't have a backup plan to keep you safe. She's got this incredibly lame soft spot for you."

She sniffed slightly, and her voice shook in a way that told him Laney wasn't the only one with a lame soft spot for their safety.

"Anyway, Tremble is insane. I know Laney likes the twin-soul, and I do too, but I don't like her enough to let her take over my ride, not in actual flight. I don't mind her manning the controls when we have a destination preset, or when we're within the gravity of someplace, as long as it's only for a minute or so, but she's not stable. If Googool takes over, she'll run us into an asteroid belt—on purpose. Amar is just old, and who knows what a guy who's been hanging around the universe over the amount of centuries Amar has thinks about stuff. He's so by-the-book about everything. You know . . . letter of the law. Sometimes the law needs . . . tweaking, but he doesn't get that kind of stuff. Tara would work, but she's also so straight-laced about everything too. She's coming around, but she thinks too much."

"So you're choosing me 'cause I don't think at all? That's not exactly a compliment, so you know."

Svarta laughed as if he'd made a joke. She took a readout on her link key and held it to the tube. She blew lightly over her link key, which brought up her holo projection. She played with equations, numbers, letters, and symbols Hap didn't recognize. He hoped he didn't have to know this stuff to fly the ship, because even though Svarta only wanted him to know for some serious backup plan, *he* wanted to do it simply because it sounded like a blast.

Svarta blew the hair out of her eyes and waved her hand over her holo, bringing up an entirely different set of numbers, letters, and symbols.

She repeated this several times. Hap got bored watching and went over to a panel of circuitry next to an old hatch like the kind found in submarines. He wanted to turn the hatch and see what was behind it.

Without looking his direction to see what he was up to, Svarta warned, "Don't even think about that."

The warning only served to make him think about the hatch a lot more. Of course he didn't touch it, because if he did, Svarta would chop off his fingers, he was sure.

Hap felt pretty attached to his fingers.

Svarta inserted her link key into a terminal and tapped some buttons. She removed the link key and turned to Hap. "It's official, you're legal to fly my ship."

"Awesome!" Hap said.

Svarta put a finger in his face, "But let's get something very clear. You ever take Nana without it being an emergency, or under express orders, I will hunt you down, and it will *hurt*. Nana's one of the few things Laney and I have left from our dad. We take the ownership of her very seriously. Got it?"

Hap swallowed as though the finger in his face was a knife at his throat. He'd seen Svarta in a fight and knew her hands were a deadly weapon all by themselves. "Got it," he said.

"Good, let's teach you to fly." She led the way back to the control room. Hap didn't care how much Svarta threatened him. He was now authorized to fly the ship. *Him.* The kid who wasn't even old enough to get a driver's license! And he could fly a spaceship!

He couldn't wait to tell Tara, but Svarta stopped walking and whirled on him as though she were reading his mind. "And no, you don't get to tell anyone. Not anyone. Not even Tara. Not even Laney when we get her back—especially not Laney, because she'll make me reprogram Nana. This rule goes for you too, Nana."

"I assumed as much," Nana said.

"And now you know as much. No loopholes. You've been directly ordered."

They went from the airlift to the control room.

"Keep watch, Nana," Svarta instructed.

"I always do." Nana's chirping, cheerful voice made her sound like she wasn't really taking her job seriously, but Svarta didn't reissue the command.

With Svarta being so intense about everything now, Hap felt let down that this little venture wouldn't be nearly as fun as he'd first imagined.

He was totally wrong.

Flying a ship was the *awesomest* thing ever! There were tons of things to know, and it wasn't anywhere near as easy as it looked. Svarta grumbled a lot and dragged her hand down her face a lot and lightly cuffed the back of his head when she didn't think he was paying attention. But after a little while he felt like he had some idea of how to enter coordinates and how to change speeds.

"I think I can do this!" Hap said, feeling exultant. At least he felt exultant right up until the moment Nana announced, "Amar is coming!"

Svarta shoved him out of Laney's chair so that he ended up on the floor rolled up against the wall with the symbols.

Amar swished into the room. Hap couldn't really see from where he'd ended up on the floor, but he scrambled to get up in a position that at least looked like he was doing something productive. He put his face close to the map as if he'd been studying the symbol of the big hands.

Amar stood still for a moment. "What are you up to, Svarta?"

"I'm babysitting the kid. What does it look like I'm doing?"

Amar considered this a moment before saying, "I thought you were against babysitting."

"Yeah, well, we were the only ones awake. I was bored. He's been entertaining me with stupid jokes, right, Hap?"

"Yeah. Jokes." He nodded, hoping Amar would drop it. Hap hated lying.

"I could use a good joke. Tell me one," he said, not dropping anything.

Hap groaned inwardly. He was terrible at jokes. He was great at pranks but not so good at jokes. "Joke?"

"Yes. I could use a diversion." And the guy really did look like he needed something funny. He looked pale and tired—as if he hadn't taken his own advice when he told everyone to sleep.

"Right. Funny. Remember, Svarta said I was telling her *bad* jokes, so don't expect to actually laugh or anything."

Amar smiled, which encouraged Hap a little.

He sat up straighter. "Okay, why do seagulls fly over the sea?"

"I don't know, why?" His lip quirked to the side.

"Because if they flew over the bay, they'd be bay-gulls."

Amar pressed his lips together and pondered this. "I don't know what a bagel is. Is it a new sort of bird?"

"Um . . . no. Let's try another one. Okay, how about . . . how does the man on the moon get a hair cut?"

"How?" Svarta asked.

"*E-clipse* it!"

They stared at him. "I don't get it," Svarta said finally.

"You know . . . *e*-clipse it . . . *He* clips it . . ."

"Ohhh, yeah, that was bad too. That's it. You're fired as the court jester," Svarta said.

Amar merely blinked, his eyelids heavy, in Svarta's direction. "How many more drops until we hit Koda's range?"

Svarta checked a reading. "Three." Hap looked at the readings but couldn't see how she got the number three out of that mess of figures.

Hap stood and nodded to Svarta. "I think I'll see what's in the pantry. Can I get you guys something?"

No one wanted anything, so Hap left, making his way to the ship's center. It felt weird to enter the supply room and find it empty, More often than not, Mosh was in there trying to find something else he could eat. Hap couldn't help but wonder and worry about what was happening to the big guy. Would Nova really keep him as bait or just do away with him?

The pantry was still a mess from when the lemsk had been locked in there. Tremble had caged the thing and declared she'd keep it in her room.

Would Nova really want a little rat-cat-looking lemsk bad enough to give Mosh back?

Hap couldn't think of one logical reason anyone would want that nasty little animal around.

"What are you doing?" Tara side-stepped her way into the pantry, dodging the boxes Amar had been bringing up from the cargo hold to restock the pantry.

"Nothing zane." This information was not technically true. He'd learned to fly a *spaceship*. That had been pretty cool.

"After getting shot at while on stage for an intergalactic rock star, will anything *ever* seem zane again?" She shoved aside some of the trash in the pantry bins to see if anything remained still in its packaging. "Everything's ripped up so much, I can't even tell what it was supposed to be. That thing has some vicious claws on it."

"Makes it a perfect companion for Googool." Hap smirked.

"Amar said we could link home again. He said we needed to do it before the next spiral drop." Tara's smile widened as she gave the news that only twisted Hap's stomach into knots. "It stinks that we're always saying good-bye to people. I feel bad we didn't really get a decent good-bye with Confucian, but knowing we can always link to those people is really cool."

"Are you going to use up your link home credit to link to Confucian instead?" He said it as a joke, but it bugged him to think she might be willing to forego talking to her mom just so she could talk to some guy who already had a girlfriend.

She made a pshaw noise. "Of course not. Don't be stupid. I'm just saying the ability to do it is cool—not that I'm actually going to." She untucked her hair, probably to hide the fact that her ears were reddening. She leaned against the wall and studied Hap a moment.

She finally narrowed her eyes and said, "Why don't you ever seem excited to call home? You always look green like Gygak when they tell us we can do it—like you're going to be sick or something. You never seem very happy. Don't you like talking to your family?"

So she'd noticed. Hap had sort of hoped he'd hid his fear of linking behind the jokes and information that needed to be relayed when he talked to his grandfather. Apparently, he hadn't hidden anything.

"I love talking to my family. I don't know why you'd say that." He turned his back on her so she couldn't see how much her question bothered him.

"Don't act all offended. This isn't an insult. I'm only trying to understand why you act like that."

He closed his eyes, even though he no longer faced her and didn't have to meet her gaze. He hated that she read him so easily—hated it even while being grateful for it. He *did* feel dread whenever Amar said they could link, because Hap was terrified to link. What if that nightmare/vision came back? He didn't want to feel the fear in the air. He didn't want to feel the glass grind under the heel of his shoe. He didn't want to watch the world explode.

It hadn't happened again, and he knew it was lame to be afraid of a little dream. But that little dream had scared the snot out of him, and he knew it for what it was—a possibility. That dream was a possible future. It had felt like the cosmos were warning him what could happen if he failed to find the missing books of the nine unknown scientists.

Hap couldn't fail.

The price was too high.

And he hated the reminder that the dream had given him. But he wanted to call home more than he feared it, so he handled it.

At least he *thought* he'd been handling it.

Tara had proven otherwise.

For a brief moment Hap considered telling her about the dream he'd had when he'd first linked home. Would it scare her the way it did him? Or would she make fun of him for going all psycho-psychic about a silly dream?

"It makes me a little sick," he admitted. "You know, the whole energy-getting-sucked-from-our-toes thing. But it isn't like I'm not excited or anything. I love talking to my family." He turned back to her, but she was sifting through the scraps of metallic packaging trying to locate some food.

Tara liked to really overeat before a link. It made sense since linking took so much out of them that no matter how much they ate beforehand, they were always starving after.

"You'll probably have to open the new supplies. Who knows? Maybe we've got some real food in those boxes." Hap smiled, hiding his discomfort over their previous conversation—at least he hoped he hid it. Tara's returning smile gave him the feeling that she felt sorry for him. He hated pity but mentally pushed himself past it, focusing on the boxes. He pressed his thumbs into the indents at the sides of the top box, making the top open with a whir and a hiss as the pressure was released.

Hap waved away the pressure fog until he could clearly see into the box. "Look at all this stuff! Awesome!" he shouted.

"What? Did we get good stuff? Please let it be pizza; please let it be pizza!" She elbowed him aside so she could look.

Then she hit him, her little knuckles digging into his shoulder muscles. "It's more of that protein paste, you bonehead!"

Hap rubbed his arm and chuckled over his joke at the same time. "Well, duh. All the nutrients to keep a carbon-based life form alive can be found in one tube of peanut buttery paste. It weighs next to nothing, takes up no room, and it's cheap. What else is going to be in those boxes?"

"I was really hoping for pizza." Tara sighed and absently opened a tube of the protein paste. She slid down the wall until she was sitting with her legs stretched out in front of her. She still looked tired, in spite of all the sleep they'd had between the drops. Hap decided not to tell her she looked tired. Girls were weird about stuff like that.

"Sorry. If I could abracadabra that into pizza, believe me, I would do it."

"If you could abracadabra things into pizza, I'd rent you out to parties. We'd make a fortune." Her words were a little slurred because of the paste in her mouth, which she ate with the most bored expression Hap had ever witnessed.

Not that he blamed her. The food that sustained their lives was genuinely boring. He opened one for himself, settled in next to her on the floor, and they slurped their protein packs in silence.

The silence wasn't the uncomfortable kind where you shift and try looking at anything but the person you're with while wondering what to say. Tara and Hap didn't do that anymore. Hap felt like Tara had been around his whole life. She was as comfortable as a T-shirt that had been through the washing machine a lot.

She was about the perfect best friend.

Amar found them after a while. Hap had been through three of the tubes and finally felt full as the paste expanded in his belly.

Amar snorted a laugh as he stared at them. "You two look fairly pathetic surrounded by empty protein packs and sitting like contented, fat cattle."

"We didn't eat all of this." Tara hurried to make it known that most of the trash was because of the lemsk, not because she'd been grazing. "I only had two." She scrambled to her feet.

Hap did too, picking up several of the slashed packages from the ground before getting up. "I had three and make no apologies." He laughed to himself that Tara claimed to have only had two when she had a third in her hand ready to be opened.

She put it back in the storage box and helped Hap pick up some of the litter. It had been in a single pile before the last spiral drop, but everyone had been too tired to dispose of it properly. Now the whole room was a mess. Hap swept up some more debris into his arms and hauled it to Nana's waste receptacle at the back of the ship. He actually liked taking stuff to the waste receptacle because when he placed the trash in and closed the gate, the metal warmed up almost to melt-your-skin-off temperatures.

Svarta had teased him about giving himself third-degree burns, but he couldn't help it. The warmth in comparison to the frigid air inside the ship felt great. Hap really liked warmth. He would've spent more time in his bed with the sheet that Nana could warm up except then he'd miss out on all the information in the ship. If he wasn't there to eavesdrop on the information the adults were discussing, they'd never tell him about it later.

He held his hands to the metal until it became too hot to bear then leaned his face close enough to feel the heat but not close enough to risk touching it.

"I hope Koda has a beach," he muttered under his breath. He thought he said it too low for anyone to hear, but Tara's voice made him jump.

"Not likely. You trying to get a sunburn off the trash compactor again?"

"Just warming up a little," he said.

"I do not compact trash," Nana said, sounding a bit put out to have Tara so blatantly misspeak.

"Oh, I know, Nana. It was just a figure of speech."

Tara huddled closer to him, moving her hands to hover just over the metal as if warming her fingers over a campfire. "Amar's ready to link now that he's done restocking the pantry. He told me to find you."

"Sure. I'll be right there."

He hoped she'd go ahead without him so he could have a minute to steady himself for the experience of linking, but she waited for him to be ready so they could go together. Not that they had far to go.

"Well?"

"Well what?" he asked.

"Are we linking or not?"

"Yes. We're going." He took a deep breath and reluctantly left the warm space next to the waste incinerator.

He really hated it when Tara got bossy.

Traveling the universe did not get him out of peer pressure or doing things to save his ego.

The universe was as unmerciful as puberty.

17. Swimming with the Fish

THE LINK TURNED OUT TO be okay. Nothing weird happened. The world hadn't exploded. Hap counted himself lucky. With Laney and Mosh missing, there were enough things to worry about.

He'd been given a list of chores. He could have sworn he was the only one who ever did any cleaning on the ship, but Tara insisted she did more work than he could even dream of, so he tried not to complain where she could hear. She turned everything into a competition. After all the chores were done, Nana called a two-minute warning to the rest of the ship that the next spiral drop was coming.

Hap felt his insides spinning and his mind whirring before they ever hit the actual drop.

He really hated those things.

And there were two more to come after that one.

It surprised Hap that he'd somehow managed to fall asleep somewhere in the middle of that drop. He must've been entirely exhausted, because he didn't see how that could be in any way possible. But then . . . a lot of things that weren't possible before had suddenly become his reality.

He woke up with the side of his face soaked in his own spit. "Yuck," he muttered as he used the sleeve of his shirt to clean off his cheek.

Nana informed him that they'd landed to refuel but were taking off again immediately so not to get out of bed. Hap nodded and tried to smack his mouth to get rid of the morning taste and finally gave in to getting out of bed and brushing his teeth.

"You finally up?" Tara called through the thin wall that separated their rooms.

"I guess."

"It's about time. Nana said she'd never heard of anyone sleeping through a drop."

"Yeah well, the *Book of World Records* better spell my name right when we report it."

"You mean the *Book of Universe Records*," she reminded him.

"Right, that too." He gagged a little on the toothpaste, still not used to swallowing it when he was done brushing. The toothpaste was designed to be consumed. It was perfectly safe to swallow. It was another way to conserve water in deep space. If only Hap could get his gag reflex to agree that water conservation was a good idea.

"We're taking off in just a minute. You better get back in bed," Tara warned.

"I am getting back in bed. I just needed to stretch a little."

"Get up on the wrong side of the universe? You're a little grumpy today." Tara sounded a little bugged by his attitude.

He poked his head around the door to her room. "Is there a right side to the universe?" He was glad to see Tara still strapped in her bed with her hair all knotted and snarled. Maybe she didn't have spit on her cheek, but she didn't look like a supermodel when she woke up either. He considered going to the control room to get a look at where they'd landed, but he was still too tired.

Which worried him a little.

He'd never been too tired for curiosity before.

"Get strapped in." The command came from Nana this time, and where Hap was willing to ignore Tara, he wasn't willing to do the same to Nana.

He hopped into his bed and let the straps do their thing. The engine hummed underneath the ship, making things inside the ship shudder as it prepared for takeoff.

Tara waited until the engines quieted enough to talk over them before saying, "Amar said we're only a few days from Koda. He loaded some information on your holo disk. He said we had to study that information if we wanted to even hope to use our space suits to check out the planet with the rest of them. He doesn't want us going out without studying what we're going into first."

Hap groaned. "Figures. Everything with these guys is study this, and learn about that."

"Education is part of good preparation," Nana interjected into Hap's whining.

That shut Hap up. If he argued, it would mean all of his free time would be taken up with lectures. *Lectures!* From a ship's computer!

Hap settled deeper into his bed. "Warmer, Nana," he said, adding the word *please* after thinking about it a second.

The takeoff didn't last very long, and soon the ship had settled into its speed and trajectory for the next spiral drops—though they had more than a full day of travel before they got there.

With the ship settled and gravity completely stable, he slid his link key out of his pocket and up to his face where he could breathe over it to power it up. Might as well get started with the homework. And he might as well do it in bed where at least it was warm. He waved his hand in the air over his personal files box, and it opened to reveal pages and pages of stuff he had to read.

"Ugh!" he said out loud.

"You opened yours, too?" Tara asked from the other side of the wall.

"Why do we need to know about the history of Koda?"

Nana answered the question even though Hap hadn't really been asking with the intent of getting an answer. He'd been asking with the intent of whining over it. "To prepare you to be on the surface of the planet."

"This is the price of exploration," Tara said.

"I guess." So he propped his head on his arm and scrolled through the information, knowing he had to pay enough attention to pass a cursory questioning from all the adults. Even Tremble quizzed him. Part of the deal she had to make to be able to leave the planet Delat was to be well educated in all kinds of crazy stuff. Hap got the feeling that she liked knowing more than anyone else on the ship. Twin-souls were pretty weird. Maybe she learned twice as fast because she had another person to help her—though Hap doubted Googool was actually very helpful with anything intellectual.

He stayed in bed for most of his "morning" studying. He and Tara conversed a little when they came across something interesting in their studies. Mostly Tara came across the interesting stuff and wanted to talk about it. Hap didn't think much of it was interesting at all until Tara explained it to him. They finally got out of bed when Hap declared he was hungry enough to eat the walls.

Nutty paste wasn't appetizing, but it did keep his stomach from growling at him.

Amar and Tremble were already in the pantry. Tremble had even brought the lemsk along in its little cage. The lemsk was locked in with a light lock. The actual black disc that made up the light lock at the top had a handle that made carrying the cage easy for the owner. It had been made with pets with claws in mind. The light kept the creature from being tempted to slash out at the person carrying the cage since the light would burn those claws right off.

The lemsk seemed to understand, because it didn't even try to poke a claw out near the red glow.

Tremble spoke to the lemsk in cooing words, her voice almost melodious.

"I trust you're well rested," Amar said when he laid eyes on Hap.

"Well enough, I guess." He opened his tube of paste and slurped it down, frowning when the paste hit his tongue. He turned the package over in his hands to look at it closer, even though he still couldn't read the glyphs that everyone called Universe Basic. Tremble made fun of him for not knowing Universe Basic—well, actually . . . Googool had been the one making fun, but Hap held it against both of them.

"What is this?" he asked after swallowing the first taste down.

Amar smiled, glad to have had Hap notice something was different. "I worried your taste buds were growing bored. I purchased the variety pack."

"But what is it?" Hap had never tasted this flavor before in his whole life. It was minty a little, but fruity a little too. He couldn't place the flavor at all.

Amar glanced at the package. "Deggort cream."

Tara opened her mouth, probably to ask Amar to explain what the heck deggort cream meant, but Hap shook his head. The flavor wasn't bad, and he liked that it gave some variety from the nutty stuff. He didn't want Tara ruining the moment by finding out that it was the insides of some alien toenail pounded down into paste.

Better not to know.

They spent the rest of the day studying, talking, and getting fake exercise. Well, the exercise was real, but Hap called it fake. The airlift tube that led to the control room had a holo program that allowed it to become more than just a way into the control room. The holo today was the ocean. Hap and Tara had to swim the false ocean to the false island. The island was really just the ramp that accessed the door.

It creeped Hap out that it looked and felt exactly like a real ocean, except for the getting wet part. He looked wet. If he lifted his hand, he could see the drops and feel them but when it was all over, he was dry. The waves pushed and pulled against him, and if he put his head below the holo surface, he could see all kinds of fish and plant life.

"Why do we have to do this?" He'd asked this question a couple of times already, not really seeing the point of it no matter how important Laney and Svarta felt exercise to be.

"It's to get our heart rates up," Tara said with a smirk. "Because we apparently don't do enough of that when we're running from the bad guys." She splashed some water at him.

She flinched away when he splashed her back, in spite of the fact that the holo water couldn't really get her wet. "Forget running from bad guys. My heart rate goes up every single time we go through a spiral drop. I think that each drop should count for a month's worth of exercise."

"Oh, I know!" Tara panted a laugh alongside him. But then she lowered her voice. "But we better stop whining. Svarta said she'll introduce sharks and darbons to the waters to motivate us if we whine."

He took a break, treading the fake water. Tara stopped with him. She looked glad for the chance to rest. "Do we even know what a darbon is? Maybe it's like a dolphin, and it'll let us ride it to the island. She might be offering us a favor."

At that moment, a mouth bigger than Hap's whole body broke the surface of the water beside them. Tara screamed and splashed around behind Hap. All the oxygen left Hap's lungs as he stared in wide-eyed terror at the monster in front of him. Water droplets rolled down each of the serrated edged teeth as it opened its maw even wider as if prepping to chomp down. Hap didn't see anything besides the teeth before it disappeared entirely.

Svarta's laughter crackled over the sound system. "Now you know what a darbon is."

"Not funny, Svarta!" Hap yelled. Though, in spite of Tara screaming and moving behind Hap, she was laughing too.

"Are you kidding me? That was hilarious!" Svarta called back. "That was even better than the time I filled Tremble's toothpaste with jitters.

Hap wasn't sure what a jitter was except that his mom said scary movies and Halloween gave her the jitters, but he didn't think it was the same thing. He didn't ask Svarta to explain in detail because he didn't want to tempt her to show him personally by messing with *his* toothpaste.

The more he thought about it, the better it seemed to find a hiding place for his toothpaste and toothbrush.

After exercise time, Tara read Hap a little from the book Amar had given her. Amar had been helping her to translate it so she could understand the stories. Hap actually liked the stories and really liked listening to Tara's voice when she told them. After she finished reading as far as she'd translated, the two of them talked way past typical lights-out time for the sleep cycle.

Nana turned out the lights and gave several reminders to them that they needed to sleep, but they talked on—remembering things about their families, school, town, and lives—as if by speaking the memories out loud, they were keeping those things safe somehow.

The next day, Amar had said he planned on placing various trackers all over on Nova while they had him unconscious so that when the exchange was made, they might have a way of keeping tabs on where the guy went after that.

Chances were good that Nova would have all of his stuff cleaned for trackers, but there was the hope that if they put enough of them on him, he'd miss one.

Hap was in bed reading more about Koda as he waited for Amar to come get him. Hap was going to help him place the trackers, since Amar wanted to reward him for exercising restraint when he wanted to paint Nova's face. Tara was still asleep, so Hap had to entertain himself while he waited. At that moment he heard a strangling noise coming from Tara's room. "You okay in there?" He wondered if she'd gotten sick again.

She didn't answer but instead began groaning and jabbering like she'd gone entirely mental. "Tara?" he called to her.

She still didn't answer. He called twice more without getting a response before he finally grumbled and swung his legs over the side of his bed to get up and check on her.

Her back was to him, and her hair lay over her pillow in long, damp clumps. Her shoulders shook, and she seemed to be talking to the wall.

"Tara?" Hap touched her shoulder, but she didn't react to his touch or his voice. He grabbed her shoulder next and used it to roll her over to face him.

He fell back in shock as soon as he saw her.

Her eyes were open and leaking tears.

The tears were black.

18. A Pool of Black Tears

SHE SPOKE RAPID GIBBERISH, AND her pillow was stained with dark circles from her black tears. She stared right at him but didn't seem to see him as she cried her black tears and said her strange words.

"Time . . . darkness . . . stop the light's expansion . . . You're failing. You've allowed yourself to be captured . . . Hired someone else to do the job . . . Wait! We're being watched . . . Someone else is watching us . . . watching us . . . Fool! Fool! Fool! You've led her right to us!"

She kept repeating the word *fool*, shouting it at Hap as he stumbled back even farther from her. She terrified him in every way.

"Tara! Tara! Stop it!" he yelled back at her. "You're freaking me out!"

He scrambled out of her room and into the narrow hallway to get help. He ran to Mosh's old room where they kept Gygak and Nova tied up and under observation during the voyage to Koda. Hap skidded into the room, panting and frantic. Amar was bent over Nova. "Amar! You gotta help. Tara's sick or something! She's—"

He stopped short when Amar straightened in response to the urgency in Hap's voice. Amar moved to the side enough that Hap had a good view of Nova.

Black tears streaked from Nova's eyes and his mouth moved to the same nonsense string of words Tara had been muttering and then shouting.

Hap fell back into the door way. "Holy Houdini," he whispered in horror. "What's going on? Do we all have some kind of disease?" Hap felt around his own eyes, fearing he'd find the oily black liquid leaking down his face too. He didn't.

"No," Amar said, "it's much worse than that. The Dark Ones opened up communications with Don Nova, but with him unconscious . . . the communications have been altered to what you see now. They had to find a way to reach him—even in his sleep. If Tara is in this same state, then apparently they tied her consciousness into the communication as well. They likely latched onto anyone who was in a sleeping state on the ship." Amar frowned. "Nana, was anyone else asleep on board? Is anyone else experiencing this?"

"No," Nana answered. "No one else slept when the communications link opened between Nova and the Dark Ones. No one else is affected."

Amar nodded, looking grateful it hadn't been worse.

But Hap couldn't imagine anything worse than Tara being connected like this to the Dark Ones. "What do we do?"

"Listen to Nova's mutterings. See what we learn, though they mentioned they feared they were being watched. The Dark Ones will be more cryptic in their messages to Nova. They won't want to say anything too helpful for us."

"Holy Houdini," Hap said again for lack of anything else to say. He raked his fingers through his hair. "What about Tara? What if it kills her?"

"It shouldn't," Amar answered. "But you need to go back and be with her. I didn't realize she'd been pulled in when I found Nova like this. Go back. She needs you. Hurry!"

"What am I supposed to do?" Hap demanded to know.

"Go back to her. Stay with her. Hold her hand and talk her back to us. We don't want her trapped in a mind link with *them*."

Hap didn't move, unsure of his instructions, until Amar shouted, "Go!"

He darted back to her room. "I don't know what to do . . ." he said to himself.

"Amar said to take her hand and talk to her," Nana instructed.

Hap hurried to comply, sitting on her bed and taking her hand. Her mouth moved, and her eyes, ringed in black, stared. His own hands shook as he held hers. "Tara?" The black streaks on her cheeks freaked him out big time. "What am I supposed to say?"

"You need to dispel the darkness in her mind," Nana said.

"How do I do that?" he asked.

"Increase the light. Talk to her about good things."

So he rambled. He talked to her about things he used to make himself feel better—like teaching Alison to fly her kite or hiking to the falls with his dad or learning a new magic trick from his grandpa. As he talked, he incorporated stuff he remembered from when he and Tara were in grade school together—like the time she beat everybody in the spelling bee and the mathlete competition, the time the whole school had made snowmen during recess and she broke buttons off her coat so their class snowman would have bigger eyes than all the other snowmen who'd had to use the gravel. He talked about how he really didn't mind that she was smarter than he was and liked having her around to help get him out of trouble. He confessed to thinking her jokes were funny, to thinking she looked pretty in her flash costume on stage, to thinking she was brave because she was the one willing to make the hard choices and do the right thing. He talked until his throat scratched, trying to make himself heard over her mutterings and outbursts.

"How's she doing?" Svarta asked, startling Hap enough that he jumped.

"I don't know. It's been like a half hour, and she's just the same."

"Nova's the same too. We need to break the link." Svarta sat on the other side of Tara's bed, closer to her head.

Hap swallowed hard. "I can't lose her."

Svarta smiled, though she looked anything but amused. "I know exactly how you feel."

That statement from anyone else would have felt like a lie. But of course Svarta knew how he felt. Hadn't she lost everyone she'd been close to? "I'm sorry about Laney. We'll get her back."

"You bet we will. We aren't losing anyone, not *anyone*." Svarta looked down at Tara and used the cuff of her sleeve to wipe away some of the black trails on her cheek. Hap had been afraid to touch the oily tears. "So you and Tara . . . were you very good friends before all of this?"

"No," Hap confessed. "Not really. But we're good friends now." He quickly added the last part to make sure there wasn't any mistake on the subject. "Now, Tara's like my best friend in the whole universe. I'd do anything for her."

Svarta cocked her head to the side. "Tell her *that,* Prince Charming. She'll wake up for that. Any girl would wake up for that." Svarta stood. "I gotta check on Amar and Nova. If Nova dies from whatever this is that's going on . . ."

She didn't have to finish her statement. If Nova died, they'd no longer have very much worth bargaining to get Laney and Mosh back. Hap tightened his grip on Tara's hands, her mutterings growing louder, as if Svarta's moving had disturbed her in some way. Svarta's breath caught as if she'd stifled a sob as she left the room.

"Come on, Tara," Hap whispered. "Wherever you are can't be better than dragging through all these crazy star systems with me. You really are pretty cool sometimes—even if you do think I'm your personal punching bag. Come on back . . . from wherever you're at. We have a lot to do still. We're not done stamping our names on this universe."

She twitched and her face contorted as if she was sobbing, and the black tears fell faster over her cheeks like miniature rivers of inky oil.

The increase of tears and the look of anguish on her face ratcheted up his fear and frustration. "Tara! I mean it!" he shouted. "You're my best friend and I need you!"

Her mutterings came to an abrupt stop.

Then she sat up straight, opened her mouth wide, and screamed.

19. Hiding in the Junk

Hap nearly jumped out of his skin at the primal shrill coming from Tara. Not knowing what else to do, he grabbed her shoulders and pulled her into a tight hug, hoping to squeeze the scream right out of her. "Stop! Please, stop!" he begged, as he rocked her the same way he'd seen his mom rock his sister when she had nightmares.

The scream did stop, cutting off as abruptly as it had started.

And the sobs started.

Hap held Tara for a long time as she cried. He didn't ask any questions—afraid of what the answers might be, and Tara didn't volunteer information. She just cried. Nana must've told the others that the connection with Tara and the Dark Ones had been severed, because they showed up to check on her. They didn't ask questions either. They came in, affirmed that her real tears were washing away the black sludge on her face, and then quietly left again.

Hap didn't ask them about Nova's condition. He hoped Nova had suffered ten times what Tara had suffered. Twenty times. A zillion times. He deserved it because he had let the Dark Ones near someone like Tara—someone who was good and decent, someone the Dark Ones never could have reached without Nova's presence.

The sobs subsided after a bit, and Hap finally dared ask, "Are you going to be okay?" He didn't ask if she *was* okay because that would be stupid. Of course she wasn't. But he needed to know if she *would* be.

She shivered, her whole body damp with sweat. "I don't know," she answered. "It . . . was awful." The hollowed, airy words felt like a gust against his shoulder, where her head rested.

He had questions—like how such a thing had happened or what Tara saw and heard—but he still couldn't bring himself to ask. He tightened his arms around her. "I'm sorry," he said. "I'm so sorry. But you're safe now. I've got you."

When he was little and constantly breaking various bones from falling out of trees and using his skateboard in ways the manufacturer never intended, his mom had always held him and used the phrase, "I've got you." Until the moment he used those same words with Tara, he really hadn't known what they meant or why they'd been said.

But now he knew.

They weren't to comfort the injured person. It was a declaration that even though things were scary for a minute, the injured person was still alive, still okay. The phrase "I've got you" meant exactly that. It meant Hap still had Tara.

Reluctantly, he relaxed his grip on her and moved her far enough away that he could see her directly. Her face was mottled gray with the black and clear tears mixing into a freakish sort of mud mask.

"Let's get you cleaned up." He moved to get a couple of dampened cloths, but Tara gripped his shirt.

"Don't leave me!"

"I'll send Tremble to help you," Nana declared, which allowed Hap to ease back next to Tara. She rested her head on his shoulder and continued to shiver.

"She appears to be in early stages of shock," Nana informed Hap. "Use the blanket to cover her, and I'll warm it up."

Hap hurried to wrap Tara up in her blanket and then helped Tremble clean Tara's face and hair when she showed up with the needed supplies. Svarta checked in again—updating them on Nova, who had survived the ordeal and was now sleeping normally again. Svarta refused to waste water on cleaning Nova up. "Let him sit in his own mud," she insisted.

Amar showed up and cleared everyone out. He wanted to talk to Tara alone.

Hap waited just outside, trying to catch snippets of the conversation, but they talked too quietly. Amar came out looking grim and sent Hap back in to sit with her. She didn't talk while they sat there, which bugged Hap because he knew she'd told Amar everything.

Didn't she trust Hap enough? But he didn't press for information. He didn't want her to start crying again or anything like that.

She didn't ever tell him what had happened to her, not even a clue during the several days it took to get through the final drops. He tried not to resent it as they passed the time with more studying, more exercise, and a refreshing variety of pastes for food. He spent time training his paper dragon to sit up on its back legs and to strike a bored pose ending in a huge yawn, which actually looked a little scary since Confucian had been meticulous at filling that tiny paper mouth with wicked looking paper teeth. At least, it would have been scary if you were only a couple of inches tall looking into that mouth of pointed teeth. Hap thought it was cute and was glad to see that it made Tara smile when he showed her. Hap also had chores, but he didn't mind them. They gave him something to do while he felt like he was just waiting for something to happen.

Just before the final drop that would lead immediately to Koda, everyone was on edge. Through the muttered communications from the Dark Ones, they'd learned that someone else had been hired to do the job Don Nova had failed in. That meant someone else would be out there—looking for books.

The question that plagued everyone was, who would they send next?

Svarta ran checks on every aspect of Nana's capabilities. Svarta worried at the door that had been dented in and shot up by Nova's thugs. She'd suited up and gone space walking to try to repair things from the outside but determined they really just needed a new door. She had taken up Tara's habit of nail clicking when she thought about it too long.

Now Hap had two girls to try to get to break that annoying habit.

Tremble and Amar weren't much better. They secured items in the pantry and in the store room. They helped to repair anything that looked even remotely damaged, and they discussed flight patterns, quietly arguing about details when they didn't think Hap or Tara could hear.

Everyone was afraid.

And from Hap's reading, which Svarta was more insistent about than ever before, Hap understood the fear. It was much more than just a new bounty hunter after the books.

The planet Koda had its own issues.

It wasn't anything like the Lizard Comet, with its casinos, bars, and recreational atmosphere.

Koda was a dark, cold, messy place.

And the only people who dared enter that place were the salvagers, who were scarred, big-muscled sort of people who lived dangerously as a rule. But even the salvagers didn't ever land on the planet. They only picked off the leftover machinery and satellites in orbit around the planet, left over from the planet's mining days.

No one dared land on the planet anymore for a very good reason.

The Raksha.

The lessons and history on the planet were a little unclear on where the creatures came from only because no one ever returned alive from the planet to explain anything.

Except one.

One man left the surface of the planet alive and made it back to civilization.

But he'd returned a lunatic, muttering out nonsense and cringing if anyone went too close to him.

He'd been placed under observation by a medical team, and they were able to piece together his mutterings enough to form a story. Something lived on Koda that sucked away the light and energy from living things. He'd said they lived on intelligence. The creatures were terrible, ruthless, evil, without mercy. He said they could attach themselves to the ships leaving the planet and not be bothered by the vacuum of space as they tore into those ships and fed on the beings found inside. He never said how or if the creatures ever made it back to the planet's surface or if they just hung around in space. No one knew if they died out there or even if they could die.

No one knew where such creatures had come from. Some guessed the miners had unearthed a dormant species that ended up wiping them out. Others guessed it was another species who'd arrived on Koda with the intent of using the blue stones for their own purposes.

Another mining company moved in and tried to do their work by using robots on the surface with the actual miners living in orbit around the planet. But eventually they'd had to touch down on Koda's surface, and no one heard from them again. Their ships orbited Koda until orbital decay took over and plunged them to the surface, where they contributed to the planet's debris. Through the years many mining companies tried—feeling the prize to be worth the threat—but ultimately they'd all failed.

Salvagers took advantage of the miners' losses. They staked claim to many of the abandoned ships and equipment before orbital decay dragged them to the planet's surface and towed them home to rebuild or recycle. Salvagers have made a lot of money off the ships that orbited Koda. Those ships were like tombstones marking the loss of their previous owners.

Hap shuddered. And they were going to this place? On purpose?

Everyone was a little on edge while preparing for the final countdown to the spiral drop that would land them at the edges of Raksha territory.

"That's the last thing on the list. We're ready to go," Tremble announced to everyone as she and Svarta entered the control room. They were dressed in their space suits. Svarta's black suit always reminded Hap of the first time he'd ever seen her. She'd looked like an alien to him at the time. But everyone often reminded him that when he wasn't on his own planet, *he* was the alien.

Tremble's suit was all lavender. She was a pastel kind of girl, though Hap suspected that Googool wasn't. Of course, who knew what nonhumans associated with different colors? Maybe lavender was a color of strength for twin-souls?

Svarta nodded at Tremble and directed them to their seats in the control room. Everyone had to be in the control room and suited in their space suits.

"Pink," Tara whispered to him as she pointed at his space suit.

"Shut up, Tara," he whispered back. It *was* red, dang it! *Not* pink—no matter what she said about it, though he was glad to see she could joke again. It had taken days for her to break out of the silent trembling, and she didn't move anywhere on the ship without her blanket.

She didn't have it now, though, and Hap took that as a great sign of improvement.

"Once we enter the drop, I expect silence from everyone," Svarta said.

"Why?" Tara asked.

"Because we don't know what's already there."

Tremble, Svarta, and Amar wore visors over their helmets, and the holos just in front of their faces were different from the much larger holo flashing in front of the wall with the Nazca lines. Each had a different angle of the ship and its surroundings. They were prepared for attack.

Well . . . as prepared as they were going to be.

They entered the spiral drop.

When they exited the drop at last, Hap worried that they might not be prepared at all.

20. THE BLACK HOLE

As soon as they'd come out of the drop, everyone tensed, trying to readjust themselves and prepare for the worst.

Nothing happened.

Though everything was horribly quiet. Nana ran all sorts of data on all the various holo screens, but nothing out of the ordinary showed up. The adults scanned their screens . . . searching.

Hap eyed the big screen in front of him. "What are we looking for?" he finally asked, hating the feeling of helplessness.

When everyone glared at him and hissed, "Ssshhh!" he shrank down into his seat in shame.

So he sat still and watched and waited, wondering if all of the adults were finally as crazy as Tremble. Nothing was out there. The holo display showed the planet with a ring of what looked like scrap metal orbiting it.

Hap hadn't been prepared for all the debris. Out the big window in the front, Hap saw nothing but garbage. Broken-down ships and random parts, along with personal belongings that must have been tossed aside when salvagers went through the old corpses of those ships to find what they needed. Old shoes and worn out bits of clothing, wrappers from food and packaging from all kinds of crazy stuff floated past the windows. He couldn't identify most of it.

Tara grabbed Hap's hand and let out a gasp when a creepy face floated past the front window.

"It's just a doll," Hap whispered.

Tremble hissed him quiet again.

The doll was more than just creepy. It might have been smiling with that circular fanged mouth. Might have been. And the large single eye took up the center of its forehead. Hap almost expected it to blink.

He wondered what race of beings created dolls that looked like that.

And he hoped he'd never run into one.

"There," Svarta whispered, pointing to something Hap couldn't see because Svarta had a different view in her visor holo. She made a few quiet movements with her hands, making her visor holo flash with a variety of colors. As she did so, the ship changed direction again and silently pushed its way through to the dirty army-green planet. It was the sort of planet that would have made his mom wash her hands just from looking at it. Some of the junk had been pulled into the orbit of the planet's two moons.

Nana moved slowly, trying to keep the ship's engines quiet.

Everything was so painfully quiet that Hap wanted to shout just to prove he hadn't gone deaf.

And then Svarta swore. Out loud. So loud that everyone jumped in their seats. "We've been tracked!" she announced.

Everything changed with that announcement. Stealth was no longer a thought as everyone talked and barked orders.

"What is it?" Tara asked over the mess of chaos. "Is it the Raksha?" Tara's eyes were riveted to the front window.

"Nope. It's a hunter," Svarta yelled in answer.

Hap shrugged at Tara. He had no idea what that meant either, but the word *hunter* sounded bad.

"Bounty hunter," Nana clarified in between answering questions regarding distance to planet and the probability of outrunning the hunter ship.

"It's Kala Cheeda!" Tremble announced when Nana explained that they would have to reach a speed Hap didn't understand in order to escape the event horizon of the bounty hunter.

"What?" Svarta shouted, as she adjusted the schematics on the holo in front of her. The ship moved and lurched around debris floating in space as Svarta and the others worked within their holos. "They sent Kala Cheeda? No one can afford her fees!"

Amar shook his head while adjusting his own holo visor. "The Dark Ones have much at stake in this matter. And as for money?

The Dark Ones have the book that transmutes metals to gold. But they don't need it—not really. They have powers of persuasion that override mere currency. This was what the whispers meant when Nova and Tara were connected to the Dark Ones. The game has just become much larger."

"This isn't a game, scientist!" Svarta yelled. "This is a job! We save my sister, get the books, get back the crystal, and *you* find our father. That was the deal! You never said there would be other hunters after us!"

"We knew there would be others because of the connection between Nova and the Dark ones. Why are you surprised?"

Svarta growled. "Because you never said anything about *Kala Cheeda*!"

"We'll enter Kala Cheeda's event horizon in eighteen seconds." Nana's computer voice remained eerily calm in spite of the fact that the ship was executing crazy maneuvers that the grav stabilizers couldn't keep up with. With all the garbage, Nana and Svarta had to compensate—at the expense of the rest of the crew. Debris clanged off the hull of the ship as they skirted too close to another derelict ship hanging lifeless in its elliptical orbit around a moon.

The ship rocked and banged and sped up and braked and pretty much replicated all of the movements Hap hated about the spiral drop.

Tara still held Hap's hand, and even through the gloves of their suits, he felt her squeezing tightly enough to cut off his blood supply.

In the holo display in front of the wall, Hap saw that a trail of debris behind them was being sucked away and then disappearing altogether when the ship that followed them came closer to it. It was like the ship was *eating* the debris.

"How is that happening?" Tara asked. "How is all that stuff disappearing?" She'd swiveled her head to the nearby windows to verify that it was disappearing and not just being blown up, but there were no fireballs, no explosions. The stuff seemed to simply melt away before their pursuer.

"Kala Cheeda is what they call a 'black hole,'" Nana said. "She's not really a black hole, as in the phenomenon. She's simply able to compress all the empty space around electrons completely. She has a storage unit on her belt that can pull in and imprison or contain the miniaturized person or object. She can fit the entire human population of Earth into something the size of a sugar cube. Her storage unit is large enough to hold fifteen sugar cubes, and she likely has more storage units at home. She's a formidable enemy."

"Nana!" Svarta shouted, her voice shrill and furious. "History lesson later, getting out of here now! Focus!"

Nana shut up and flew, though the information she'd given didn't exactly inspire confidence as Hap watched the debris dissolve behind them. The trail of cleared space seemed to be racing toward them, trying to snatch them up as well.

"You're not fast enough!" Svarta yelled at Nana and took over the controls entirely.

"I'm taking you through the safest route—"

"We need fastest! Not safest!" and with that, Svarta steered the ship into the heart of the debris, swinging into trash and ripping through scrap metal and other garbage. A dirty old tube sock floated past the front window. Hap briefly allowed himself to wonder where a tube sock would come from when they took a nose dive and the ship shook with exertion. Amar and Tremble used the guns to try to blow up the ship chasing them. They came close a few times, but their laser blue fire failed to ever reach the hunter. Svarta had managed to put better distance between Nana and the hunter.

Hap felt the ship shudder around him as Nana absorbed a blast.

"Kala Cheeda has opened fire on us as well as trying to pull us into her event horizon," Nana said, but her voice no longer sounded calm. Nana did not like getting shot up.

"Thanks for the update," Svarta growled as the ship shuddered around them again. "What's the damage?"

"Superficial," Nana said after a brief pause.

"You closed access to damage assessment. You wouldn't do that without a reason. Nobody likes a martyr, Nana. Tell me what's wrong."

"The hatch took a direct hit. It's still holding and oxygen levels remain stable."

"That's good information to have to those of us who breathe oxygen!" Svarta yelled.

"I didn't want to cause you alarm," Nana said in her own defense.

"We can't outrun Kala Cheeda!" Tremble said as she manipulated whatever schematics must have been showing up in her visor.

"Yes, we can!" Svarta insisted.

"No, we can't!"

Svarta growled something so foreign, even the translation crawler couldn't make it sound like anything more than gargling. She snaked between two ships that were much larger than Nana and headed straight for a hulking mass of wreckage.

"What are you doing?" Nana demanded to know.

"Driving through that wreck."

"A very poor decision!" Nana said, sounding alarmed.

"That's why I took over. Sometimes it isn't about the good decision or poor decision. Sometimes it's the hard decision." She closed her eyes as she completed her sentence and drove them straight into a wrecked ship that was very likely to turn *Nana* into a wrecked ship.

Tara squeezed her eyes shut and let out a little yelp.

Amar blinked in disbelief as he realized Svarta really meant to endanger them.

The only sign that Tremble even noticed what was happening was the fact that she gritted her teeth in preparation for impact.

Hap wondered why he didn't feel the panic he knew he should feel before a crash.

It might well be the *last* thing on his coolest-things-ever list, but crashing into wreckage floating in an orbit of junk while being chased by the humanoid equivalent to a black hole? *That* was pretty cool.

Svarta started firing at the same time Nana plowed into the wreckage, creating a tangled mess of metal and sparks. Then Svarta made a hard turn, hiding behind the mess she'd just created and attaching the ship to a large chunk that had blown off, using its momentum to carry Nana away from the explosion.

Svarta cut the engines. The lights in the control room went out entirely except for the little glowing lights on each of their face shields in their space suits and the ghostly holo display that showed Kala Cheeda the hunter taking a different course through the debris until she disappeared entirely.

Svarta sighed in relief.

"Don't be too proud of your escape," Nana said, her voice a mixture of scolding and relief.

"Why not? We'd be lost somewhere in the black hole of that crazy bounty hunter's belt pouch if I hadn't done that." Svarta sounded proud.

"The hatch is hanging open and the oxygen is depleted. With the door swinging out into the vacuum of space, it is impossible to enter the atmosphere of the planet previously coded into our registry for landing. You would burn up on entry."

That was definitely bad news.

21. SYLLO-G

THE ADULTS WERE OUT OF their chairs to investigate the broken doorway leading to the vacuum of space. "Stay strapped in!" Amar and Svarta ordered the two teens as they swished out of the control room.

"As if," Hap said. He made a raspberry as he pushed against the straps that held him to his chair and instantly regretted it, since it left spit speckling the inside of his helmet. The straps didn't retract. He pushed a little harder.

"I distinctly remember our first in command ordering you to stay strapped in," Nana reminded him.

He scowled out from his helmet. The bad thing about scowling at Nana was that it was difficult to find exactly what to scowl at. She was the ship—the whole ship. Where did you direct the scowl?

"I have a right to see what's wrong," Hap insisted. "And to help fix it, if I can. I don't want to stay in this chair until my suit runs out of oxygen. That's lame, so let me out."

To his surprise, she did. The straps zipped back into the seat, and he was free to check things out for himself.

Tara grabbed his hand. "We'll get sucked out if we go by the door." Her eyes were so wide that they nearly filled her entire helmet.

Hap considered Tara's concern. He'd seen movies. It seemed valid to worry about getting sucked out into the vacuum of space. But the others had gone to check it out. Maybe they had a rope or harness or something. He was about to suggest they go look for some rope in the supply room when Tara yelled his name and pointed at one of the windows.

He turned to see what she pointed at, and his legs wobbled underneath him with the shock of it. Svarta—all suited up in her black outfit—was floating past the side of the ship.

"Svarta got sucked out!" Tara shouted and fought against the straps in her seat until Nana released her. Tara jumped from her seat and hurried to the window.

Svarta wasn't waving her arms wildly or trying to get back inside the ship like Hap would've done if he'd been sucked out. Her face was lit by the lamp inside her helmet, and the lights on the cuffs of her suit sleeves cast a brighter glow on all the garbage she was wading through.

From the look on her face, she wasn't worried about being outside the ship at all. She seemed to be searching for something. She turned a little, and Hap finally saw the cord connecting her to the ship. "She wasn't sucked out," he said with a lot of relief and a little bit of irritation at Tara for freaking him out so bad. "She's just looking through the trash."

Svarta stopped, bent over, and wrestled some huge sheet of metal out of a pile that had been orbiting the muddy green planet off to the side of them. The planet cast a sickly green glow around them, which made Hap think of a flu commercial.

"It's a new door. She's found a temporary replacement." Tara sounded relieved.

Svarta grinned inside her mask and gave a thumbs-up to Amar and Tremble, who must've been off to the side where Hap couldn't see them.

Someone reeled Svarta in by pulling on the cord that tethered her to the ship.

Hap and Tara hurried to the hatchway to see what they would do with the door. Svarta floated through the hatchway holding on to the rungs of the sheet of metal plating. She slammed the metal up against the hatchway. She tsked through the commlink in her helmet. "It's got a bulge keeping it from sitting flat against the top," she called out. "We'll need to scrape it down. Tremble, get me my tools."

Tremble ran off and returned with Svarta's tool chest. Svarta removed what looked like a huge potato peeler and began scraping away curls of metal around the door. She grated, trimmed with big metal clippers, and sawed through the metal until she'd made something that would sit flat against the doorframe.

She welded it all together while everyone else looked on.

"Is it airtight?" she asked Nana after a considerable amount of time had passed.

Nana directed Svarta to the few gaps in her welding work. Svarta then coated the entire hatch area with a silicone spray that hardened into a rubbery sheet after a few seconds. "Just in case," she said.

"We're good to go!" Svarta announced. "Let's get some airflow in here!"

Hap touched it to see if it would move, but the thing seemed pretty solid. He heard fans blowing, which meant Nana was trying to replenish the oxygen inside the ship.

"Let's get to the planet!" Tremble insisted. "I don't like being out in the open."

Svarta agreed and everyone returned to the control room. Hap barely managed to get seated before the ship entered real gravity. Everyone acted like they were still being chased, but Kala Cheeda had disappeared, and Hap had yet to see anything that resembled the creepy space zombies everyone acted so afraid of.

"According to the clue on the last box and the findings of the society on Earth, the next one should be in the cave system here . . ." Amar pointed to the Multi-D holo display which had formed into a topographical map of the planet instead of a map of the solar system.

They'd landed on the dark side of the planet. Sunrise wasn't for another hour. The sky had a lighter cast off on the horizon as the sun made its way to their side. Svarta said all reports from the mining operations through the years led her to believe that the Raksha were only active at night. Because of this, she made them wait until the sun had fully risen over the horizon while Hap and Tara kept watch through the windows.

If Hap thought there was a lot of flotsam in orbit, it was nothing compared to the mountains of debris on the ground.

"Are we seriously supposed to find a book in this disaster?" Hap looked doubtfully out at the terrain. "My room is cleaner than this. Under my bed is cleaner than this. Buildings that have been condemned due to health code standards are cleaner than this."

"We know the general region. It shouldn't take us too long to find it and to make the trade for Laney and Mosh. You two *absolutely* will stay here. We won't be gone long. An hour or two . . ." Amar wasn't really paying attention to Hap as he spoke. He stared intently at the holo display and gave Svarta quiet instructions as to where to turn and how far to go before the next turn.

"You mean like on the comet," Hap reminded Amar. "Where we spent almost two whole days with no sleep and with criminals breaking into our ship and with getting shot and with Mosh and Laney getting taken hostage?"

Amar held Hap's gaze. "You're right. You shouldn't be left on your own in the ship. I suppose you must come with us."

Tara scowled. "Nice going, Hap. Now we have to deal with Raksha, who are waiting to feed on my brains."

"Naw. They feed on intelligence. They'll totally leave *you* alone."

"You're so not funny." She lightly punched his arm.

He grinned at her. "Nice to have you back."

They'd landed in a recessed area between several piles of wreckage covered in moss and vines. Amar made them stay suited up just in case they ran into anything poisonous. The suits were made of good, thick stuff that made them pretty sturdy. Most things would have trouble getting through.

Most things. That didn't exactly sound encouraging.

Amar had awakened Nova enough to move him. He said that this drugged state for Nova was like sleepwalking. Amar didn't feel safe enough to awaken Nova completely.

"Stay close by. Kala Cheeda is likely out there too," Tremble insisted, her voice several octaves lower as if she grappled with Googool for control. Googool was always close at hand when it came to danger. She really was a better fighter than Tremble.

They exited through the cargo hold since the hatchway was sealed by the new door. A hole dilated in the middle of the room, revealing a circular light.

Amar stepped out first. Hap wanted to warn him that walking into nothing but light seemed like a bad idea, but Amar didn't fall to the ground like Hap expected. He hovered just over the light.

"It looks clear. Let's go." Amar lowered into the light.

Hap stepped into the circle carefully. He didn't fall through, but he didn't feel anything underneath him either. He gave a little jump, and though he came to a stop just before the light, he didn't feel the jolt of landing on, or of connecting with, ground again.

Weird.

"Stop messing around, Hap," Tremble said.

The light lowered him to the ground, the intense heat and thunderous pulse almost as difficult to deal with as the spiral drops.

Hap wasn't all that fond of a mountainous terrain of metal and broken machinery—the skeletons of lost colonies. Everywhere he looked, the junk appeared to be some sort of monster. And since he didn't know about the creatures that lived on this planet, anything really could be a monster.

"I think we made it here before Meg and Nova's people," Svarta said. "Even if they did leave before us. Nana's the best."

"So what's up with that Kala Cheeda—the black hole?" Hap figured if he kept asking questions and kept the conversation going, it would take his mind off the shadows all around them and the weird feel of squishy rusted muck under his feet. He'd definitely need his suit cleaned after this little excursion.

"She's a bounty hunter." Svarta's voice crackled through the headphones in Hap's helmet.

"Does she work for Nova too?" Tara asked.

"Nope. She's his direct competition. We're probably on the hit list of every bounty hunter in the universe." Svarta sounded irritated, which seemed pretty mild considering she'd just announced that lots of people were gunning for them. This was definitely something he wouldn't want to share with his family when he linked home.

"What if they know where all of the books are already, and now they're hiring locals to get them? What if Kala Cheeda already got the book that's here and has already gone?" Tara asked. Hap hated that she always asked the good questions—things he'd never think of on his own.

Amar's voice came through the headphones. "If she already had it, she wouldn't have been bothering with us. But that means she'll be coming planet-side as well."

Well, that was cheery news.

They hiked around all kinds of creepy stuff: rusted-out metal bodies of what looked like train cars tipped onto their sides near twisted tracks, housing that had been broken into by the looks of the way the domed portions still had bits of dirty glass like jagged teeth clinging to the frames, and bits of satellites that had once been orbiting the planet. It looked like the original settlement had been there a long time before they experienced a full-on attack.

"How long were the original mining colonies here?" Tara asked the question Hap had been thinking.

"Over a couple of generations. Long enough that people were settled. They'd had children here and those children had grown up and were starting families of their own. They'd been very profitable with the urja deposits during that time, and many others moved here to help with the mining. That is why I agree with those who think the Raksha must have been unearthed during the mining. They wouldn't have waited to attack."

"Can we *not* talk about the Raksha?" Svarta asked as she shot a glare at Amar.

Amar fell silent.

Varying kinds of robotic faces stared out of dark, lifeless eye sockets. Hap hated how the faces seemed to watch his every step. A moldering sort of smell clung to the air. A whole planet that smelled like rancid tomatoes. He was tempted to switch to the oxygen provided by the suit instead of breathing the oxygen provided by the planet, but Svarta had told him not to waste resources. This was Hap's idea of torture. He almost asked what was rotting, but they'd come across enough shredded clothing that looked like it had been pulled straight off a person. Hap didn't think he really wanted to know.

Evidence of actual families once living on the Koda existed in the forms of rusted bicycles, dolls, and metallic things that looked like action figures.

"Children . . ." Tara whispered. "Children were here." Her tone was filled with dismay and horror. Hap worried she was going to sink into the depression she'd experienced after she'd been trapped in the mind link with the Dark Ones. "When were the last miners here?" she asked, obviously not caring that Svarta didn't seem to much want to talk at all.

"Two hundred fifty-seven Koda rotations ago," Tremble answered. "The urja stone is a powerful temptation. You'd think they would look at the history of losses and make better decisions, but they all seem to believe they are the exceptions and they will succeed where everyone else has failed."

Hap took a deep breath. "What makes us so different from them? Aren't we risking our lives to come here to get something from the planet the same way all the miners did?"

Amar turned and offered Hap a brief smile. "Very wise, young Hap—to see the similarities between our current mission and the others' who have been here before. Yes. Of course there are similarities. But there are differences too. The difference is our cause is not one for personal gain. We fight for life itself—not merely our own lives but for the lives of every sentient being in every inhabited star system. Our cause is just. Besides, we won't be here very long. Those mining companies were all here long enough to settle down before they ran into trouble. They were also here at night, when the Raksha are active. We'll be long gone before night falls."

They hadn't gone far when Svarta jumped down into a pit of muck and squealed, "Awesome!"

"What?" Everyone gathered around the lip of the pit to see what had Svarta acting crazy.

"It's a Syllo-G 42! I haven't seen one of these in forever. They stopped making them years ago."

Hap looked doubtfully at the bits of scrap metal in her hands. "And that means what?"

"I've always wanted a robot." She messed with something inside what almost looked like a head, and a faint hum came from it. "And he still works! Look at him! He's adorable!"

So the thing was supposed to be a robot. Adorable really wasn't the word Hap had thought of when he inspected the stuff hanging from Svarta's fingers. She adjusted it so the face turned out toward Hap.

Freakish described the machine much better. One electric eye hung from circuitry down over the robot's face. A light glowed red in the center of the dislocated eye. The good eye had a blue glow. The thing's left arm hung by a few scant wires of copper, and the right arm and left leg were totally missing. It was like a robot zombie. Forget the zombie Raksha that wanted to eat their brains. Hap figured the thing in Svarta's hands was more likely to kill them all while they slept than Tremble when she was having an "off day," as Nana referred to Tremble's split personality days.

Svarta wrestled the thing up and out of the pit. "A little help here, Happenstance."

Hap moved to help her. "Here." Svarta shoved a bunch of greasy odds and ends into his arms. "Help me carry these back to Nana."

Hap agreed only because saying no to Svarta made you a target for her practical jokes—the kind where she would be the only one laughing.

Nana opened the light and sucked the ugly little machine into the cargo hold before Svarta and Hap returned to the others. "He'll be useful after I fix him up. Laney will be glad I got him."

Hap doubted Laney would ever approve of that hunk of junk coming onto the ship, but he didn't argue. It was the first time Svarta had been genuinely happy since Laney had been abducted.

Hap's legs were tired, and his feet hurt after a while—not that he dared mention it to Svarta, because she'd think her exercises weren't good enough, and she'd make him do more.

Amar had led them to the entrances of two different caves, but they ended up being mining caves—not the original caves that the scientist would have used when he dropped off the box and its book before the mining operations began. Before the Raksha.

Amar led them away from the second tunnels, grumbling about how he couldn't go any farther away because then his coordinates would be entirely off from what his contacts on earth had given him.

"If those are the coordinates, then we should at least check it out." Svarta waved her arms back in the direction of the cave.

"But there were no signs on the walls. And there's a rail system leading into the cave. My brother would never have been so careless as to leave the book in a place heavily trafficked enough to require it's own transportation system."

"Maybe the miners tunneled into the original caves," Hap suggested. "Maybe they're interconnected now."

Amar stopped. "Yes. Of course. I should have thought . . ."

"I warned you that you weren't sleeping enough," Svarta said. "You're not thinking. You gotta get your head on straight, scientist."

"You're right." His agreeing with Svarta took them all by surprise. Amar and Laney agreed on all kinds of things. Amar and Svarta? They never agreed, or at least it was so close to never as to be a minor point. "You're right," he repeated. Let's try the miner's tunnels with the coordinates we have and see where they take us."

Amar held his link key in front of him, the little holo above it pulsing furiously, indicating that they'd arrived at the X that marked the spot. "It does indicate this as the place to begin," Amar said.

Tremble stumbled on one of the railroad tracks, and a spiteful Googool laugh came from her throat. "Clumsy."

"I am not," Tremble's sweet voice responded.

Googool must have retreated, because she never argued further.

Amar pointed the cuff light on his wrist into the cavern. He pointed to Nova. "We can't search properly while dragging him with us."

"I'll stay," Tara volunteered after darting a quick glance down the long dark corridor of the tunnel.

"Sorry, Tara," Svarta interrupted before Amar could agree or disagree. "If Kala Cheeda finds us or Meg shows up for the trade off, you aren't exactly the person who should be standing guard. I'll stay. Tremble will back me up."

Tara nodded as though she expected that answer.

Farther into the cavern, the rancid smell of tomatoes faded into the mustiness of damp earth. Hap decided he loved the smell of damp earth. He retracted his helmet so he could feel the cool air of the cave on his face. Amar and Tara had done the same, enjoying the break from breathing recycled air on Nana and the nasty air of Koda.

"Stay with me," Amar instructed as he led them farther into the dark. "Keep your eyes open. We're looking for symbols like this . . ." He flashed a holo similar to the one they'd seen on the Lizard Comet door that led to the cave system with the book.

Tara edged closer to Hap as they walked, and he felt glad that she did. Not that he expected Tara to be able to save him or anything if a native creature should lunge from the darkness, but her presence made him feel better.

"When Emperor Ashoka's kingdom was attacked, why didn't you and the other nine scientists just destroy the books? Why go to all the trouble and danger of hiding them?" Tara asked Amar after a while.

He turned, a swath of light moving up the wall as he did. "It's knowledge. It's blasphemy to even think of destroying knowledge."

"But you and the others obviously hid your books in really good places, or we wouldn't be having so much trouble getting them back. How are you going to keep Nova or the Dark Ones or anybody else from getting them once we've gathered them?"

"Don't you worry yourself, Tara Jordan. I know what I'm doing. They will be safe once they are gathered."

She was busy shooting him a doubtful sort of glare when she stumbled. She fell into Hap, which made him trip over a rail and land on his face. "Ow! Tara!"

"Sorry," she said with a cringe.

His ankle throbbed, and pain shot through his foot and ankle when he tried to sit up. "I think I twisted it," he said.

Amar grumbled something about not having time for antics as he leaned over and touched Hap.

Hap felt the energy between Amar's hands flow through his whole body. The warm energy went straight to his toes. It almost seemed that he could now see his injury. He saw the ligament hanging by a few threads. He saw the red burn of pain. Then things started to "click" into place in his ankle. He felt the adjustment as if someone had moved his ligament back into place and reattached it.

The red burn of pain melted into something cooler, calmer.

Amar removed his hands. "Be more careful." Amar turned back to the dark corridor and kept moving.

Hap got to his feet, testing the ankle carefully, but it seemed fine.

"Are you okay?" Tara asked.

"I'm . . . fine. Really. Weird. That guy could make a ton of money working for the NFL as a physical therapist."

"Keep up," Amar called.

They hurried after him.

The tunnel split a short time later. Amar stood at the split, shining his light down both options several times as he rubbed his chin.

"Which way?" Hap shined his own light down both corridors. They looked identical. The railroad tracks had split off and now trailed down both sides. The tunnels were cut with the same sort of precision that left the walls with a ridged texture like it had been drilled out. No symbols existed to tell the direction they should go.

Amar looked at his link key with the coordinates flashing. "I can't really tell. Technically, the coordinates say we're there—just not deep enough. I can't tell which one of these will wind back around to this location underneath us—or even if either of them will."

He stood there for several moments longer before Hap said, "Go to the right."

Tara laughed, not mockingly but in a genuinely amused way. "Might as well. It's Hap's solution to pretty much everything. We can't just stand here wondering."

Amar smiled briefly. "Yes. Might as well pick one and move on. We can backtrack if we need to. But we need to hurry. We don't have much time before sunset."

With a choice made, they started down the right tunnel at a trot, deeper into the ground.

"You know, you're doing pretty good, Tara," Hap said after a while.

She laughed. "What? At keeping up? It's all that fake swimming Svarta makes us do. It's like she's training us for some Olympic event for when we get back to Earth."

He smiled, thinking back to a few school races where Tara had pretty much stomped on any competition she had as she sped past them. "Yeah, but you were always a better runner than me. I mean, you're not freaking out about being underground."

"I must be getting used to no sunlight and cold, damp air." Her eyes widened, looking like white moons with the reflection from her helmet light.

"Hap . . ." she said slowly.

"I found something!" Amar yelled, drawing Hap's attention away from Tara. He stood near the wall, peering into the carved surface. Bits of the glyphs they'd expected to see were still visible where the drill hadn't scratched all the way down. It was fuzzy and tough to read, but Amar acted alert for the first time since they'd stepped foot on the surface of Koda. He was excited by the find. They'd come to another crossroads with three different options, but Amar didn't hesitate at this one. "Left," he said.

No railroad tracks went left so they were walking on soft earth, and the tunnel didn't have the same ridged, drilled-out texture. It took an immediate turn back the direction they'd come and sloped down at an uncomfortably steep angle. The walls narrowed drastically enough that Hap felt like they were squeezing in on him.

Amar didn't pause at all before crouching down and sliding his feet down the slope. He tried to keep his hands against the rock walls to slow his descent, but gravity took over, and Amar was tumbling down before Hap could reach out and try to make a grab at him.

"You okay?" Hap yelled down the shaft.

"Fine!" Amar called up. "Get some of that rope from your pack. Tie it to something secure, then throw it down. It'll keep you from getting hurt on your way down, and we'll likely need it to get back up out of here.

Hap hurried to do as told.

"Hap . . ." Tara said again, her voice carrying a sort of urgent plea.

"Hang on a second." Hap pretty much tuned her out while he went in search of a secure place to tie the fibrous rope. It had been a gift from King Anansi. It was really an incredibly strong webbing that Hap knew would hold his weight if he secured it properly. It had, after all, held the weight of Tara, Laney, Mosh, and him all at once back on Anansi.

He found a stalagmite that was as thick around as Mosh and tied it to that. He gave several tugs before determining it was ready, and he started off down the slope using the line as a way to keep himself from falling to the bottom like Amar had.

"Hap!" Tara yelled.

"Come on! Tell me when we're down! We can talk while we move."

She grunted, but he felt the fibrous rope strain a little as she added her own weight to it and followed him.

While they'd been climbing down, Amar had used the time he'd been waiting to see which direction to go next. There were several darkened corridors leading from the place where the slope settled into flat ground again. Symbols decorated the stone floor and the walls all around them as if they were standing in the middle of a huge ancient drawing.

This way!" Amar practically shook with excitement to finally be on the right track.

Tara followed along behind Amar and said, "We're not in daylight."

Hap looked around him. "Are you sure? Because I'm pretty sure I saw some light glowing and . . ." He looked down at his flashlight then blinked in mock surprise. "Oh . . . right . . . just my flashlight. Sorry, you were saying something about sunshine?"

"You're impossible," she said, shaking her head. "I'm trying to tell you guys that we're worried about getting to the ship before sunset because the Raksha come out at night, but what if they aren't nocturnal, exactly . . . what if they just don't like light? What if they're—"

Amar had stopped, and Hap and Tara nearly ran into him as he finished Tara's sentence in a hoarse whisper. "Down here." He pointed. "With us."

Tara inhaled sharply as Hap instinctively reached out and grabbed her arm—whether to steady her or steady himself, he couldn't tell.

Coffin-shaped recesses had been carved into the cave walls, and inside each one of those niches leaned a creature that turned Hap's legs to mush. Their hairless skins were albino pale and seemed to glow with a sickly gray light. They didn't really have mouths, which freaked Hap out big time. Where mouths should have been was stringy skin roped over and over itself. They didn't have hair but instead a mass of snakelike appendages writhing back from their heads Medusa-style.

The creatures' eyes were all closed. At least they looked closed. For all Hap knew, the creatures could see through those closed pale flaps of skin hovering over the spaces where eyes should be.

The floor was littered with pale blue chips as though someone had smashed thousands of blue china plates to the ground in a huge tantrum.

They'd accidentally stumbled into a hive or something.

But it wasn't that they could have avoided it, because at the middle of the room sat the stone box.

Holy Houdini, he thought, not stupid enough to say the words out loud.

Amar rested a hand on Hap's shoulder and waved his other toward the box, then he pointed to the ground as if indicating that Hap and Tara needed to stay put while he went and opened the box.

That suited Hap just fine.

He had no desire to put himself in the dead center of a room surrounded by sleeping creepy guys.

Amar inched forward a little a time, careful to watch his step so he didn't stumble or step on the blue shards.

Tara and Hap tracked his movements. Hap wasn't aware he'd been holding his breath until Amar finally reached the box, and he finally realized he was feeling dizzy from the need of oxygen.

Amar glanced back and gave a nervous sort of smile, his teeth flashing against his dark skin in the light of Hap's flashlight. Amar turned back to the stone box and removed the silver flower pendant from one of the pockets in his suit and fitted it into the carved-out lotus flower on the box.

Nothing happened.

The drawer that should have hissed and grated open remained closed. Amar jolted with the shock of it not working, and Hap saw the sweat beading up on Amar's forehead.

Amar removed the pendant and then carefully placed it back. Everyone waited.

Nothing.

Hap wanted to howl in frustration. How could it not work? Why right now when they were surrounded by sleeping zombies?

Could they carry the stone box out? It looked incredibly heavy, but maybe . . . then he remembered the slope and the fact that they'd have to pretty much climb out. There would be no way to climb with it.

Pulling free from Tara's tight grip, Hap moved to see what he could do. She made a noise as if about to call him back, and he and Amar shot looks of horror at her. She already knew she'd made a mistake, because both of her hands flew up to cover her mouth, her eyes even wider than they'd been. They needed to get out of the nest fast. Hap had to help, but he shot her a look as if to say, *We'll be fine. I'll be right back. Trust me.*

She nodded as if to say, *I do trust you, but if you get yourself killed, I'll be so ticked off at you.*

Hap carefully picked his way over the blue bits to get to Amar. He managed to reach Amar's side without stepping on anything that made noise. Amar nodded in approval. They faced the box together to puzzle out what could be the problem. Hap took Amar's pendant and placed it in the carved-out lotus flower—not because he didn't think Amar knew what he was doing but just because he had to try it for himself. Amar rolled his eyes and spread out his hands wide as if to say, *See, it really doesn't work, you know-it-all kid.*

Hap jiggled the pendant a little bit but still nothing. While he jiggled it, Amar pressed the carved stonework at the middle of the box—the place where the compartment holding the book *should* have released from.

They poked, prodded, and pressed until Hap's fingers hurt from the friction of his suit rubbing on his fingertips. Hap even tried to lift the box, hoping maybe it wasn't as heavy as it looked.

He thought he might ask Svarta for upper body exercises because he felt like a complete wimp at that moment. The box didn't budge under his efforts. No matter what they tried—nothing worked.

Hap kept telling himself to focus on the box, to not look at the creatures, but he couldn't keep his gaze from slipping back to where the notched out spaces held those pale-glowing faces. It was weird the way the creatures stood in kind of a leaned-back position. So unnatural.

And the fact that they didn't move, no twitches, no signs of a chest rising and falling with the motion of breathing, nothing—like the dead artifacts of some long-extinct race—made Hap's skin crawl.

Were these even the Raksha? Maybe these creatures were something else. Maybe they were as kind as bunny rabbits.

But he knew they weren't. He could sense it in the musty rot smell in the air, feel it in the energy that surrounded him. These motionless things were what had wiped out several generations of colonies. And if he accidentally woke them up . . .

Bad things would happen.

Focus on the box. Get the box to open. He forced himself back to the task at hand, moving his hands over the carved details of the stones, trying to find anything that would click this thing open the way the box on the comet had opened for Amar.

Hap grabbed Amar's arm and almost gasped aloud. Thinking of Amar opening the box reminded Hap of something he hadn't even thought about since he'd done it.

He'd stolen the pendant that Nova had tried to use.

He'd put it around his own neck.

He tugged at the collar of his suit, trying to keep the hard plates of the suit around his arms from clacking against the plates on his chest as he did it. He reached into his collar and fished around until he got hold of the chain. He pulled it out and with a triumphant flourish showed it to Amar, who smiled briefly, snatched it from Hap's hands, and hurried to use it to replace the pendant that was already sitting in the spot carved out for it.

The carving of the flower recessed into the stone with a grinding noise and hiss.

Hap couldn't help it.

He looked up to see if the Raksha had noticed the noise.

Everything about them looked the same . . . except for one thing.

The flaps of skin that had covered their eyes were up, and Hap was staring directly into the black pits of the Raksha.

Amar removed the steel-banded book and shoved it inside the satchel he had slung over his shoulder and under one arm. The Raksha had yet to move out of their beds or whatever those recesses were. Hap and the Raksha closest to him stared at each other, unblinking.

Amar pulled Hap gently back toward where Tara waited. He flicked his hands in Tara's direction, indicating she should start climbing like crazy up the shaft. She wasted no time arguing and disappeared around the corner. A high-pitched whine came from the creatures—a noise that seemed to gather together in the middle of the room.

"Time to go. Now!" Amar said.

Hap turned and bolted for the rope, pulling himself up on the rope as fast as his arms would move. Amar was right behind him.

Hap chanced a look beneath him to see only Amar. The creatures weren't following. Not that he slowed down or anything, because creatures capable of wiping out an entire civilization weren't things to take lightly.

"Why aren't they chasing us?" Hap finally dared ask.

"They're coming out of stasis. They'll be fully active soon enough. Keep climbing."

Hap climbed.

A hand reached out over the lip of the entrance into the shaft, making Hap yelp until he saw Tara's head pop over the side. "Take my hand!" she demanded.

He grabbed it and let her help him over the top.

They both grabbed at Amar and pulled him up and out of the hole. Hap turned to gather his cord, but Amar shoved at him. "Get moving!"

"But King Anansi gave me that!"

"Priorities, boy! It won't do you any good dead. Leave it and move!"

That was enough to convince Hap.

They ran.

They made it pretty far—they were already nearly to the entrance. Hap felt the air change as they moved closer to the outside air.

The high-pitched whining of the Raksha got louder, more aggressive. The Raksha had finally woken up.

Hap heard the skittering of claws against the cave walls, as though the creatures were climbing the sides of the tunnels rather than using the softer dirt floor. But he didn't dare look back.

"Svarta!" Amar yelled. "The Raksha are coming! Call Nana to get us out of here!"

"Svarta! Tremble!" Tara yelled.

But no one answered.

Everyone was gone. Svarta, Tremble, and Nova had disappeared.

22. Attack of the Space Zombies

THE TUNNEL THRUMMED WITH THE vibrations of the horde racing behind them, quickly catching up.

The light from the tunnel entrance wasn't the way Hap remembered it from when they'd entered. It was angled wrong, like the sun was setting.

Had they spent the whole day in those caves?

No. They hadn't really been there that long, and most of their time had been eaten up in trying to open the box, but even that hadn't taken a whole day, even if it did feel like it.

"We can't outrun them!" Tara yelled, her voice desperate as her feet pounded the ground.

"Don't stop!" Hap yelled, fearing she might give up, that her legs might burn in the same way his burned, that her mind had seen the uselessness of running anymore when the creatures were obviously faster.

"Don't stop!" Amar agreed.

Both Amar and Tara had outstripped Hap by a little.

Hap felt the creatures behind him, their energy, their noise, their *closeness*. They were almost right on top of him. He felt it in every cell in his body. He was so close to the entrance. Maybe when he got out, he'd see Nana there waiting and she'd pull them up in a light capture and save them all.

It was with this hope that he took a giant leap toward the entrance, out into the rays of the waning sunlight, hoping that Nana would save the day.

But he wasn't caught up in Nana's light. Instead he hit the ground hard, knocking all the wind out of him. He'd expected one of the creatures to grab his ankle and drag him under the mass of the horde, but though he sensed them behind him still, he also sensed they no longer gave chase.

He opened his eyes and wiped at the dirt that had covered his face when he'd landed.

The creatures whined and clicked in the tunnel—hovering at the edge of light and shadow. He could feel their anger, their desperation, their *hunger*.

He crawled over the ground, cutting up his hand on the blue stones that had been buried under the dust, to distance himself from the Raksha.

"They're photosensitive," Amar wheezed, his hands on his knees as he tried to suck in oxygen. "I should have been thinking. I led you into a death trap. I'm so sorry . . . so sorry."

"So they aren't coming out because of the sun?" Tara asked between great shuddering breaths.

"So it would appear. We're saved by the light," Amar said.

"Hate to be the voice of negativity here, but the sun is on its way down." Tara pointed at the horizon.

Hap finally figured out why the sun was already setting. Small planet . . . short days.

And no sign of Svarta, Tremble, or their prisoner Nova.

No sign of Nana.

"This is bad," Tara said slowly, still catching her breath, looking around to find any sign of their missing party.

"And getting worse." Amar nodded his head toward the distance.

Hap stretched his neck to see.

A woman ambled over the wreckages and useless junk toward them. Her face was beautiful and terrifying all at the same time. Her angular, narrow features gave the illusion of her being sharp in all things, like a knife. Her face made Hap feel like he was looking through a kaleidoscope. He almost adjusted the controls on his mask to clear things up but realized he'd pulled it back from his head before he'd ever entered the cave. He saw her with his own eyes, exactly as she was. She was just hard to focus on. She was all in black, from the tips of her boots to her dark eyes, which were visible because she wore no helmet. She had *four* of those dark eyes, slanted upward on the sides of a sharp widow's peak hairline that led to a bushy mane of black hair. Her ears came to sharp points, and her hands ended in needle-fine claws. She looked like a panther, especially considering how she moved over the wreckage piles without difficulty, whereas Hap had tripped his way through most of it.

She was far enough away that it would take her several minutes to get to them.

"Kala Cheeda," Hap guessed.

"That's Kala Cheeda? The black hole thing chasing us?" Tara asked.

Amar nodded grimly. "She's pulled in her event horizon. She's not compressing anyone right now. But that doesn't mean she can't cast her net out again. It's time for us to go."

Hap didn't argue.

Tara did, though. "We can't leave. We don't know what happened to Svarta and Tremble!"

Hap almost asked if Amar thought Kala Cheeda had taken the others, but that didn't make sense. If she had, she would have gone into the caves after the book already.

A thrumming noise filled the air above them, and Tara's hair was blown back from her face. Hap felt like the force of wind would pull his hair right from its roots. It was Nova's ship.

Meg had arrived to make the trade.

"Just in time for the party," Hap said, shielding his eyes from the debris flying around in the wind. Several small blue stones skittered over the dust against Hap's hands. He looked down at them and, out of habit more than anything else, pocketed a bunch. He might need to throw them at his enemies as a last-ditch defense effort if his drubber gave out.

The question was, who did he aim at when enemies were on all sides?

Hap moved out farther from the cave, putting a lot of distance and wreckage between him and the creatures who waited on the other side of shadow. Tara and Amar followed.

Nova's ship landed close by. Meg stomped down the ramp dragging a pitiful Laney behind her. Laney's legs wobbled underneath her like they would collapse at any moment.

Mosh was led out by several muscle guys. He looked a little better than Laney. His legs didn't waver under him, at least. Several other guards had moved out of the ship faster and now surrounded it with their guns held at the ready.

Meg had a drubber tight against the skin at Laney's forehead. Laney lifted her chin, proving that though she'd been weakened, she was not weak. "We're here for a trade!" Meg shouted. "Where are Don Nova and the book. There's no deal without both."

"Hap," Tara whispered his name in a breath and edged closer to him. The sun had become a sliver of light over the horizon. Within another few moments, it would be lights out.

He glanced at her but realized her focus wasn't on him. It wasn't even on Kala Cheeda, who moved toward them, or on Meg, who threatened Laney's and Mosh's lives if they didn't cough up Nova and the book fast.

The noise from the cave now filled the air outside the cave—the humming, thrumming sound, almost like a cicada's buzz.

Now everyone's attention had been diverted beyond the threat of each other—beyond the threat of Kala Cheeda. Even Kala Cheeda had stopped moving toward them, her ears twitching like a dog's when honing in on a sound. She looked worried. Hap suspected everyone was worried.

He wasn't.

He was terrified.

The Raksha were coming out.

"Run!" Amar shouted as the sliver of sun melted into something less than a sliver.

They all sprang into a sort of inaction—no one sure exactly what to do now that they realized the Raksha were a part of the rendezvous.

Meg held her ground and demanded the return of Nova and the book as she jostled Laney, making Laney cry out in pain.

"We don't know what happened to Nova!" Amar yelled. Though he had told Hap and Tara to run, he had stayed to contend with Meg. "He was gone when we came out of the cave. You should just give us Mosh and the girl and save yourself. We're all in great danger!" His dark eyes were filled with desperate pleading as the last bit of sunlight disappeared.

"I'm not leaving without Nova!" she yelled.

"He'd leave without you."

Her mouth hung slack for a moment as if the truth of this was too much to bear, but the moment of deciding and bargaining and trading was gone. The Raksha were loosed from the cave and closing in fast.

The henchmen holding Mosh abandoned him and dove back into the ship. Mosh stood alone and confused for a moment before he came to his senses and moved to grab a hold of Laney, but Meg jerked Laney's arm and yanked her out of Mosh's reach. He ended up stumbling off the ramp to the ground. "Not without a trade!" she yelled.

"You're a fool to risk yourself in worry of trades!" Amar yelled at Meg, who looked uncertain.

"Yet, you don't run either, scientist! Are we both fools, then?" Meg answered.

With a growl, Amar turned from Meg, rounding on Hap and Tara. "Get to where we left Nana!" Amar demanded as he shoved them forward. "Run!"

Hap didn't need to be told again. He dragged Tara along with him, back toward where they'd left Nana. "Holy Houdini!" Hap breathed, feeling the blood leave his extremities. His watery legs barely held him upright.

Kala Cheeda had arrived at the wrong moment.

The Raksha came upon her first.

Most of them had surrounded Kala Cheeda. They seemed fascinated with her and unwilling to move away from her. A clearing had formed around her as all the debris melted into the air around her in a cloud of dark emptiness. The Raksha hovered at the edge of the clearing unwilling to enter it for whatever reason. And for whatever reason, Kala Cheeda seemed unwilling to widen the clearing to compress them down and lock them up in her little storage box.

Hap thought it might save them all a lot of trouble if she did, but then, he didn't want to be miniaturized down with those things in a small box.

And then Nana appeared over the mountainous horizon of debris. Hap saw Svarta through the large window and about started crying in relief. Svarta had gone back to get the ship! They'd be rescued!

But Nana didn't pick them up as she swooshed past them and came to a stop near Nova's ship. Instead, Svarta, Tremble, and Nova were dropped to the ground in the beam of light. Svarta hit the ground at a brisk walk, shoving Nova forward on unstable legs. He looked as helpless as Laney.

"Hurry, Meg! There's no time! Give me my sister, and I'll give you Nova, and we can all focus on getting out of here alive. Just let her go!"

Tremble had moved to where Hap and Tara had been fleeing the Raksha. "Get to the ship, fool!" It was Googool, not Tremble, who was in control as she insisted he move and tugged on his arm forcefully. Tremble had likely been too scared to face the onslaught of these creatures who seemed to be everywhere. Hap stumbled with Googool's tug but stopped again as several of the creatures took down one of Nova's guards who'd been surrounding the ship.

He couldn't help it. He stared and watched in mixed fascination and horror. The first creature to have pounced the guard raked a long, razor-sharp fingernail into an X shape over the guard's forehead. Then the creature placed its palm over the X-shaped welt. A white glow seeped from between the creature's palm and the man's forehead. It was so white that it blinded Hap. He had to look away and blink several times to try to clear the spots from his vision. The creature's dull-gray glowing skin now shone in absolute brilliant white.

Googool propelled Hap forward again. "What are you doing? Move!"

Hap moved alongside Tara to Nana, readying himself to be pulled into the light capture.

He turned in time to see Mosh wrestling with two Raksha. Mosh growled and shouted at the creatures as his huge beefy hands batted away the claws reaching toward his forehead.

No! Not Mosh! Not again! Not when they were so close to him—not when he stood within their reach. This might be the only chance to rescue Mosh. Hap veered off toward Nova's ship. He heard Tara call for him to come back, but he didn't look back. He put on more speed to catch up to Mosh. He nearly stumbled in shock when the Raksha bounded over Nova's ship and rained down on top of Meg and Svarta. The Raksha were everywhere.

Hap pressed harder, making his legs work faster than he'd ever made them before. "Mosh!" he yelled. He whipped the drubber from his utility belt and shot down several of the creatures that had targeted Mosh so they couldn't feast on him.

Hap shot them away until a creature tackled him from behind, knocking the gun from his hands.

He managed to throw the creature off of him so that they faced each other. The Raksha blurred, and the hammering pulse in his head vibrated with pain as though he'd been electrocuted. It would attack again, and he had nothing left to fight with.

The creature sprung, tumbling Hap to the ground close to where one of Nova's thugs had dropped his drubber and been consumed by the Raksha. A claw traced an unsteady line over his eyes. It felt like acid had been wiped over his forehead, and he screamed as he reached until his fingers gripped the hilt of the drubber. He jerked the drubber up and shot. The creature fell away from him. Hap stumbled back toward Mosh and shot at the creatures that had tackled Mosh on the ground. Nova had somehow been awakened and was no longer being held prisoner by Svarta. Meg no longer held Laney either. It had become every man for himself under the barrage of the Raksha attack. Hap watched Nova barrel up the ramp. He'd made it inside the ship and closed the door before Meg had the chance to reach it.

Nova had left Meg, just like Amar had said he would.

She had three creatures hanging on her, trying to drag her down to feed. She roared and swatted and took aimless shots at them.

Hap almost left her. One less enemy to fight. It seemed the smart thing to do.

He nudged Mosh toward Nana but held himself back.

Hap grunted in outrage at himself. Why would he bother saving her when she was the enemy? When she'd been the one to shoot Laney and take her hostage?

Meg let out a scream of pain. One of them had made the mark. It was moving its hand toward her forehead to feed off her intelligence. He charged back, close enough to have a good shot, and fired. They shrieked in a way that echoed in his head along with the hammering. But he was slow to get away, and as he turned, another creature had managed to trip him. He fell, and with the creature's weight holding him down, Hap's arm was pinned underneath him.

"Hey!" Meg yelled. The creature and Hap looked up at her at the same time as her fist connected with the creature's head, knocking the Raksha over and off Hap. Meg shot it before it could recover from the blow.

"We're even now," she said, turning away from him.

Hap blinked in surprise but didn't stick around to ponder the whole situation. He scrambled to his feet and ran to the ship, kicking up trash and metal and trying not to fall on his face as he went.

He made it to the ship, where the beam of light waited to pull him up into the cargo hold. He charged toward the light, dodging around a creature and diving inside the light before anything else could lay hands on him.

"I'm alive!" he yelled out, as much surprised by this information as he was elated. "Tara? Are you here?"

She was there with Mosh.

"It's just us," Tara said, her voice filled with concern.

Hap moved out of the cargo space.

Tara followed, telling Mosh to go to his room and strap in while they figured out what to do.

"Not leaving you anytime soon," Mosh insisted as he lumbered to his feet and followed them to the control room instead. Hap surveyed the scene outside the ship from the portholes and the front window. Even with Nana's weaponry firing into the fray and Nova's ship joining in as well, the Raksha were everywhere, clambering over the ships, trying to burrow their way down to get at the people inside.

Svarta, Tremble, Laney, and Amar stood with their backs to each other, picking off the creatures as they closed in on them.

The thumping, digging, and scratching at metal overhead as well as the hands and feet that dangled into view every few moments through the portholes was enough to let Hap know they'd overtaken the ship. Even if the others made it to Nana, they'd never get on board without bringing hordes of the creatures into the ship with them.

Svarta was surrounded and, for the first time ever, looked panicked—like she had no idea how to get out of her current situation. This terrified Hap more than anything. Svarta was the queen of courage. If something scared her, it would be outright stupidity for Hap not to be scared as well.

And then Svarta made eye contact with Hap—as if sensing his evaluating eye. She mouthed something to him and pointed to the front of the ship.

"What?" he yelled. "I can't hear you!" He still hadn't put on his helmet, so he couldn't communicate through the headphones.

"It looks like she's saying, 'Drive' and 'Get out of here!' But that doesn't make any sense." Tara's voice had that high pitch Hap had come to recognize as her I'm-terrified-but-let's-find-a-way-out-of-this voice. She whirled on Hap. "Why would she tell you to drive? Drive what?"

"Nana," Hap whispered. "She wants me to get us out of here." He moved into Laney's seat.

"And leave them? No! No way! We are not leaving them! And you can't drive Nana! Laney will kill you, and then Svarta will kill what's left of you! Besides, you need to be biocode—"

She grabbed a hold of the back of the seat as the ship lurched forward under his command.

"We're not leaving them; we're just going to shake off the things on the ship, then we can go down and beam them up or whatever it is that Nana does," Hap hurried to say over all of Tara's protests.

"We cannot technically perform a light capture because we are unable to isolate them," Nana interrupted. "We would end up bringing the Raksha on board with us. I was strictly instructed not to use this method unless I was given a clear shot. Bringing you up was the last chance I had at a clear shot. Svarta gave the command that I was not to take Raksha on board no matter what the outcome or alternative. I cannot go against a direct command."

"Get strapped in," Hap informed Tara and Mosh. They both leaped into seats and were barely secured when he shot the ship straight into the air and rolled it.

Several of the creatures flew past the window and to the wreckage piles on the ground, but many stayed attached, and the digging at the metal above them became more persistent.

He rolled and rolled and rolled, basically imitating the spiral drop. He almost threw up with the motion since Nana's grav sensors couldn't keep up with the constant shifting. He watched several of the creatures fly off into empty air through the windows. Tara looked sick, but Hap ignored that. "Is the cargo entrance clear?" he demanded to know.

"The cargo entrance is clear at this moment," Nana confirmed.

He rolled a last time to set them on the course straight back to the place where he'd left the rest of Nana's crew. He nearly crashed them into the ground. Tara screamed, and Mosh bellowed out his own cry of terror before Hap pulled out of the dive and managed to remember how to make Nana hover over the place where he'd last seen his friends. "Bring them up!" he commanded to Nana.

"I cannot. Svarta gave orders to not do a light capture if there were Raksha within the range of the light."

"*I'm* in control now. Svarta said I'd have total control. So I'm overriding anything anyone else said. I take full responsibility. Do it! Now!"

Nana complied. The capture sequence commenced. Hap pushed out of his straps, grabbed his drubbers, throwing one to Mosh, who up to this point hadn't been armed throughout the conflict, and bounded to the cargo hold where the light brought people into the ship. He prepared to fire on anything that wasn't someone he cared about.

Tara came too, with her own weapon shaking in her hands. She still hated using a weapon, but Svarta had made her take it before letting her leave the ship when they'd arrived on Koda.

Laney showed up first. The giant sizzling X marking her forehead glowed faintly as the creature that had materialized with her moved its palm over her head. Hap shot it before it could touch her directly. It fell to the side. Laney shuddered where she lay but made no move to get up. Others began appearing—but just creatures. There was no sign of Svarta, Amar, or Tremble. The creatures were only confused a moment about their new environment before sensing Laney's weakness and turning to attack. Hap picked them all off before they could press their palms to Laney's head.

He almost shouted in relief when other beams of drubber fire joined his. Mosh swayed slightly next to him but managed to hit whatever he aimed his drubber at. Tara's aim was a bit shakier, but she managed to not hit Laney, which Hap counted as a good thing.

Svarta materialized in front of them. She was in a struggle with one of the creatures—wrestling it to the ground and striking a vicious blow when she realized where she was. She glanced up at Hap, alarm and fury fighting for the same space in her expression. A ragged single welt sizzled on her forehead.

"You didn't!" she bellowed at Hap. But then she looked away and took inventory of the cargo hold. Laney lay unconscious near Svarta. A couple of the Raksha were now at the wall with the jewels and ancient writing embedded into the coppery surface. One of them was reaching out to place its palm on the wall. Svarta screamed, "No!" and vaulted across the room to the creature. She yanked it away from the wall by grabbing into the mass of slithering snakelike things at the back of the creature's head.

Tremble and Amar appeared and within seconds had shot down the remaining creatures, including the one Svarta had by the "hair."

She piled the bodies of glowing creatures at the center of the cargo hold. "Get them off my ship. Now," Svarta said to Nana, who quickly obliged her by opening the light and lowering them into it.

Svarta didn't bother hiding her anger with Hap as she helped Laney to her feet. "What are you staring at?" she asked him. "Fly us out of here while I clean up your mess."

Hap jumped to action, not certain why she thrust so much venom into her words. What made her so mad? They were all aboard the ship. They were all alive, which he felt was a good thing—a thing to be praised. He'd saved them! That should at least merit a little bit of gratitude. But her cold glare and furious tone indicated she'd break both of his legs before giving him any praise. The sound of digging grew worse as more and more creatures scrabbled to get atop the ship and get to the people inside.

He had to get them off the planet before any of the creatures actually gouged their way into the ship. He took off, trying to fly straight enough not to knock anyone off their feet, but crazy enough to knock the Raksha off the ship.

But he couldn't seem to shake the creatures off.

He didn't want to try reaching escape velocity from this planet being orbited by all that debris. What if he crashed? What good would it do to get everyone safely on board the ship if you ended up blowing that same ship up a few moments later? But what good would it do to get them all on board just to have the ship invaded by the space zombies trying to suck out their brains anyway?

But he did as told and took his place in Laney's seat.

He geared up the engines while Nana informed the passengers to get buckled in wherever they were at. Hap shifted into high gear, the readouts on the Multi-D display flashing as the ship prepped itself for escape velocity. Nana was fast. It didn't take her long to clear the planet's atmosphere.

"Holy Houdini!" he roared as the ship broke into space. He breathed deeply, panting with the need for oxygen. "I did it! We're out of there! The space zombies didn't get us!"

He glanced over at Tara, hoping she, at least, would be proud of him. He needed someone to tell him he did okay in saving everyone.

Tara wasn't looking at Hap, though. Her eyes were on the front window. "I don't mean to mess up your moment of glory or what-ever, but Hap . . ." Her eyes were round and filled with horror as she pointed. Hap followed her gaze to the window and felt his heart and stomach and all other vital organs sink into his toenails.

Leaving the atmosphere and flying into the vacuum of space didn't bother the Raksha at all. Legs and arms still hung in front of the window. The scraping continued on all sides of the ship, the desperate clawing filling Hap with the dread of knowing there was no way out. A face of one of the Raksha flashed into view from the front window, meeting Hap's gaze with those pitted black eyes. Hap involuntarily took a step back in horror. There was no way out—no way to escape.

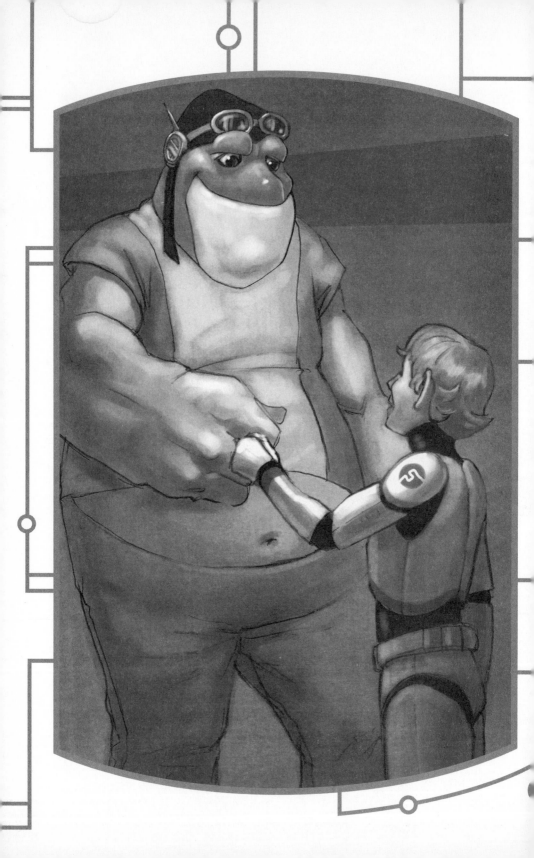

23. Squeaky Clean

"We're going to die," Tara whispered.

"Can you at least pretend to have a positive attitude?" Hap growled. As he checked all the readouts to tell him where the Raksha were located on the outside of the ship, he considered how Svarta had flown them into a wreckage to hide them.

What if he could try the same thing?

"You're not a skilled enough pilot," Nana said as if she'd been reading his mind.

"Then we're dead either way." He maneuvered close to a hunk of what might have once been part of a space station. He didn't think he could actually hit it and survive the crash, but he hoped to get close enough to knock the Raksha off the ship.

He dove in as close as he dared, but not close enough.

"This is a good idea," Tara said, watching the Multi-D display at the front of the ship. "Do it again. Closer."

"They've almost breached the hull," Nana said. She sounded sad, almost as if there was a "goodbye-it-was-nice-knowing-you" in her words.

Hap moved in closer and actually made a direct hit. The Raksha had been scraped by the piece of wreckage, but it had managed to keep its grip. Hap hadn't accomplished anything.

"We lost," Tara whispered.

Out the front window, the vision of the creatures clambering over the ship in thick masses like bugs made Hap feel a little sick, kind of like the time he'd accidently let the scourabs out of their box and they—

"Crettles!" Hap grabbed Tara's hand which made her jump. "Scourabs! The scourabs chew crettles off the ship! They're indestructible! Get the box and let them out onto the ship's hull!"

"You're not going to roll the ship again, are you?"

He shook his head. "If they made it into space, rolling them isn't going to do anything." She took a deep breath, nodded once, pushed free of the straps, and ran from the control room.

"Let's see how *you* like being chased," he muttered to the alien creatures raking their claws over the metal, working to break through.

He tried hard to fly straight so Nana's grav sensors could help Tara do her job. It was difficult to keep things steady when the creatures kept popping their heads over into the windows. A few of them actually touched the plasma and burned themselves off the ship entirely. They floated away into deep space. Hap wished they'd all do that.

They weren't carbon based life forms; they were something else. They were like energy bundled up into skins.

Tara showed back up, out of breath like she'd run a mile when there was no such distance to be had on a ship as small as Nana. "I did it! Let's hope it works!" she said, focusing her attention on the windows and Multi-D display with mixed terror and hope.

Scourabs skittered into view over the windows, completely unbothered by the plasma burns. Nothing bothered scourabs. Laney had taught him that the scourabs didn't actually eat the crettles, because scourabs didn't eat. They merely sawed through the connection that held the crettles to the ship. He hoped they'd do the same thing with the Raksha.

He held his breath. In spite of Svarta's protests, Laney staggered into the control room and slumped down into the seat Hap had vacated, but Hap didn't even look at them. He held his breath and watched out the windows. Amar and Tremble joined them—each one looking grim and lost. They heard the scratching. They knew it was game over for all of them.

Hap still held his breath. *It has to work. It has to work!*

And that's when he saw it, several creatures floating away from the ship trying to force their way back as the ship moved away from them.

Then scraping above them stopped abruptly. It was replaced by a low pattering—like rainfall. The scourabs were forcing their way over the ship. Raksha floated into view as they were detached from the ship and carried off into the space debris.

"It worked!" Tara yelled, making everyone jump and Laney about fall out of her chair.

"Well then. It's time to go," Svarta said, taking over ship control since Laney seemed too out of it to maneuver through the debris. Svarta sped off as fast as Nana could fly, racing to the spiral drop that would take them away from space zombies and human black holes and Don Nova.

Hap didn't even mind the way the spiral drop whirled him around until he felt like he'd been through a garbage disposal. They'd made it out. They had Laney and Mosh back. They had another book. They hadn't died.

Svarta glared at Hap as she pushed against the straps and got up out of her chair. "Do you realize what you could have done letting those Raksha come up in a light capture?" she demanded to know.

No one said anything. Hap definitely didn't say anything because Svarta had never been mad at him like this before.

"A Raksha feeds off of intelligence! The core of Nana's intelligence is in those crystals in the walls in the engineering room and the cargo hold. If they'd touched one of those crystals, she would have died!"

Hap blinked, baffled by the way Svarta used the term *died* when talking about a machine. "I'm sorry," he said quickly. "I didn't know what else to do. You guys needed help. I was just trying to help . . ." He felt pathetic. Pathetic because Svarta was being a complete creep over the fact that he'd saved her, and also because she was mad enough at that moment, she actually scared him.

"But they did *not* touch the crystals," Amar interjected before Hap blew up yelling at her for being ungrateful—or before he ran off to hide in his bed. Either was possible. "And we cannot dwell in might-haves. We are all alive. For that, Hap, I thank you." Amar unbuckled himself and slid out of his chair and over to where Laney sat as if that settled everything between Hap and Svarta. Svarta grunted but scooted out of her chair too, turning away from Hap, so she could take Laney's hand and smooth back Laney's hair. Laney's eyes were clenched closed, and her lips were pressed firmly together.

Amar took Laney's head very carefully into his hands. "Elaine? Elaine, you're skin is burning. Can you tell me where the pain is?"

"Everywhere." The word escaped past her lips in a groan.

"You can fix her, right?" Svarta asked.

"She has an infection, which is causing a fever. I can't rid her of the infection because that's microbiology—it isn't what I know. But I can mend where her bone has splintered, and mend the muscles that were seared in the laser fire and by the Raksha. I can fix her, but I cannot stop the foreign contaminants. But by healing her, it will allow her blood cells to focus on the infection. Right now her body is fighting infection *and* trying to mend itself."

Amar gently straightened Laney's head and coaxed her to open her eyes and look at him. He mumbled words to her. She shivered like someone had dropped an ice cube down her back. He stayed there holding her head for a long time. Hap's whole body had tensed while waiting to see what Amar could do for Laney— remembering the way his own ankle had clicked into place under Amar's touch.

Finally Laney gasped and Amar released his hold on her, letting her rest her head against the back of her chair. The X on her forehead scabbed and then smoothed away into new skin all while Hap watched in amazement. Amar stood and turned as if to go away, but Laney grasped his hand and gave it a light tug.

"You're handy to have around," Laney said weakly.

"Not handy enough to keep you out of trouble. Charging after Nova by yourself, Elaine Sanchez? You found more trouble than even Hap usually does."

"Hey!" Hap protested, but no one paid any attention to him.

"Will she be able to fight off the infection?" Svarta asked.

Laney's pale lips turned up in a smile. "I borrowed some medical supplies when we were Earth-side. They're in the supply room."

By *borrowed,* Laney usually meant "took without asking." Hap cringed every time she said it. He'd been taught some pretty hard and fast rules on taking stuff that wasn't yours. But he wasn't in a position to judge. Hadn't he been the one to take a crystal pyramid that wasn't his? And worse, he'd handed it off to the guy working for the Dark Ones.

"I'll get what's there. We'll see if we have anything she can use." Tremble, who was genuinely Tremble again, hurried out on her errand.

Tara and Hap had unbuckled from their chairs as well. Amar healed the marks on Hap's and Svarta's foreheads too so they didn't leave scars. It would be a while before the next drop. Hap wanted to sleep before they got to it, since sleeping through it was not an easy thing. And he was exhausted.

"You okay, buddy?" Hap knuckle bumped Mosh's huge knuckles.

Mosh smiled, his stumpy yellowed teeth showing between his blue lips. "I am now. You always come back for me. You're a good friend, Hap."

Hap grinned. "Yeah, you just remember that next time Laney and Svarta give me chores I don't want to do. Just kidding, man. I'm . . . glad you're okay." It could've easily gone the other way. Hap could've easily lost everyone in that little trip. But the trade went as planned. They'd gotten rid of Gygak and Nova. And Mosh and Laney were safe again. Tremble had never brought out the lemsk carrier so he suspected they still had an extra passenger.

"You were worried," Mosh confirmed.

"Yeah, I was worried."

Mosh smiled even wider. "Good friend."

Hap patted Mosh's shoulder and moved to leave the control room when Laney called out weakly, "Hey, Hap?"

He turned.

"I personally think that was some nice work."

He stood a little straighter at that. She had yet to yell at him about flying her ship, or disobeying orders by not lying low on the comet, but he figured once she healed up a bit, she'd remember to be mad at him for all that. For now, he was simply glad, and he decided it was okay to live in the moment of glad for a little while. He went to his room, fell into his bed, but before he could fall asleep, he said, "Sorry, Nana. I didn't mean to put you in danger. I didn't know."

She whispered through the speaker in his bed so only he could hear. "You did what I would have chosen to do if I had been given the choice. I did not deny you out of self-interest but because I was held by command. You did right."

He nodded at her and fell immediately into the deep sleep of the totally exhausted.

He woke up to Tara nudging him. "Wake up, lazy-bones," she said. "Amar said we could link again. He said we deserved to talk to our families after all we've been through. Isn't that awesome?"

Hap scratched at his head. "Yeah, awesome."

He got dressed into his Hazzard's Magical Happenings shirt and the black pants he'd acquired at the comet and followed her to the comms room which was so small it hardly could be called a room at all. But Nana did call it a room, and did so proudly, so Hap made sure not to make fun of it where she could hear.

The CME link plate was small but prettier than the one in Nova's lair. It had a cool pattern of stars and solar systems molded into the metal plating. Instead of gutters to drain off the melting ice on the plate, it had pipes. The coppery pipes were also decorated with stars and planets.

The cabling that ran the CME link plate was hidden inside other big copper pipes.

Amar looked up from the holo screen where he revved up the link plate. "Oh, good. You're here. Why don't you hop on up, Hap?"

"You sure? Tara might want to go first." He really wanted a few minutes to talk himself into getting on the plate. After the whole experience on Koda, he felt a little weird about doing anything that might cause more stress.

"I always get to go first," Tara said. "It's your turn." Tara smiled encouragingly as if she seriously wanted to do Hap this favor.

Her favor made Hap panic.

"No, really. I insist. Ladies first. Grandpa Hazzard would be really ticked if he thought I took your place. You know how he's always talking about men of honor and all that. What kind of honorable man goes in front of a lady?" Hap smiled. Sweat slicked between his shoulder blades in spite of the cold of deep space.

"C'mon, Hap. Just get up there. You like being the center of the universe." Tara shoved him forward a little, but because he hadn't seen the shove coming, he almost fell face first onto the plate. He caught himself, barely, and tossed back a scowl at Tara, who smiled her take-it-like-a-man smile. She frequently referred to standing on the plate as being the center of the universe because when a person stood in the dead center, it appeared as if the stars and planets were in orbit around them.

"Hurry, Hap." Amar encouraged. "We don't have much time before the next drop. You don't want to be in the middle of an energy link when you go through the spiral."

Hap resigned himself to climbing up onto the coppery plate. "What would happen if I was in here during the drop?" He now stood in the center of the plate, the metallic stars and planets surrounding him.

"I don't really know," Amar said. "But I would not want to test it to find out, do you?"

Hap shook his head no and then held his breath—waiting for Amar to begin the process on his holographic screen.

The plate froze over, the ice cracking and splintering right up to where Hap's shoes connected with the metal. Then Hap felt all of his energy drain down his body like a drop of water slicking down an icicle on a warm day. The energy drained out his toes, making them tingle. A jolt of electricity arced through him as he made the first link. The arcs came faster until they flowed into each other—one long jolt of electricity. Each star on the journey back to Earth captured his energy into its fiery grasp and held it until the pressure built up enough the star couldn't hold it anymore and had to spit the energy back out in the form of a coronal mass ejection.

When Hap could no longer bear the constant flow of links from each star, and his head started to fuzz with exertion, everything on the plate around him sprang into the clouded shapes of Hazzard's Magical Happenings.

His grandfather stood behind the counter punching keys on the antiquated cash register. Grandpa Hazzard had refused to update the cash register to an electronic one because he loved the melodious cha-ching noise the old one made.

Grandpa Hazzard and the surrounding area of Hazzard's Magical Happenings looked ghostly to Hap. And Hap and Tara had discovered that to everyone they linked with on Earth, *they* were the ones who looked like ghosts. Hap had long since suspected that the ghosts people thought they saw on Earth were really just people out in the universe trying to make a link.

Hap took a step forward to say hello to Grandpa Hazzard but almost accidentally walked into the customer he was ringing out. If the customer turned, she'd see Hap and then the rumors would start about Hazzard's Magical Happenings being haunted.

The magic shop received enough bad publicity because Grandpa Hazzard quite vocally and forcefully believed in aliens. Everyone in town thought the guy was whacked.

Hap used to wonder about Grandpa Hazzard's mental stability when it came to the whole alien thing, but once Hap had been abducted aboard a real spaceship and then imprisoned by a couple of aliens, he felt a little ashamed of doubting his grandfather.

Alison was straightening some of the snowstorm fans and mystic smoke tubes when she turned, saw Hap, and broke into a huge grin. "Hap!" she yelled. She nearly fell on her face trying to reach out and hug him. She shivered deeply as she passed through him and now stood between him and the customer.

Hap ducked behind Alison, hoping no shadowy parts of him stuck out.

"What's the matter, darling?" the customer asked. "Did you remember something about the day your brother disappeared?"

It was then Hap noticed the badge attached to the customer's belt loop of her black slacks. A weapon was holstered near the badge.

"Umm . . ." Alison's whole body tensed in front of Hap.

Grandpa Hazzard leaned to the side and caught Hap's eye. Though a variety of silent signals, Alison scooted herself so she leaned against the display of D'lites. Hap ducked behind the display and peeked through the packages to see the customer who he'd figured out was a detective investigating the disappearance of him and Tara.

"No, ma'am," Alison said loudly. "I haven't remembered anything new. He was out cleaning the garbage the last time I saw him . . . that day." She added the *that day* part likely so she didn't have to lie. She'd seem him a couple of times *since* that day.

"Well, if you remember anything . . . anything at all, you know how to call me, right?"

Alison nodded.

The detective gave Grandpa Hazzard one last accusing sort of look and then clicked out on low heeled boots.

"Hap!" Alison rounded the display, looking happy again. "Are you okay? Have you seen anything cool? Have you bought me a present yet?" The questions tumbled out in rapid succession.

"I've seen all sorts of cool stuff. I did get you something. But you'll have to wait 'til I come home to see it. How are Mom and Dad? Are you taking care of them?"

Alison rolled her eyes and grunted. "They're driving me crazy. They almost never let me go anywhere anymore because they're afraid I'll turn up missing."

"Just because I ended up on a space flight doesn't mean you will. Tell them they're being paranoid." Hap said. He tried to lightly tug at her hair, but his hand passed through. He knew he couldn't really touch her, but old habits were hard to kick.

"They're not really." She lowered her voice and glanced back to the curtain. "Weird things have happened. I've seen strange people in town. And at school. I could've sworn I was followed home one day. That's when Mom started driving me to and from school. I'm not allowed to go anywhere any more. It's been awful. But even with it being awful never being able to go anywhere alone, being alone would be worse than awful."

Grandpa Hazzard nudged Alison's shoulder. "Hey, Ali, why don't you go tell your parents that Hap's here to visit?"

She nodded but looked reluctant to leave Hap. She stared at him as though she expected him to figure out what to do over the new situation. After another gentle nudge, Alison hurried off behind the red curtain that separated the storage room and office from the store front.

As soon as she was out of earshot, Hap turned to Grandpa Hazzard. "What's going on?"

"Nothing we can't handle." Grandpa Hazzard scratched at his head. "I had to reinstate myself fully with ICE, which was less than pleasant. They have agents crawling all over this town. It isn't like it could be helped, I suppose, since the two ICE razors crashed in our canyons. The moment they entered the airspace over our community, it was inevitable I'd get called back into the mess they've created."

"What mess?" Amar asked—his voice clear and loud on purpose. He stood close to the plate. Hap had learned that in a weird sort of way, the people he linked to were also linked to his senses. If he saw or heard something, then his links could see hazy images of those things, and hear fuzzy voices. Amar had to be loud and had to enunciate or his words would sound garbled to the links.

"The Dark Ones have allies here on Earth. They've wormed their way into the ICE networks. They suspect I know something. I've felt the darkness closing in on me a couple of times—a pressing so horrible against every molecule of my being, I feared I'd be crushed under the weight of it. Their terrible voices demanded answers of me."

"Answers?" Amar asked.

"They believe I know where the books are hidden. They believe Hap has told me this information."

"Have you told him anything about the where the books might be?" Amar demanded of Hap.

"No!" Hap said loudly. Though he felt slightly foolish, because he *would* have told if he'd been given the chance. He'd planned on telling Grandpa Hazzard everything when he heard they could make another link home.

"And you never will," Grandpa Hazzard said. "Who knows who's listening here? And even if no eavesdroppers overhear our conversations when you come, who is to say what I would do if I'd had the information the Dark Ones want. I'm ashamed to admit I would have told them anything they wanted to know if it would have made that horrible pressing stop." Grandpa Hazzard frowned. "Now I know what an orange feels like when it's being juiced. And the cold of hopelessness seeping into my pores . . . Awful." He shook his head. "Don't tell me where anything is. That is information I cannot be trusted with."

If Grandpa Hazzard felt like he wasn't up to the task, how could Hap hope to be? "Are you guys in any danger?" Hap needed to know. But if they were, who would help them?

"Not that I know of. ICE keeps close tabs on us, but those who aren't on our side haven't done anything because the ones who *are* on our side are watching each other as closely as they're watching us. They do their fair share of following Alison, your mother, and me. But I've no doubt that whoever these strange people are . . . they *aren't* friends—not any of them."

"And Houdini's inner circle? The trust of Ehrich Weiss? The society? Have you contacted them?" Amar asked, interrupting the conversation again. Amar interrupted Hap's visits a lot more than he interrupted Tara's, not that Hap minded exactly, but it took time from him talking to his family.

Grandpa Hazzard shook his head. "I have not contacted the society. I know they're helping you locate the books. I truly do not want to know that information—not when I'm being watched as I am. Tolvan has gone to them, and though I tell him all I know, I don't want to know all he knows. But we worry. Even the trust is in jeopardy, Amar. Ehrich Weiss left his share of enemies and some have them have found their way into the inner circle of the society, under the guise of seeking apprenticeship into the magician's guild. They learned magic fast, grew in the ranks, and then still wanted to know more. They've broken off from the original group and started their own guild, one that practices a much darker art of magic, but we believe they still have spies. The trust is broken."

Hap interrupted this time. "Darker magic? Magic isn't real. Magic is tricks. Illusion." He could feel his energy waning. The link wouldn't last much longer.

Amar answered. "Magic is science, if you look at it from the perspective of one who understands the science. The books of my brothers would seem like magic to most. But those who understand the science behind it would see it for what it is."

Hap turned to look at Amar. "What is it?"

"Intelligence."

Grandpa Hazzard nodded in agreement.

Hap's mom rushed through the curtain with his dad close behind her. "It's so good to see you! We worry when you go so long between visits!" his mom declared. Her arms were lost between reaching out to him to pull him into a hug and knowing she couldn't.

Just knowing she wanted to hug him made Hap feel like he'd been wrapped up in one.

"Everything's great, Mom! Don't worry about me." He made sure to smile wider as evidence that he was fine. He didn't bother telling her that he'd been shot at *again*. And that two members of the crew had recently been abducted and recovered. Or that all of them had been under attack by things that would likely give him nightmares for the rest of his life. Some things were not good for moms to know.

"I told you to stop worrying, Jessica," his dad said. "He looks like he's doing great; aren't you, buddy?" Dad smiled wide too, but Hap could see the exhaustion behind the smile. He could also see that in spite of Dad's assurances to Mom, he'd been worried too.

Hap was quick to answer. "Totally perfect. I got to go on stage with an intergalactic rock star! And I got to explore the caves on a comet in the Elektra star system. Everything's fine. And we're getting closer to being able to come home every minute."

Everyone nodded and agreed and smiled wide. Well, everyone except Alison, who scowled. "Hap always gets to do the cool stuff," she whined.

"You wouldn't want to be doing any of this," Hap said. "You'd be crying your eyes out to come home immediately." He was only sort of teasing. She'd be crying but not because she was a baby. She'd be crying because some things were terrifying enough to be worth crying over.

"Would not!" she insisted, but they both knew she lied. Alison hated being away from home, even for the week long girl's camp. She did it, but with much drama and tears and promises to write—as if there were postal services in the mountains.

But Hap didn't tease her any further. His energy was draining fast, and he didn't want to leave Ali upset.

"Are you feeling okay, Dad?" he asked, needing to know before the link was over. "Fit as a fiddle," Dad said.

"Really? How many push-up-doing fiddles do you know?"

Dad finally gave a genuine smile. He loved that joke. "I keep my fiddles on a rigorous work-out schedule."

"Where are you going now?" Mom interrupted the joke before anyone could go off on the pig's fiddle that pulls a *ham*-string while doing warm ups. "When is *home soon*?"

Hap looked at Amar, who shook his head. "I . . . can't tell you," Hap said. "If you guys don't know anything, then no one can ask anything. I—"

His family and the store around them flickered. "It's ending!" he yelled. It always panicked him when the world flickered, when the connection to his family withered to nothing.

His mom's eyes swam in tears. "I love you, Hap!" she yelled back. Hap's announcement of the link ending panicked her too. She reached out to him, though she couldn't touch him as his family all chorused their love and pleadings for him to be careful.

"Take care of each other. Hang on, Dad; I'll be home soon!" The magic store disappeared like vapor, his family disappearing with it. The ice on the link plate cracked and melted into the copper piping. Hap collapsed where he was, drained of all energy.

"I've never seen a link last so long from such a distance." Amar's voice sounded like fuzz. Hap felt hands grab hold of his arms to help him up, but he never stood, not even with the extra help.

Hap blacked out.

The nightmare again.

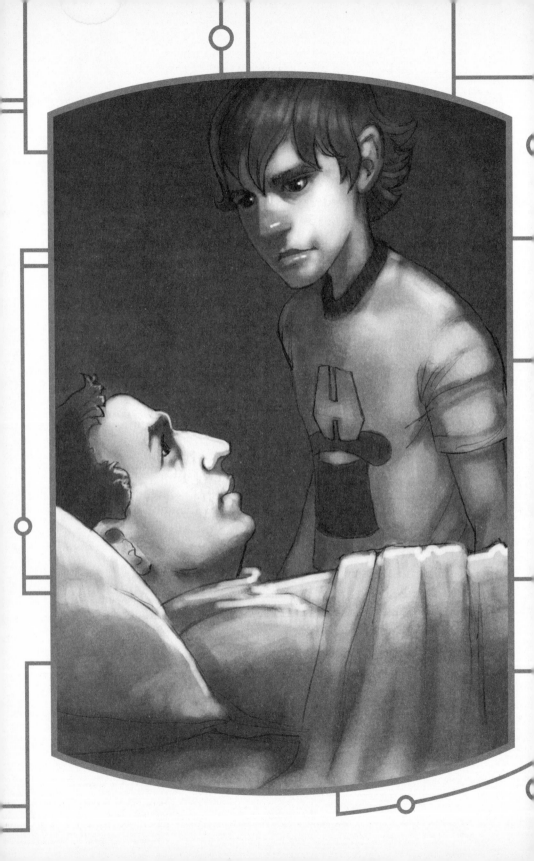

24. A MESSAGE FROM HARRY HOUDINI

HE KNEW HE WAS IN the nightmare, but he couldn't force himself to wake up. It's not a vision of things to come, *he thought to himself.* It's just a dream.

But he'd never had a dream where all of his senses were involved, where everything felt so real, where his whole being was consumed by the dream. He took a step and closed his eyes at the feel of the crunching glass under his shoes. No. Not again. No more.

He tried to think of himself in a field by his house, teaching Alison to fly a kite. We're running. I'm in a field, *he thought.* Alison's with me. We're flying kites.

But when he opened his eyes, he was in a city. He'd never been to this city before, but he instinctively knew his location.

Michigan . . . Detroit.

The glass wasn't from broken windows in broken buildings. The great tragedy of the earth about to explode hadn't happened in this dream and, oddly, didn't feel like it would. This dream was . . . something else.

The glass was from an A-frame sign standing next to two sets of double doors underneath a wide awning that reminded Hap of an old theater he'd visited when he was in New York with his parents for a magic convention. The glass had been broken on the sign and little bits of it littered the sidewalk. The poster underneath the cracked glass was an announcement for the greatest magician of the age: Harry Houdini.

Hap blinked.

There was no way possible he could be at the Garrick Theater. That was in 1926. Hap could not possibly be in 1926.

It was the middle of the day, but Hap had to wrap his jacket tighter around him as he moved. The sun shone in dappled spots on the street, trying to break through clouds that looked dark and heavy with rain. The air smelled wet. The water from the recent rainfall shone on the street, and people had to sidestep puddles to cross the road. A man with an umbrella walked past him, crunching the glass even more.

Hap closed his eyes again. "I am not at the Garrick Theater," he said out loud. His voice sounded like he was speaking into a tin can, muffled and echoing at the same time.

He took another breath and found himself in a hallway. He jumped out of the way, falling against the wall to avoid getting run over by a woman with a white apron and a white cap. She carried a tray full of silver things that looked like torture devices. She didn't say excuse me or anything. Rude, Hap thought. He put his hand behind him to push off the wall, but found he was pushing against a door instead. He turned and looked.

Room 401.

His heart hammered against his ribs. And he pushed the door again until it swung open for him.

A man sat in a chair next to another man lying in the narrow bed.

The man in the bed looked up. And Hap knew who it was—the same way he knew the city in which he stood. He just knew.

Ehrich Weiss. Harry Houdini himself.

A small smile curved over Houdini's lips. And he tilted his chin as if beckoning Hap inside the room.

Houdini focused on the man in the chair, in spite of Hap edging closer. "Be prepared, Theo . . . if anything happens," Houdini said.

"Stop it, Ehrich," the man—Theo, replied. "First you tell that to Bess, and now to me. It's like you're trying to frighten us with your ethereal warnings."

Hap was close enough he could touch Theo on the shoulder, but he didn't. He stayed quiet. He didn't move any closer, waiting to see what Houdini wanted him to do.

"I mean it. Listen. Be prepared . . . if anything happens."

Theo grunted, but Hap felt the fear rolling off Theo. "And what's going to happen? You'll be fine. You'll get through this." Theo said.

Houdini's eyes flicked from Theo to Hap. "Anything can happen. And a wise man prepares for anything. A man of honor prepares for every-thing."

Hap jolted at those words. He knew the message wasn't for Theo. Houdini meant the message for him.

How was that possible?

"Ehrich, Bess won't like hearing of you speaking this way. And don't think I won't tell her how you're carrying on. You mustn't give up, brother."

Houdini whispered something both Theo and Hap had to lean in to hear. "You know I believe it is possible to contact the living from the other side. It's simply a matter of timing. And now that I've made contact, I'm saying . . . no, I'm demanding! Be prepared! So much rests on you. Protect the secrets in the boxes."

Houdini's eyes stayed on Hap as he said this, but Theo never turned to see what Houdini stared at. Theo nodded as if understanding. He likely thought Houdini meant to protect the secrets of magic. Houdini had several magicians' boxes.

But Hap knew what boxes . . . what secrets.

Houdini had learned his best tricks from a book in the box that linked to one of the nine scientists. That box was still on Earth. Houdini knew what power lay hidden in those boxes.

Houdini looked calm then—peaceful, if a man in a hospital bed could ever be described as peaceful. "I'm tired of fighting . . ." were the magician's last words.

Then Hap heard something else.

Someone was crying his name.

"Hap! Wake up!"

Someone jostled his shoulder. His clothes were soaked clear to his skin. He lay on something hard. He blinked the blurriness out of his vision and found Amar, Svarta, Tremble, Mosh, and Tara hovering over him staring down at him. Their faces—all pinched and lined in worry wrinkles, showed they were in the midst of panic.

He shivered violently from the cold as he tried to prop himself up on his elbows, but he was overcome immediately by dizziness. He put his head back down, and Svarta stuffed a tube between his lips and started squeezing the nutty protein paste that served as food into his mouth.

He gagged and Tremble helped him slowly up a little so he could eat the paste Svarta was forcing on him without choking on it. "He can't eat lying down. He isn't a Mazer, Svarta! You're going to kill him trying to feed him like that!"

Svarta didn't stop squeezing the tube of paste though, in spite of the fact that Tremble was right. "He needs nourishment! He was in that link longer than anyone I've ever seen—longer than *anyone* has seen, longer than should be possible! If we don't get some food in him, he could go into shock!"

"You're not a doctor! You're just making that up!" Tremble said, her voice going gruffer as she tried to keep control of Googool, who always hovered on the brink of that control. Svarta had been walking a fine edge with Tremble lately, and Hap suspected Tremble was tired of being pushed.

"Well, it makes sense!" Svarta shot back, not denying the accusation of her making up the bit about Hap going into shock.

"Well done, Tremble!" Nana and Tara said at the same time.

Hap assumed Tremble had managed to keep control but couldn't verify for himself since she sat behind him and held his head. He really hoped she didn't let Googool take over since she *did* have a hold of him.

His head pounded, but he took deep breaths of air, feeling relieved.

The world hadn't exploded in this vision. He didn't even dare call it a dream anymore.

But he'd seen something impossible . . . he'd seen something as impossible as the future of the world ending. He'd seen the past.

How had he seen the past?

He hurried to slurp down the nutty paste so that Svarta would move away, and he finally managed to sit up on his own. He was still on the plate—encircled by the planets and stars as if he really were the center of the universe. Nana's small crew hovered over him.

"His vitals are leveling to normal," Nana said. She sounded relieved. Being that she could monitor every aspect of his breathing, heart rate, and everything while he was on the link plate, she would know better than anyone how he was doing. The fact that she felt relief meant that he had to have been in a really bad way.

"I feel fine. Why do you guys all look like I died?" he said, not really feeling fine. He felt like someone had used his head as a drum and had beat on that drum for hours. And he was freezing!

"Your heart stopped," Tremble said. Her voice was soft and more melodious than he'd ever heard it. She spoke to him as if speaking in lullaby.

"You just . . . flatlined. Nothing would wake you up. We thought . . ." Tara's voice cracked and she looked away.

They thought he was dead.

He really didn't feel dead; sure, he had a headache, but a headache wasn't usually a sign of dead, was it? "I'm fine," he assured them again. "Really." He offered over a shaky smile.

Svarta laughed and ducked his shoulder lightly. "Of course you are. Strongest kid in the universe. You can do anything, right, Happenstance?"

Hap laughed a little—though that was shaky too, and shrugged a shoulder. "Well, not anything. But anything I can get away with."

Everyone laughed, seeming to be breathing easier, though they looked like they were all torn between hugging him in joy and beating him up for scaring them.

He inhaled deeply. What had happened to him was definitely weird. For his heart to have stopped? Crazy stuff. But he was with friends—people who cared. And in spite of everything, he felt safer because of those friends.

Amar caught his eye and a question seemed to sit on the edge of his tongue. Hap turned away, unsure of how to answer that question in Amar's eyes.

Yes, it's possible I just died.

Yes, I saw Harry Houdini.

Yes, I'll be prepared.

Because Hap knew that he had somehow linked to Harry Houdini nearly a hundred years after Houdini had died. And if Houdini was shooting messages across time and space like *be prepared and protect the secrets of the boxes*, it could only mean one thing.

Houdini knew the world was in danger.

And he was trusting Hap to do something about it.

He expected Hap to save the world.

And Hap was prepared to do exactly that.

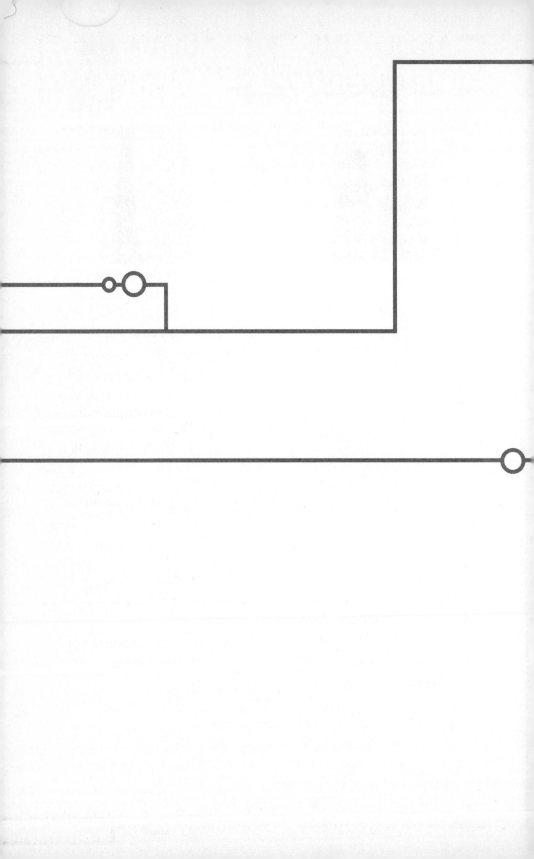

ABOUT THE AUTHOR

ABOUT THE ARTIST

Julie Wright has written more than a dozen books and especially loves writing about the fantastic. She strongly supports the cause of literacy for everyone.

She enjoys speaking to writing groups, youth groups, and schools.

She loves life and everything life has to offer except mayonnaise and mosquitoes. She especially loves reading, eating, writing, hiking, playing on the beach with her kids, and snuggling with her husband to watch videos. Julie's favorite thing to do is watch her husband make dinner. She has a profound respect for ice cream.

Visit her at her website:
www.juliewright.com

Kevin Wasden has an overactive imagination, is unable to sit still through meetings without drawing, and tends to be silly at the most inopportune moments.

He is an advocate of art and creativity in education and enjoys speaking to youth, writers, artists, and educators. He studied illustration at Utah State University and has studied figure drawing and painting from the exceptional figure artist Andy Reiss, in New York City. He is creator of the independent comic *Technosaurs*.

You can hang out with Kevin at www.kevinwasden.com.

Visit Hap and Tara at
www.hazzardousuniverse.com

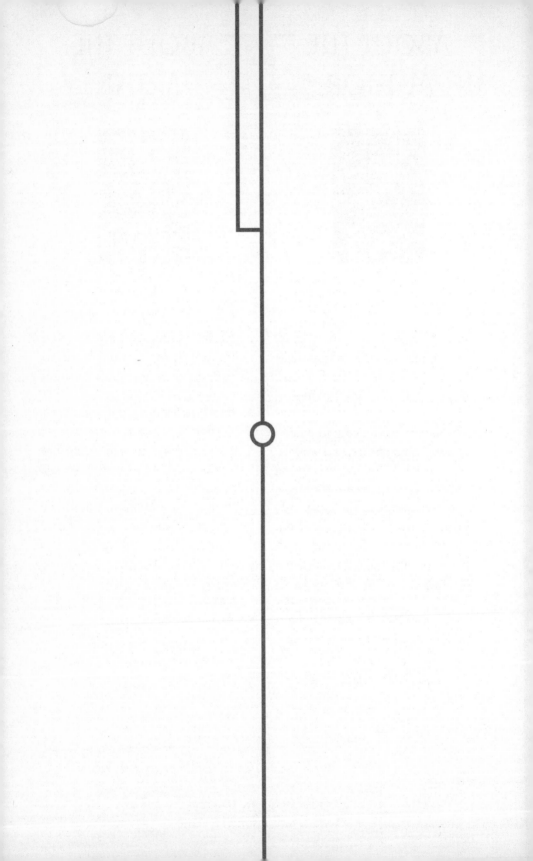